USE Somebody

BECK ANDERSON

OMNIFIC PUBLISHING

LOS ANGELES

Omnific Publishing
2355 Westwood Blvd, Suite 506
Los Angeles, CA 90064
www.omnificpublishing.com

First Omnific eBook edition, October 2016
First Omnific trade paperback edition, October 2016

The characters and events in this book are fictitious.
Any similarity to real persons, living or dead,
is coincidental and not intended by the author.

Library of Congress Cataloguing-in-Publication Data

Anderson, Beck.
Use Somebody / Beck Anderson – 1st ed.
ISBN: 978-1-623422-08-0
1. Contemporary Romance — Fiction. 2. Movie Industry — Fiction.
3. Idaho— Fiction. 4. Fly Fishing — Fiction. I. Title

10 9 8 7 6 5 4 3 2 1

Cover Design by Micha Stone and Amy Brokaw

Printed in the United States of America

To my Marcus. I am my best self when I'm with you.

ABSOLUTE BEGINNERS

The worst sound to hear in a private jet cruising at thirty-thousand feet is the rattle of two ice cubes in an empty Scotch glass.

Okay, the worst sound to hear in an airplane at that altitude might be one of the engines exploding into a million little pieces. Or the pilot shrieking in panic, that's probably not a good sound to hear, either. Of course I'm not talking about cataclysmic noises. But I'm thirsty, and I'm irritable, so this is my state of mind at the moment.

I rattle the ice cubes together again. I look for the flight attendant. She looks in the other direction. On purpose. There are only two of us passengers on the plane, for crying out loud.

Andy looks over at me. "What has you so keyed up?"

I sigh. I've clearly annoyed Andrew Pettigrew, world-famous actor and my number-one client. That's saying a lot, because the man is a saint, and the man has a toddler, and his patience is as deep as the ocean.

"I don't know. I just want to get there," I say, trying to focus on something besides the empty glass in my hand.

Andy doesn't let it go. "Are you sure it's not about Ashley?"

I scoff. "Definitely not. I'm done seeing her, anyway."

"Why?"

"She has this weird, baby-fine hair." I feel more annoyed now.

Andy shakes his head. "So? I can't believe we're talking about her hair."

"So, I'm not dating anyone with hair like that. It's finer than baby Quincy's hair. She'll probably be bald before she's thirty."

This comment does not sit well with Andy. He rolls his eyes. "You are not exactly knocking it out of the park on the hair business, Jeremy."

"Shut it, Andy." I self-consciously run a hand through my hair. For the record, Andy teases me about this because he knows it's a sore spot. My hairline may have receded a bit, but that's it. I promise, I'm not even close to a comb-over.

He takes a deep breath and closes his eyes, opens them, and points past me. "Just look out the window so I won't be forced to throw you from the plane at thirty-thousand feet."

I do as I'm told. I never follow directions. Never have. But my best client is also my best friend, and I'd like to keep it that way.

Does he know he's my best friend? I think so. Yes. I'm pretty sure. I don't fucking know. Yes.

My name is Jeremy King, and I am one of the most powerful agents in Hollywood.

I may or may not have a best friend. I may not have any friends past that at all.

Don't feel sorry for me, or I will kick you in the balls.

This may be why I have no friends.

But let me tell you what I do have.

I own a Tesla Model S, white. I paid cash for Marlon Brando's house in the Hollywood Hills. If you don't know who he is, you are a dumb ass and should go look him up right now if I am supposed to put up with you for the rest of the story.

I'll wait for you to put some of his movies in your cart on Amazon. You can watch them later.

I mean, really. He was the star of *Streetcar Named Desire*, for Christ's sakes. A complete bad ass. Please don't tell me you haven't heard of him.

You should stop reading now, too, if you have any illusions that in finding any kind of love, I will change in some way and sprout a heart of gold. The only gold I have is on my wrist – Rolex Cosmograph Daytona, thank you very much.

I am a loyal friend. I take care of people who take care of me.

I am fierce, and I am the fiercest in my field. Do not cross me.

And I have everything I want.

Go away if you think I'm going to have one of those moments where I look out at the ocean and feel all hollow and run through the rain to knock on some chick's door and profess my love to her.

I rep movie stars, but never once for a minute have I ever thought that life works the way movies do.

"You can stop pouting now, J," Andy says. He must be speaking to me again.

"Pondering, not pouting. But if you say anything about my hair thinning again, I will cut you." I loosen my tie and swallow the last of my Scotch.

"We're on vacation. You need to lighten up."

I wave a hand, dismissing the comment. "I'm never on vacation. I'm working from the field."

"Cell service is shitty on the South Fork."

"I can survive without it, don't you worry." I change the subject. If I don't, I'll break out in hives. "Anyway. How's the fam? You talk to them before we left?"

"Kelly was putting Q down for a nap. She couldn't talk very long. Hunter had a birthday party to go to, and apparently some older kid was going to pick him up and they were driving together to it. Kelly was worried about it. I told her not to."

I shake the cubes in my glass one more time, hoping the flight attendant catches the hint. She just shoots me a glare and crosses her long legs the other way. Maybe I shouldn't have made that crack about the mile-high club when we got on.

I look at Andy. "Kelly should be worried. A teenage driver she doesn't know is a risk to Hunter, bro. Plus if she drives him she can check and see if the parents are home and that Hunter isn't lying his ass off."

Andy smiles at me. "That almost sounds like you care about the well-being of my step son, J. Nicely done."

"Whatever. Did you read that script that I sent you?"

He shakes his head. "I didn't like the synopsis. Ghost of Al Capone and a modern-day accountant track down his hidden money? Rotten idea."

"I don't care if it sucks. Take the meeting to meet the director, Rye Burnsides. What you want is to take a pass on the weak script, but get in line for his next project, the one where he gets a decent script. This one's going to die on the vine, anyway. The financing is looser than your grandma."

"That is the weirdest metaphor I've heard from you yet."

I change the subject again. "Take the meeting. And is this plane ever going to land? The river's going to dry up before we get there at this rate. Or Todd'll have drunk all the beer."

"Thank for your consideration on that front, by the way. I love it when you drink in front of me."

"You're always welcome to go in another room."

"You're drinking right now. We're on a plane. There is no other room."

"Now I feel guilty. Jesus." I set the glass down and stop trying to get a refill. But only because he's my best/only friend.

"Exactly the point. I promise to smoke Cohibas with you, though."

"You have to on the river—it'll keep the mosquitoes away."

"That's Alaska. Idaho isn't overrun. This fishing lodge is paradise, I swear to you. When Kelly took me and her dad there, it was like heaven on earth. Cool, not humid, not terribly buggy, and best of all, in the middle of nowhere. I went to the c-store at the crossroads almost every night to get doughnuts just because not a single person recognized me. It's heaven. I'm not even kidding."

The plane lurches to the right.

I clutch at my armrests. "I guess I'll get to see heaven one way or another. I don't like bumps like that when I'm flying."

"I'm sure it's nothing."

"Whatever. Let's just get on the ground and get to the fishing and bonding and cigar smoking. It's way overdue."

Finally we put down in Idaho Falls, Idaho, of all God-forsaken places.

Andy seems pretty relaxed. A private plane means a private terminal, and no commotion.

Last summer Andy got married to Kelly. He's got a kid. Quincy, a little girl. She's cute if you like drool. He's got kids, really, counting the two stepsons he's got. He's thirty-three, a year younger than me, and he's a family man.

I don't know if it's to celebrate or what, but he planned this trip out, told us about it on the bachelor golf trip we took. Tucker, his bodyguard, and Todd, his childhood friend, are coming, too. They took a different flight in from the East Coast, so they're waiting for us there already.

We'll fish, hang out, chill. I'd say drink, but Andy's been sober for more than three years now, so I'll drink, but try not to be too blatant about it. No sense in pissing him off.

Todd I don't like much, but Tucker's a good guy. I can always fish farther down the river from Todd if he starts working on my last nerve.

Part of me freaks when I think about being this far away from the office for a full week, but I pay people to freak out for me, so some junior agent can do my bidding while I soak up a little peace and clean air.

I've got one deal cooking, but I think it's not going to gel until I'm back. It's with Amanda Walters, Andy's old co-star, who just about blew all her chances of everything when she got mixed up in harassing Andy. But he forgave her, so I didn't have to drop her as a client the second I signed her. And that stupidity never made the press, so she was able to save face. What jealous ex hires a paparazzo to slash a co-star's tires, just 'cause he's banging somebody who's not you, I don't know, but that's what Amanda did to Andy. I don't know why anybody would obsess like that.

But I'm not a chick. So, there's that.

But maybe it's not a girl thing. It might just be a Hollywood thing. This business twists people's brains. Any grey matter that might have helped a star make good decisions, LA fries it to a pulp. Quicker if you live there full time. Hell, if I went to twenty million auditions and heard how they didn't like the bump in my nose (I have a great nose, that's just a hypothetical) or that I needed bigger tits (obviously not me), I'd be warped, too.

Anyway, crazy Amanda might just get a very big deal and it might happen soon, but I don't think it's happening this week.

And I can always fly out early.

Andy and I pick up the rental car, and it's a big Yukon beast of an SUV. We have a little ways to drive, east toward Jackson and Yellowstone.

I'd stay right in Jackson, if it were my trip, but I get it—Andy wants secluded. The South Fork of the Snake River in BFE, Idaho, definitely qualifies for secluded.

I'd just like a bar besides the one on the property, and I don't know if either town nearby is worth the drive. Plus, from my experience, when a bunch of LA types show up in a cowboy bar, they get their asses kicked (Not me personally; okay, me personally. I'm not welcome in Amarillo, Texas, anymore. Long story.).

"Tell me again about this place," I say.

We're driving. Andy drives. He never gets to drive himself around, so he gets a kick out of it. I don't give a shit.

He looks at me. "We have a whole house. Thirty feet from the river. There's a lodge, a fly shop, a restaurant, a bar for Mr. Insensitive, world-class guides, brown trout and rainbow and Yellowstone cut-throat, and the fly hatch right now is crazy, which means we'll be catching fish like you catch wannabe starlets at Coachella."

I nod. "I like the idea of the house. I hate being forced to eat dinner in a little restaurant with a bunch of heart surgeons from San Jose or litigation lawyers from Chicago."

"We might have to share the river with them, though. I might be a movie star, but I wasn't movie star enough to rent the whole resort out. There'll be other people there."

"I don't care, and I'm glad, by the way. I like you to keep some of that money—I may need to swindle you out of it at some point. When your career cools off, you know."

Andy slams on the brakes. "Shit."

"What? Jesus, you're going to kill us." Maybe I do mind that he's driving. Not doing it very much may be making him suck at it. "Did you run something or someone over?"

"No, I think I missed the turn for the highway."

I pick up my phone, prepared to navigate. "What exit was it supposed to be? What's the GPS say?"

"Exit 311."

"It's not supposed to be very long from here. Like forty-five minutes. Are you sure you missed it?"

He squints his eyes for a minute in the growing dusk and then shakes his head. "Oh, no, there it is up ahead."

"Do *not* get us lost. This is Donner Party territory."

"No, it's not. That's California at the top of the Sierra Nevada Mountains in the middle of a blizzard. We're in Eastern Idaho in June. Cool it with the drama. The people around here are very nice."

"Whatever you say. I don't plan on meeting any of them anyway, so what do I care?"

Andy shoots an eyebrow up. "No plans to meet anyone? Say it ain't so, Jeremy King of the horn dogs."

"What girl would I meet when I'm landing a brown trout? Summerteeth, and though there may be an advantage to no teeth, it doesn't outweigh having to look her in the eye in the morning."

"I'm going to regret asking this. Summerteeth?"

"You know, she's got some of her teeth."

"Jesus Christ, Jeremy." But then he laughs, so I'm happy.

We drive down the single-lane highway. The night's getting darker and darker. I spot a couple elk on the right side of the road, but I don't say anything to Andy. I don't want him to freak out about them and drive off the side of the road.

One of my clients hit a moose driving up in Alaska and totaled his car. He damn near died. They have moose around here, too. I grip the door handle a little tighter and silently bless the rental car agency for the Yukon.

"Here it is. This is the loop. Hang on." Andy brakes and makes a hard left.

I grab the dash and my door handle. "We're going fishing, for Chrissakes. Can you not give me a heart attack? This is supposed to be relaxing."

The lodge's sign looms large in the headlights, and Andy pulls into the parking lot.

We get out. There are four other cars in the lot.

Andy looks left and right. "I don't know which way our house is."

"What's Tucker driving?"

"Todd was supposed to text me, but he didn't," Andy says.

"Surprise, surprise."

Andy raises an eyebrow, a caution. "Attitude."

"Fine."

"Just come in with me, and we'll get up to speed."

I tag along behind him. It's not too late. I wonder how busy the check-in desk will be.

Here's the weird thing about hanging out with world-famous, impossibly good-looking, movie-star-of-the-decade Andy Pettigrew: I brace myself anytime we go anywhere in public.

It's gotten to be a reflex, I swear. We walk through a doorway, and basically one of three things will happen:

1. They know he's coming. Glass-shattering squealing ensues. Tucker has to save all of us from being crushed. I always wish I was wearing earplugs.

2. They don't know he's coming. Someone spots him, and everybody freaks out. Nine hundred people ask to take their picture with him. If we're quick enough, we get out of wherever we are without the squealing.

3. Some miracle occurs, and we fly through whatever location it is as fast as we possibly can because how fucking lucky are we, no one has noticed him, so hurry the hell up and don't push our luck.

It's a weird thing, though. At first I had these jealous fits about it. You know, like, no one ever in the history of ever will make that big a deal over me.

Then I kind of figured out that most of us go through our lives with no one making a big deal if we walk into a room. Us normal people, we don't cause a commotion.

Except I guess what I'd like to experience is when there is one person who does care when I walk in the room. One person who does make a big deal out of it when I arrive. One person whose face lights up. Some woman, when I walk in the room, her face will light up.

I'm still waiting on that one.

Andy waves me on. "Leave the bags. Let's go check in."

"Lead on."

We enter through a door with antlers on it, and into a lobby with animal heads. Not a surprise, I guess. It is Idaho.

No squealing. Thank God.

There's an old grandpa-type sitting in front of a fireplace, reading a newspaper. No fire, though, since it is June. It's late, but the sun didn't go down too long ago, so it's not cold or anything. Andy always goes on and on about Boise and how light it stays in the summer. I never listen but I guess I get it. Long twilight is cool, more time to play.

Besides Grandpa, the lobby is empty. There are voices drifting from the restaurant and bar, but that's it.

The front desk is deserted.

"Hello?" Andy stands there, and I can see his hand over the bell on the desk. His nice brain is going over the whole, "Ring it? Don't ring it?" dilemma that nice people with nice brains do.

I have an impatient brain who would like me to feed it a beer, so I give the bell a nice, hearty ring.

"Jeremy, for crying out loud. Give them a minute to come out front."

"Why? There's a bell on the counter. Pretty sure that means it's there to be rung."

We stand for another second. Andy shifts his weight from foot to foot uncomfortably. He's probably starting to feel like a sitting duck. Too long in a lobby, he's bound to get spotted.

"Hello, we need to check in!" I yell. Andy throws an elbow.

There's a loud crash from the back room. It sounds like a big piece of metal.

"MOTHER of PEARL!" Someone didn't expect that crash. Someone who is a girl.

I smile and raise an eyebrow. Now, I'm interested.

She comes in the room backward, ass first. She's dragging two metal lids, and one of those buffet dishes that they always have at weddings.

It's a nice ass. In jeans, faded and without any of that sparkly crap on the pockets.

She hasn't turned around yet when she speaks. "You didn't hear that, did you?"

I speak up before Andy can. "Every word."

She drops the lids and the dishes. "Guess I'm fired." She turns around.

I get a good look at her for the first time. Petite. Nice rack, nice-shaped hips. Blonde hair, but she's dyed the ends dark brown. She looks straight at me. Big hazel eyes.

I smile, hold her gaze. "Hi. You got fired? For what?"

"Scratch that. Can I help you gentlemen?" She licks her lips and pastes on a fake smile.

I wait. Here's the part where she goes all ape-shit over Andy, finally looks at him and loses it. Then I listen to nine years of her reminding him of all the movies he's been in (What? He was in *Redcoats Rising*? Oh my guh!).

"We need to check in." I say it. Andy's just standing there.

"Okay. Sorry again." She just looks at me. "Have I seen you somewhere?"

I stand a little taller. "What?"

She's still looking right at me. "Have we met before?"

This is new. She must've noticed Andy. "I don't think so. I'd remember someone who used that curse."

She casts her eyes down on her mess and shakes her head. "Sorry. I'm way off my game. I sliced my hand open this afternoon, helping a guest." She holds up her left hand, bandaged around the palm. "I shouldn't be telling you this. Or talking to you. But you do look familiar. Let me check you in. Sorry, sorry, sorry."

"It's no problem. You're human. I'm Jeremy. Jeremy King. But the room's under Tucker Caldwell, I think."

She digs through a box full of receipts with keys attached, finds what she's looking for, and takes a huge breath. She plucks a key out and looks up at me. "Here we are. You're in The Residence, just follow the lighted path at the east end of the lot. Your friends are here already. You're all taken care of, Mr. King." This must be what her hospitality is supposed to look like.

"Got that game face back on. Good on ya', way to rally." I smile again.

The phone in front of her rings, and she answers it.

"Front desk." Someone tells her something that makes her frown. "No chafing dishes? Fine. No, I can put them away. Fine." She hangs up and turns her attention to me again, pasting the smile back on her face. "Sorry for the interruption. If you gentlemen need anything else, let me know."

I consider a line, but nothing really good comes to me. "Just hoping your night improves."

She crinkles her brow. "I guess. Have a good night. Thanks for being understanding."

She turns around and kicks the chafing dish, the lids, kicks them back into the back room. As soon as she's out of sight, the curses erupt again. "SCUM-SUCKING WEINER DOGS! FOR THE LOVE OF READING RAINBOW AND ALL THAT IS HOLY!"

I take the key and turn around to pick up my bag. "Well, that was interesting."

Andy looks stunned. "She never even made eye contact with me."

"Oh, poor neglected movie star boy. Not every girl with a nice ass is going to fawn all over you."

"Excuse me?" She's back at the front desk. She heard that last thing. She looks like she might punch me with that bandaged hand.

"We were just leaving. My apologies." I turn tail and get out of the lobby as fast as I can.

But, *but*, she never once freaked out over Andy Pettigrew. Maybe there's hope for me after all. After she gets past the wanting to punch me part.

We get out the doors and carry our bags down the path the girl mentioned.

I'm still thinking about her. "I didn't see if she had a name tag. Did you see a name tag?"

Andy looks at his phone. "What?"

"The girl at the front desk. Did you see if she was wearing a name tag?"

He shakes his head. "I was too busy watching the two of you."

"What do you mean?" I feel something clench deep in my gut. I ignore it.

"The two of you, staring at each other. Batting eyelashes at each other, you smiling your pearly, toothy, sharky smile."

I wave a hand. "Whatever. What I noticed is her ample ass."

Andy smiles. "And she noticed, no, actually, heard you talking about it. Well done, my friend."

We are at the end of the pathway, and a large log lodge rises above us.

"No worries. I'll charm her. Plus, it was a compliment. I'd say a woman should be glad to know if a guy admires what she looks like."

Andy leads us up the stairs to the front door. "Jeremy King and charm are not two words that come up together very often."

The front door is open, and Todd is in the doorway. "Snake charming and Jeremy King, yes. Charming and Jeremy, no."

Todd. Fuck him. I've never liked him, and he always acts like because he was Andy's friend first, he's Andy's best friend. Bullshit, I say. And the poser rocker thing? It's old. He needs to own up to the fact that he and his smug face and self-referential band name (Oxford Comma? Yeah, you're hilarious) are a flash in the pan that flashed two years ago.

But my biggest complaint about Todd Ford, alleged best friend and supposed musician? When Andy was struggling with alcohol, Todd was clueless. He took Andy out to clubs, encouraged the drinking. Total dumb ass. Andy says that it was his own decision to go out with Todd back then, but let me tell you, I'm not a pro at letting things go. Having a long memory has served me well in my business. History in Hollywood can sink a movie deal in a heartbeat, so I make sure I know the history.

I acknowledge him. "Todd."

He does the same. "Jeremy."

"Hey, brother." Andy smiles wide as he comes up the stairs to the door.

Todd gives Andy a "bro-hug"—you know, the handshake with one hand and the hug with the other. They part, and Todd takes Andy's suitcase. Suck-up.

I sigh and go inside to find my bedroom.

"That was quite a sigh." Tucker, Andy's bodyguard, sits on the couch in the living room. There's a huge fireplace, and river rock surrounds it and climbs to the vaulted ceiling. Tucker takes up the whole couch. He fits right in to the oversize décor. He's a beast.

"Could be a long week. Just sayin'." I think back to the front desk and wonder if I'd get slapped if I went back over to talk to her.

"A long week of choice fishing." Andy drops his backpack by the stairs. "Tuck! Come here, you."

Tucker springs from the couch in a way that scares me—he's too fast for a guy that big. I've seen him lay a guy out who came at Andy from the crowd at Cannes once. Don't try that. Trust me.

Now, though, he just hugs Andy. He claps him on the back, and I can hear it from over by the couch.

I get down to the details. "Did you guys pick rooms?"

Todd opens the fridge and plucks a beer out, cracks it. "Saved the one with the hot tub on the deck for Andy."

I swallow. "And I get?"

Andy points at me. "Don't start. There's not a bad room in this place. You get the one next to mine."

I grab my bags and take them upstairs. He's right. I swing my bedroom door wide and walk into a large room with a king-sized bed and wide windows facing the river. The river's almost purple under the moonlight.

I'm not outdoorsy. I live in LA. If I was the type to pine for the pines, I'd have shriveled up and died a long time ago, choked out by the smog.

What do I love about LA? I love Indian food on Mondays, Thai Tuesdays, the Lakers and concerts at the Staples Center and driving my Tesla down the PCH. I like buying bespoke and eating at SoHo House.

LA and I just fit. I wasn't born there, but I should've been. I don't even mind the traffic. It's just an excuse to hang out in my car longer.

But tonight, I decide to walk out into the great outdoors. I hope that some pissed-off grizzly bear isn't looking for a snack.

Most mornings we're here I'll have to drag Andy out for a run. He's got a shoot coming—he's going to have to fly straight to Toronto with me after our boys' week. He needs to look lean and mean.

In LA I lift three days and run two. Sometimes I hike in the hills on Sundays. Usually it's when I'm wooing some actress. Especially if she likes dogs. Take her and her dogs on a hike early Sunday, buy her a coffee at the Coffee Bean and Tea Leaf, get a treat for the dog, offer to make her breakfast at my house—have you ever hung out with a woman on a Sunday? It's the non-date that gets you to scoring position faster than any come-on in a club will, I guarantee.

Really, I doubt you're a guy if you're reading this, but if you are, sit at the feet of a master. I can tell you how to get a woman in bed. You tell me what she likes, I'll tell you the way into her boudoir.

Is she a Midwestern girl? I bet she loves football. Find out her favorite team, fly her to their stadium, invite her dad, get a meet and greet. Ka-ching. You will score.

New Yorker? Carriage ride doesn't cut it, my friend, and don't try the cheap-ass last minute Broadway tickets thing unless you never want to get past a cozy hug. Do not pass go, do not collect her panties in the inside pocket of your suit jacket.

No, you take her with you to ring the opening bell of Wall Street, and follow it with pancakes on the roof of a penthouse overlooking the Park, then let her sit in with you on a fitting session for New York Fashion Week. Make sure the designer fusses over her and signs a first-edition charmeuse scarf for her before you go.

LA ladies love trips to surf school in Cabo for a quick weekend, sure to be followed by quickies on the corporate jet.

I am good. Make an experience for the girl, make her feel special, make her feel like she's the only one you've ever done something so thoughtful for, and you will have her where you want her. I like the little touch of cooking breakfast for her, preferably before I've had sex with her. Cooking after conquest is awkward.

My favorite parting is to woo her, bed her in the afternoon, put her in a cab or on a plane when she's got somewhere to go. Then I'm on set, busy-busy, off to a premiere on the other side of the world.

They don't usually feel abandoned or dumped. They usually feel like they've had this amazing experience. Kind of like a visit to

Disneyland. You don't live there. You just soak in the adventure and then jet back to your real life.

That's what the Jeremy King experience is like.

Sure, I've done the long-term dating thing before. They tend to be either man-eating actresses or agent colleagues, and it doesn't tend to go well. I do like the thrill of the chase with a tough case like that, but if we date for more than a few weeks, I get claustrophobic or she gets crazy. Either way it ends, and then she usually wants to bury me in the business world.

There's a half knock at my door, and Andy strolls in. "Well?"

He wants my approval. One of the reasons I dig this guy. He still wants my approval, even though he could go get another agent and pay him handsomely to constantly voice approval for anything Andy might do.

"First-rate, Andy. Still not sure how long I can take all the quiet and nature before I go stir-crazy."

He plops down on my bed, reclines. "There's still TV, still us. Still poker games, where I intend to bankrupt you, by the way."

"Not a chance." I unzip my suitcase and dig for the Cubans. "I don't know about you, but I'm ready for a beer and a cigar."

He's about to answer when his phone buzzes, and he fishes it out of his pocket. "See you out on the porch for one of the cigars but not one of the beers, my ever-thoughtless friend." He points to the phone. "I've got to take this—it's Kelly." He gets off the bed and takes three long strides out of my bedroom. "Hey, Kells. What's up?"

I find the cigars in my bag and stroll out on my deck to light up.

I mentioned a drink again, in front of my friend the recovering alcoholic. I'm an ass.

It probably would serve me right now to say that I don't always *intend* to be an ass. Plenty of times I do, don't get me wrong. Getting a rise out of someone, getting them off center, it's a brilliant business tactic. God, get somebody steamed, and he shows you all of his cards. It really works. I can't tell you how many deals I've completely scored extra packages or percentage points on the back end of the movie because I got someone so off-kilter he showed his hand.

Sometimes the deal goes down in flames because of me and my ass-ish behavior, but more often than not, the way I act is to my advantage.

But there are times when I'm not deliberately a dick. I just don't think. I forget to be considerate. Is that redundant—not considering to be considerate?

One time in college, a girl broke up with me because she was a vegetarian and I ordered a pepperoni pizza. It wasn't the ordering of it that completely drove her over the edge—it was the part where I asked why she couldn't just pick the pepperonis off. This was inconsiderate, apparently.

Or the assistant who quit because I asked her to pick up a mega-pack of toilet paper when she asked what she could do on the way out to a big after-party for a client's movie premiere. It was in Malibu, and hey, she asked, and hey, the house we'd rented was brand-new and didn't have toilet paper, and I was already there, and if she wanted to be helpful but only in ways that she didn't consider "demeaning," she should have been clear about that in the phone call.

I take people literally a lot of the time, and the rest of the time I am too goddamned busy to worry if what I say to you is going to hurt your feelings or not, or if I've thought about all the ins and outs of asking a person to do something.

Yes, I will ask my assistant to go to the animal shelter to look for a client's lost cat. I will tell a stylist to stop dressing my client like a streetwalker; I don't give a shit what her "artistic sensibility" is. If I think the dailies are coming back on a movie and my star looks like he's underwater because the color wash is so blue, I will say something.

And I forget that Andy doesn't drink anymore.

I used to say "so shoot me" in regards to my bad memory/basic lack of consideration. You know, "I forgot that you just broke up with your partner of ten years when I asked if you and he wanted to come out to the after party with me. So shoot me." Then a director told me once he'd take me up on that offer (you know, to shoot me) after the film wrapped. I reflected and decided I shouldn't push the power of suggestion.

I turn over the latest in my long string of forgetful moments as I light up a cigar and survey the river in front of me.

It's quiet. The evening is warm and still, no breeze. There aren't trees along the shore line. Just scrubby sage and bushes at the water's edge.

Across the river, I spot movement. A moose picks its way down to the water. He moves slowly, in no particular hurry, it seems. I've never seen a moose in real life.

I think to take a picture and curse my luck—my phone's inside on the bed. I look left and right, but no one else is outside on the deck.

Some moments are meant just for you and your mind: no sharing, no telling. I guess this is one of them.

I breathe in deeply as the moose slips into the river, then swims across. He takes his time, head bobbing up and down in the current through the deepest part. Soon, though, he's back in shallow waters. He walks to the water's edge on our side, nibbles the leaves off a shrub for a moment, and then climbs out and lopes away, disappearing into a stand of pine trees to the right of the lodge.

"Wow." I whisper it to myself.

"I know, right?"

I jump straight up. Where did that come from? I look down off the porch. Just below me, on a path between the house and the river, the girl from the front desk stands looking up at me. She has a fishing rod in one hand and a pack of cigarillos in the other.

"Jesus! You scared the shit out of me."

"Please don't curse in front of me," she says. She cranes her neck to look up at me. Too bad she's wearing a regular t-shirt—another shirt and I'd have a glorious view of her cleavage.

I lean over the railing to get a better look at her. "What? I seem to recall you yelling some interesting things at the main lodge."

"Yeah, but not one of them was a bad word. I'm trying to quit."

"Aren't you supposed to be treating me with the guest courtesy I witnessed at the front desk? You seem awfully casual for one of the help."

She tosses her head. "When you commented on my butt you lost your guest standing. Now you're just another jack"—she leaves off. "Crud. See? You almost made me cuss."

"You're gonna be fun." I can feel my interest in her rising, so to speak. "Come up and have a drink with me."

"You don't even know my name. Besides, I'm headed down to fish." She holds the rod up as proof.

"What's your name?"

"Macy."

"Come up and have a drink with me, Macy." She's petite, but those luscious curves, they beg to be ridden. I could have some serious fun with this one.

"No can do, Mr. King. No messing with the guests. I could lose my job." She shakes her curls. I like the blonde thing. The dyed-brown tips, I don't get, but I like blondes.

"Mr. King? That's how we're playing it? Then what's your last name?"

"Summerlin. Like Summerwind, but with an L. And no D."

"Miss Macy Summerlin, I wish you'd reconsider." I smile and flash as many teeth as I can. People tell me I have a nice smile.

"Mr. King, you have a nice night. I'm walking down to the river." She turns and starts to walk that way when she stops for a second and turns around again for a minute. "And please, if you're going to say something else about my booty, wait 'til I'm out of earshot."

"Watch out for our moose friend." I tip an imaginary hat to her.

She salutes me with that bandaged hand. "Always."

I watch her walk away, I do admire that ass, and I wonder again how she sliced that hand up.

She spoke to me, so that helps. She even told me her name. She didn't seem too chapped about the comment at the front desk. Maybe I have a chance.

I'm at a disadvantage here. In LA, my reputation precedes me. My money shows women I have power, and that usually gets some play, too. I can always tell if a woman is a wannabe actress, and depending on my mood, or how quickly I'd like to get laid, a would-be starlet is an easy date. A lot of times those kind of girls are no fun, though. I can see right through them, and I don't like to be played for a fool because I may be a lot of things, but I'm definitely not anything close to a fool. I'm the smartest guy in a room. Always. I'd be done in my business if I weren't.

Anyway, some girl who thinks she can get some play with an agent by romancing him is the dumb one. It's hard not to want to hand over some sort of pre-printed statement. It'd look like this:

The man in front of you is an agent. Yes, he's a talent agent. No, he's not seeking any more clients at this time. No, not even if you give the best hummer west of the Mississippi. Still not taking you on as a client (not disinterested in the blow job, though, if you're just giving them out). No, he won't pass your headshot along to anyone else, either. No, he won't introduce you to a director, or an actor, or a manager, or another agent. If you're still interested in getting into his pants, let's discuss that hummer.

It'd save a lot of time, I'm not kidding. I could get a "Yes, I know Andy Pettigrew, and no, you can't meet him" tattoo, too, which would also save a lot of time.

But still, in LA I've got game. Here, I guess I'm just another guy with money, which, judging by the check Andy had to write to secure this private lodge for the week, is who this place caters to. Maybe something else will appeal to Macy. Maybe there's another way in.

I just need to find out what it is.

I stroll back into the house, through my room, and go to find the other guys. Andy's off the phone, done with his domestic check-in. Tucker stands over at the stove, managing two big pots.

"What's for dinner?" I didn't realize I was hungry.

Tucker lifts a spoon to reveal a noodle dangling from it. "Spaghetti. And don't give me some paleo crap. We're on vacation, and you can eat carbs. Don't be a baby."

He's usually the one worried about his intake, but he's huge, so I try to keep the Tucker criticism to a minimum. Plus, if anything bad ever goes down on the red carpet, I want his instinct to be to shield me along with Andy, not push me out in front as a target.

Andy pulls a stack of plates from the cupboard. "Where's Todd?"

"I was out on the deck of my room. Haven't seen him." If he were lost for the duration of our trip, it wouldn't bother me.

"How was the view?" Andy asks.

"You want to hear about the moose or the girl?" I consider the girl. Macy.

"A girl? Do tell." Tucker feigns interest. He's gay. He doesn't care. Andy said he thinks Tucker might even be dating someone in LA, but he doesn't pry. I want to know, and I have no problem prying, but Tucker's never brought it up, so maybe Andy doesn't really know what he's talking about.

Andy points to a chair. "That girl from the lobby?"

I nod. "Macy." I sit down.

"You got a name, huh? That's got to be a good sign." Andy joins me. "Should we start the betting pool now? I'm betting it takes you three days to bed her, and one day after that for her to hate your guts. Tucker?"

Tucker brings a large pasta bowl with the tossed spaghetti. "No bets for me. I'd be betting against Jeremy, and he hates to lose, or against some poor innocent country girl."

Todd strolls in from the other room. "Something smells good." He looks around the table and chooses the chair across from me.

"Where've you been?" Andy hands him the salad bowl.

"On the phone. Trying to get this next tour set up." He shakes his head. "But that's boring. What were you people talking about?"

I prepare to stomp on Andy's toes to keep the Macy thing from coming up, but he gets what I want without me using brute force.

"What we need to talk about is tomorrow's fishing." Andy changes the direction of the conversation, and I relax my grip on my fork.

How to woo Macy and not show my hand to double-oh-douchebag sitting across from me preoccupies me for the rest of the dinner.

After dinner, Tucker pulls out his laptop, Todd goes out front to smoke, and Andy gets on the phone in his room to FaceTime the fam. I sit on the couch and read all the different news outlets on my tablet—Variety, Hollywood Reporter, all the online entertainment websites. I usually have Esther, my assistant, do a compilation and give me a brief on what's been said about our clients the day before. If something big has happened (one of my clients drunk tweets about an ex, one of our stars slips up and makes an off-the-cuff remark about current events—it should be illegal for actors to have opinions about global politics), then I'll make calls and get a publicist on it. Most of my clients have a team. I'm usually the lead, though some of them lean more heavily on their manager. Then they'll have a publicist, a lawyer, a stylist, an accountant, and who knows what else.

But when the chips are down or it's money on the line, it's all up to me. I negotiate. I make deals. I make movies happen for my clients. Most of the time, when an actor works with me, his only job is to do his job well and try not to screw up off-camera.

Tucker chuckles.

"What?" I'm curious. Most of the time when I see him, he's all business.

"There's just a funny GIF my aunt posted. It's a kid."

I shrug. "I'm not much for babies. I don't like children much at all. Q's the exception."

"It's not a human kid, it's a baby goat." He smiles. "You wanna see it?"

I look at him for a minute without answering. He stares back at me.

When I don't respond, he nods. "Right, I forgot. You have no sense of humor." He smiles at me and goes back to his computer.

I feel a little defensive. Not a lot, because God knows I'm not really known as the jokester of the group. If I'm not taken seriously, I'm out of a job.

"I've been known to laugh at stuff."

Tucker doesn't even look up. "Uh-huh. You keep telling yourself that."

"What's it gain me if I'm Mr. Laugh Riot? Tell me that." Now I sound a little defensive.

Tucker stops and thinks about that for a minute. "A chance at happiness? A chance to make it past forty without a heart attack? I don't know."

This is quite the dig. If it were Todd saying it, I'd use it as the excuse I've been looking for to punch his lights out.

But Tucker says it, I don't know, almost gently. Like it's advice for me, or as though he might actually care about me.

And he's gigantic, so he's a person I listen to. I listen for no other reason than he is someone who can skin me alive and feed me to the bears outside the lodge. Not attending to him might cost me dearly. "Point taken. Sense of humor is helpful at times."

Tucker nods and goes about his business of baby goat videos.

I sit staring at the screen in front of me, but only just. Happiness. I'm not sure I buy into the idea of happiness.

Really. Think about it. What's supposed to happen to make me happy? I find the right woman, and we settle down? How long is it supposed to stay exactly the same way that made me happy when I first found this so-called "love of my life"? And we'd have to change, because that's what people do. So then, would we still be happy?

Or maybe I'm supposed to be a "live in the moment, YOLO, savor the experience" kind of person.

Whatever. Most of the time, the moment is so built-up, it ends up being a disappointment. I remember looking forward to my first major league baseball game. Then we got there, and there was a loud, drunk guy next to my dad and me, and he ended up getting in an argument with my dad. The guy was cursing a lot in front of me (ironic, I know) and got all bent when my dad asked him to stop. I had no moment to "live in". There was no "YOLO-ing" going on. In fact, Dad was really worried that the guy was going to follow us into the parking lot and do something rotten.

I'm sorry, but I'm not a big believer in the "here I am having a snow cone, oh look I just snapped a pic of it in the light of the sunset while I happened to be wearing a fashionable floppy hat" kind of bullshit. Those people are lying. Instagram and Tumblr are full of people who are miserable pretending to have wonderful "YOLO" lives. I'm pretty certain 90% of them live in their parents' basements and drive shitty little broken-down cars and work at the mall in retail, getting treated like the gum on the bottom of their customers' shoes.

Tucker sighs. Maybe he's happy. Maybe I'm over-thinking it.

But I'm going for content. Content means "in a state of satisfaction." I like that. I can be satisfied. A good meal satisfies me. A good lay satisfies me. Driving a nice car, living in a nice house, closing the deal, scoring the client.

I can live with content.

I can hear Andy finishing up with his FaceTime in his room upstairs. Todd comes in from the front porch, smelling of cigarettes. Tucker appears to be nodding off in front of his laptop.

This might be a moment when I am content. I don't feel the need to be anywhere else, and I don't want to scream or kick anyone's ass, and I've had a good meal. It might be a sign to call it a night before the contentedness is lost. Come to think of it, sleeping makes me content.

"Gents, I'm headed to bed."

Tucker rouses a bit. "Good night."

Todd gives me a salute. Andy passes me on the stairs, coming down to the great room as I climb to the balcony and the bedrooms.

"Jeremy, no run in the morning. We're up at first light to eat and get on the river."

I shrug. "Not sure what kind of vacation involves waking up at dawn, but okay. See you then."

I crash out in my room, marvel at the absolute quiet of the night beyond my four walls, and settle in. I'm able to keep thoughts of business at bay, and just as I'm about to drift off, I count myself as content.

MORNING GLORY

The next morning we're all up and out early. Ass-crack of dawn early. Breakfast was eggs and bacon at an ungodly hour, but I can't eat when I'm not fully conscious.

I have a piece of toast in the zippered pocket of my fishing vest. So shoot me (don't, please, we've been through this, remember?).

"Could someone turn that down a bit?" I push my Wayfarers up on the bridge of my nose with my forearm as I make my way outside.

"It's called the sun, J. It's what's behind the layers of smog in LA. Purty, ain't it?" Andy's got his hands full, too—rod in one hand, fly box in the other, and he's added a float tube to the mix, slung over his shoulder by its web straps.

"I'm assessing whether I'm a vampire or not. That's how searing the sun is right now. Jesus." It takes me two deep cleansing breaths to not scream with all this brightness assaulting me.

"You wore sunscreen, right?" Tucker's a couple strides behind me. Todd disappeared again about fifteen minutes ago, said he had a phone call.

"Yes, Mom, I wore fucking sunscreen."

"You'll be glad for the sun when we get on the river. I checked the river temp this morning. It's 54 degrees, nice and brisk." Tucker, ever the logician.

Andy comes around the house to a clear view of the river, and I'll be damned if there aren't already four white-haired guys downstream about fifty yards from us.

"Did those guys sleep in the river?" I stand next to Andy.

A sweet voice speaks up behind us. "That's not dedication, that's old guys. They go to sleep after the five o'clock buffet."

Macy. I turn around, and there she is, blonde hair with the brown tips braided into two pigtails over her shoulders, suited up with waders, a tank top underneath, rod in hand, sunglasses on. She is damn cute.

"You fishing today?" I take a step to her.

"I'm guiding today, Mr. King."

I don't follow. "What?"

"Your gracious friend engaged a guide for the day. I'm it." She points a thumb in her own direction. She's got fingerless leather gloves on, kind of like driving gloves, and her fingernails sparkle pink.

I shoot Andy a look. "Did you know?"

"I did not." He smiles and walks away, picking his way down the gravel path to the water's edge.

Todd saunters down the path from the house. He has a cigarette between his lips, a porkpie hat on. "Did I miss the big fish yet?"

Tucker brings him into the fold. "Todd Ford, this is our guide for the day." Tucker puts out a hand to Macy. "I'm Tucker."

She gingerly offers the fingertips of her right hand. "I've got stitches. Sorry. Macy."

Tucker gently shakes, and Todd worms his way in front of him, hand outstretched. "Macy. Nice to meet you. I'm Todd. Todd Ford."

"Mr. Ford, nice to meet you." She smiles at him. I'll kill him.

"And we've met." She turns to me and smiles a different smile, and now I don't care what Mr. Cheeseball's doing next to me. The smile I'm looking at—it might be brighter than the sun this morning.

Damn. "Yes, we have. A moose introduced us, I believe." I reach out to shake her hand, touch her, and she hands me a plastic box. And grins.

"Your flies for the day, Mr. King. The caddis are hatching. It's gonna be a good day of fishing."

I give her a nod and take the box from her.

We make our way down the gravelly path to the river.

"Watch your footing, gentlemen." Macy leads. I watch the back of her neck. It's smooth, with wisps of hair lit in the morning light. I'd like to trail a finger down that graceful curve.

I want her to notice me, look at me. Like me best. I go for humor. "Unlike your typical guest, we're not a hundred years old."

She turns her head, just enough to comment over her shoulder. "All the more reason not to land on your butt, then."

Todd laughs. "You just got served. That took, what, two tenths of a second?"

God, I hate his guts.

"The lady is welcome to tease. I like it." I smile.

She shakes her head. "Let's talk casting. I think it'll be a much more gratifying discussion for all of you."

Except for Andy, we're not dressed to wade, but Macy is. She strides into the water, turns to face us.

"In the next day or two we'll all fish from a drift boat on the river. It was a dry winter, so the river's down now, but they're going to release runoff from Palisades Dam tomorrow or the next day, so the South Fork flows will be too high to wade. Right now, I want your full attention on the cast, so you're on shore for the morning." She pulls the line through her fingers, gracefully turns the rod in her hand until the tip is pointing straight to the sky.

Listen, hot girls are one thing, but a good-looking woman who is gifted at something? That is pure sex. Have you ever watched a really good female bartender? That is hot. So is a pilot, or a musician, or a painter, or a glass blower, or, gee, I don't know, a fly fisherwoman.

Talent is sexy.

Macy's talking, and I'm not paying attention. "Mr. King, was it?"

"Huh?"

Todd laughs again. "Dude, are you deaf?"

"What?"

"Can you show me your basic cast? Ten to two, nice and easy. Don't even worry about where the line goes."

I straighten my shoulders. This, my friends, is why I'm always prepared. I took lessons in LA. I always know what I'm doing. Sometimes it's just barely enough to be competent, but I'm never caught looking stupid. I hate looking stupid.

I pull the line through the eyes of the rod, feel the slack in my hand, and try my best to pull back to ten o'clock and over the top to two o'clock.

To be honest, besides casting off the rooftop deck of my house, the best preparation for this moment was watching Brad Pitt and Tom Skerritt in *River Runs Through It*. I love movies so much. You can learn a lot from some careful watching.

Our guide holds her rod across her chest, watching me.

"That's not a bad start. Try not to force it. If the rhythm's right, the line will sail along with you. Don't push it too hard, or it'll pile up behind you."

Tucker nods. "Physics. I could get into this."

Of course the bodyguard is a part-time science geek. I thank my lucky stars he's gay. He'd be impossible to ever compete with. He's a kind man, the size of a mountain, a decent cook, and, apparently, into physics.

I smile at Macy as she turns her attention to Tucker's casting. I keep practicing for a minute. I've been known to kind of get a little competitive (okay, I'm rabid), but today I'd especially like to be a star pupil.

Then my mind wanders, drifting to thoughts of star students, teacher-student relationships, then Van Halen, and that one video about the hot teacher, and then—

"Mr. King? Your line's all tangled in the brush." Macy's pointing behind me. I tug at my rod, only to discover I'm hung up in the greenery behind us on the slope of the shore.

"Yeah, man, that's a big ol' mess." Todd chimes in. He adjusts his stupid little porkpie hat.

"Shut it, Charlie Chaplin." I stay still for a minute, trying to think how to calmly untangle my line.

Macy takes a few swift, hopping steps through the river, and she's beside me. She reaches into the pocket on the breast of her waders and pulls out a pocketknife.

With the hand that isn't wrapped, she flips the blade and cuts the line in one deft movement. "There you are. You know how to splice the line back together? I can show you the knot if you want."

As much as I wouldn't mind her close to me, I don't relish looking like an idiot. And yes, the fly fishing coach in LA did actually show me how to tie two pieces of line together.

"I can do it, but thanks." I set to the task.

"You need reading glasses for that, old man?" Todd chuckles.

"Andy? Can you please take your friend to the other side of the river before I drown him?"

Andy can't hear me. Mr. Movie Star, he's been on the river a lot since hooking up with Kelly. Her dad likes to fish, and since Andy and Kelly made their home base in Idaho's capital, Boise, they've been all over the state fishing it up. So he's our gifted and talented fisher today, and he's already out in the river in his waders, casting like a pro.

I watch him. He looks like he's at peace.

I remember him when I met him. Man, he's come a long way.

He was staying at a friend of his mom's. He slept on her couch, in a little cheesy condo in Venice Beach.

We met for coffee down the street from her house. He was probably hung over, but he was so charming, it didn't matter.

He's not that much younger than me, but he puts out this aura of youth and vitality and just plain charisma. The waitress was falling all over herself to take care of him. I think we were served nine thousand waters that lunch. I've never had better restaurant service than that, I swear.

I'd reached out to him. One of my friends had directed him in a shitty little ad about taco shells, I think, but Andy had said he was looking for representation, and this friend of mine had offered me up.

At first I'd been pissed, but when I met Andy, I understood. My friend, I owed him big. Huge.

I knew it when I saw Andy that first day, but man, has it proven out. He's had his ups and downs, to be sure, but he's a good guy, and a great talent, and I'm damn lucky that he's stuck with me. A lot of actors taste success and go shopping for a new team, thinking they can negotiate greener grass.

But you know what? Andy's loyal. I'm loyal. We get it. I may be a lot of things, but I'm not a backstabber. And he's never let me down, so when he's needed a sergeant-at-arms, I'm his man.

Okay, if he literally needs physical protection, that's what Tucker is for, but I've got his back in this business.

That's probably why we're unstoppable. It's rare that talent and management don't try to screw each other over eventually, but I'll never do it to Andy. I don't care if he gains a hundred pounds and has to play Dan in a *Roseanne* remake, I'll still rep him.

On a side note, he's made plenty of money, and he's not an idiot. We won't have to do the *Roseanne* thing. Trust me on that one.

Suddenly a shadow falls on my hands, I smell something sweet, and look up. Macy's right in front of me.

"You're quite the thinker this morning. I didn't peg you for the introspective type." She checks the knot I've made, mending the lines she cut, and nods in approval.

"Maybe I'm napping behind these sunglasses. Don't give me too much credit."

"Oh, I won't. Why don't you come into the water a bit?" She takes a few steps back into the current of the river and motions for me to follow. "I think you're ready to get in a little deeper."

I know I am. I want to, that's for sure. I save the double entendre for my own thoughts, since cheese doesn't seem to be the way in with this woman. I edge into the river, feeling for my footing. I'm not interested in swimming, especially since I didn't wear waders this morning.

I'm surprised by the bite of the cold. I can feel the bracing cold through my river boots and thick socks, and I feel goose bumps raise under the sweat on the back of my neck from the rays of the sun.

I shiver. "It's cold."

Macy looks at me, serious for a minute. "Doesn't matter if it's June; this river always means business." I think she says this for the whole party's sake. "The current can catch you off guard, and if you go under, you'll get real cold, real fast. Most of the time we're not in any really challenging current, but don't ever forget the river's the boss."

I smile. "I thought you might be the boss. You're the guide, after all."

She looks across the river at where she's just floated her fly, as a trout rises to take a taste of it. "I'm the guide, that's true. Why don't you just assume that I'm the one you take direction from, and we'll be just fine."

I nod. And tell my overactive imagination to stand down, 'cause suddenly I have all sorts of bedroom applications for that last statement, and I think she's standing close enough to me to see the gears turning.

She must feel the testosterone surge she's just aroused in me, because she moves downriver to Todd, who struggles to get the line to come up off the water after landing his first cast.

Andy wades over to me. "I think I might pick my way down to just above the geezers over there. Wanna come with me?" He points towards the white-haired group fishing near us.

"Sure. We could take 'em if they challenge us." I'd love to stay close to Macy, but this is Andy's fishing trip, and my first job is to hang out with my friend.

It's not deep, but the current picks up a bit, and we edge downstream.

"Now listen, don't aggravate the Golden Girls over there. We're not trying to start a turf war." Andy points to a spot in the shade, where the current lags a bit. "That's where the fish are. The current's slower; water's cooler."

"Let's go over there, then." I take a stride.

Andy puts an arm out. "Wait a sec. The old guys are fixing to move farther downstream. I don't want them to change their minds if they see us sizing up that spot." He turns his back on them and points something out upstream to me.

I keep my eye on the group. "This is an award-winning performance." Andy's right; they are sizing us up. Andy shakes his head and points more vehemently upstream to me, and they fall for the fake-out. They leave their spot to move farther away from us downstream.

Andy doesn't turn his head yet. "Are they leaving?"

"Yeah. You called it."

Andy smiles wide, pleased with himself. "To our shady spot. The trout are calling."

We edge through the shallows to the little shady hole. I hold off on casting. Andy deserves his moment, and I can guarantee that my sloppy cast will freak out any fish in a twenty-mile radius.

He works the rod and gains the momentum on the line. With a graceful flick of the wrist, he sends the line floating and drops the fly gently at the edge of the shade. The current pulls it downstream. It twirls on the surface.

"C'mon, c'mon." Andy watches, hands still.

Then the fly disappears under the surface. And there's a flash of silver.

As little as I'm invested in the fishing portion of this trip, I can't help but be impressed. "I'll be damned."

Andy gives the rod a quick, tiny jerk up, and grins. "Did I call it or did I call it? Now I just need to not lose him."

I watch him gather line in one hand and pull on the rod, then let line out through the eyes on the rod, then gather the line in again. "What are you doing?"

"This is what it looks like to actually catch a fish, my friend." He laughs, and the exuberant noise catches the attention of our guide, who wades over in our direction.

"We have a winner over here, do we?" She comes up behind us. Andy turns, a head nod in the direction of the fish, who is apparently not interested in participating in this fishing business.

"He's a fighter."

Macy looks at Andy. "Is this one for dinner or heading on its merry way when you're done with him?"

"I think he's a formidable foe—he's earned another day to swim the South Fork."

She nods. "I'll help you release him. Maybe Mr. King can snap a quick shot of you with your catch."

I pull for my dry bag around my neck. Yes, I brought my phone. Andy's right—there's no service on the river, but I'm never far from my phone. I'm an agent. It's part of me.

I have the phone out, and Andy's pulled the trout in, and now he cradles it, just out of the stream's current.

"Take the picture quick. Fish has to get back to breathing." Macy's already freed the fly and hook from the fish's mouth.

Andy grins, the trout's scales glint silver, and I get a couple good ones. "You're good."

Macy smiles. "The first of many, I'm sure."

Andy points to me. "Time for you to land one."

I shrug, look at Macy. "It's okay if I have to bide my time. I get what I want in the end."

Macy looks at me over her sunglasses. "Some guys find they wait a really, really, really long time." And then she wades away, up the stream to check on Tucker.

Andy points the trout downstream and gently lets it wriggle out of his grasp. "You're talking about trying to land her, huh?"

"Whoever said actors are dumb is so wrong."

Andy pushes me, just enough to throw me off balance, but catches me before I swim. "Watch yourself. I'm quick. And the cute guide looks to be a pretty wily fish."

"No one's more cunning than a Hollywood agent. I guarantee."

"Ha! That sounds like a 'mark my words' declaration. Tell me how that goes for you, J." He edges a little farther downstream and readjusts his rod. "I'll just be over here fishing while you make all sorts of big promises."

"You can't tease me about the 'mark my words' thing forever."

"I can as long as you're my friend." He chuckles and turns his back to me to cast again.

I chew on my lip. Yes, years ago, when the first of the *Harry Potter* movies came out, I may have said that it was a guaranteed flop. I may have said some unkind things about Chris Columbus and maybe made a few disparaging remarks about Emma Watson's hair. And yes, I may have said "mark my words" when I declared that the franchise wasn't going to make it past the first movie.

I'm mostly never wrong. Andy remembers when I am. He remembers really well for a long, long time.

We fish for most of the morning, straight through lunch, and come off the water when the day starts to really heat up. The fish don't bite when the sun is high and the day is hot.

We retire to the lodge, and I hole up in my room for a few hours to conference call with the junior agents in the office. Like I said, I don't vacation, I work from the field.

As the call is wrapping up, I step out on to the deck to stretch my legs. One of the agents is recapping a pitch meeting she attended with one of our clients. This agent will one day be great. Right now, she's still too worried about sounding smart. So she goes on. And on.

Movement in the bright sun catches my eye. I turn and shade my eyes to see what's moving near the river's edge.

It's our guide. Macy. She picks up rock after rock and skips them out into the middle of the river. All the groups are off the river—the fish hide away in the heat of the day. The old guys would more likely catch heat stroke than a fish this time of day. Plus, it's time for them to watch some judge shows on TV and nap.

She's good at it. Skipping stones, that is. She gets at least three good hops out of each rock. I don't know that I've seen anyone like her before. She certainly is different than the LA kind of girl I'm used to. Sure, she's attractive, but there's more going on than that.

I don't even notice that the agent's stopped talking until someone on the call clears his throat.

"Is that it, then?" My voice sounds deeper than normal. Inattentive or not, I'm still the alpha. I want to remind them of that. They work for me. Even when I'm watching Macy.

Someone jumps in to kowtow. "We're done, Mr. King. Have a nice evening."

I end the call without another word.

Macy picks up her rod and gear and walks down the river's edge, disappearing behind another one of the buildings of the resort.

I decide to go talk to her. Just go and find her and talk to her. Maybe it's not the best idea I've ever had, and maybe it's not the Jeremy King experience, but I'm interested in her, and there won't be many times to get to talk to her on my own. I'm always up for any kind of advantage I can win, and right now this is the only one that's presented itself.

I slip out before any of the guys notice. They'll all figure I'm still on my conference call with the office.

Outside, the heat bakes the air and shimmers off the asphalt in the parking lot. I walk around the other side of the house and scan the riverbank for Macy.

I see her, upstream, sitting under the shade of a tree. It's at the edge of the property, and I can tell this is probably her time, her way to get some space from all of us.

So I will naturally go and interrupt that.

I can't tell what she's doing. Reading? Texting? Probably not, since cell service here is shitty. I secretly hope she's not a serial texter or Snapchatter, or any of that. I'm the first to admit that I'm narcissistic and self-centered, but I also have no time to preen and pose and take endless pictures of myself. Not when there are deals to be made.

I try to approach as casually as I can, and she catches sight of me and calls out.

"Mr. King."

"If you're on your break, I don't mean to interrupt," I say, hoping to give her some choice in the matter.

She waves for me to come ahead. "You came looking for me, so you do mean to interrupt, but I don't mind the company."

I can see now what she's working on, in the cool shade of the tree. Little fluffy flies. Her lap is full of iridescent fake insects, shiny and sparkly and meant to tempt a trout into taking a hook in its mouth. She takes each one in her fingers and adds a slick brown tuft of what looks like duck feather to the tail end of it.

I point to the one in her hand. "Nice work. You tie all of your own flies?"

"Yep. It's cheaper, and the detail work quiets me down." She deftly weaves a tiny bit of feather on the fly and places it back in the plastic tackle box next to her.

"So, what is it about fishing? You really like it?"

She shakes her head and smiles, not lifting her head from her task. "Don't let anyone tell you that you're not a master conversationalist. That's the best line you've got?"

I ignore the burn and try for funny. "I was looking to find a smooth way to work in some reference to scum-sucking wiener dogs, but it just wasn't coming to me."

She does look up at me now. "Fishing is peace. I'm good at it. I figured out I was good at it when I was pretty young, and around here you don't need a fishing license until you're fourteen."

I pick up a couple rocks and skip them into the river. I get one skip on each, and then they plop to the bottom of the river. "Interesting."

She narrows her eyes. "Were you watching me skip rocks, earlier?"

"Maybe. Is that bad?"

She gets up. "Kind of stalky, but I'll allow it." She picks up the tackle box and starts to walk back toward the main lodge. "I've got to go cover the front desk."

"Maybe we can grab a drink after," I offer.

She shrugs. "Mr. King, guests come and go, but my river is always here for me, so I'm gonna leave now. If I ever lost this job, had to leave the river, it'd break my heart. I can't mess around with our clients. Sorry."

She gives a little wave with the tackle box.

She looks back once, over her shoulder, and smiles to see that I'm still watching her go.

She calls out to me. "You're still looking at me. You're gonna get a reputation. Seriously." Then she laughs. It's musical and full of joy.

I said earlier I could wait, but she is something. I don't know what it is about her that's so tantalizing, but I intend to find out.

THE RIGHT STUFF

That evening, the guys decide we're going into town.

Town is a complete overstatement. We're going to the cross-roads, not even into Driggs, and sure as hell not into Jackson. No, we're not going there, since Andy wants to lie low.

We're just, really, this does exist, just going to the intersection of two highways. *State* highways.

"BFE, ladies and gents." I say this to the group as we pile out of the Yukon. Tucker drove. The guy can't let go of his bodyguard tendencies. Todd and Andy rode in the back, and Todd spent the whole time trying to get a signal on his phone.

He's lucky I rode up front. I swear to God he's been acting like a twelve-year-old this whole trip.

As we walk through the parking lot of the Double A Supper Club, there's a huge clap of thunder. The black clouds are piled up over the Tetons.

"Big storm moving in. It'll clear before we even drive back, what do you wanna bet?" Andy sounds relentlessly chipper. Tour guide chipper.

"It's okay if it rains, Andy. We're not made of sugar." I sound less chipper.

Tucker smiles. "Speak for yourself." He straightens his Polo out over his huge form. He's smiling because he knows he's not made of sugar; he's made of tank. Or freight train.

We follow him into the supper club. These kind of places can be two things: they really are the small-town supper club. It's where the locals come to eat and meet. It's Ma and Pa and the mayor.

Or, a supper club is a cowboy bar where I'll probably get my ass kicked.

This one looks weirdly like a little of both: dining seating on the far end, a bar in front of us.

I look for the hostess. "Dinner and an ass-kicking. Convenient."

"What?" Todd looks up from his phone long enough to irritate the hell out of me.

I grit my teeth. "Engage, son. Lord, I can't believe I'm saying this, but put down the damn phone. I'm not even that bad."

Todd slips the phone into his front shirt pocket. "Yeah, you're right. Let's get a drink."

Andy points to the booths at the far end. "And dinner, we're eating dinner. Work with me here, people."

I will make this work for him, damn it. "Of course. Why else would we be here?"

"To get blinded drunk. That's what most people are here for." A voice speaks up behind me.

Macy.

I wheel around to face her. She's on her way past me, to the bar. "Is that your plan?" Please let it be her plan. Wild Macy has to be amazing Macy. I'd like to see that.

She snorts. "I come for the dumbass-watching. You, for instance."

"For a girl who's trying not to swear, you sure do it a lot."

She arches an eyebrow at my remark. "Touché, Mr. King."

The hostess has menus in hand and is summoning us to follow her. She has rotten timing.

Macy nods in the hostess's direction. "Looks like you're eating. See you later."

Damn. "I'll buy you a drink after dinner if you're still around."

A tiny smile turns up the corners of her mouth. "That would be nice. Come find me."

I follow Andy and that damn punctual hostess and Tucker and Todd to the booth that is absolutely the farthest away from the bar possible. I can't even spy on her from way the hell over here.

"You're going throw a disc out or something." Tucker elbows me. "Our river guide's here."

Andy smiles. "We saw you drooling over her up front. You should go buy her a drink."

He's giving me permission. It's like having dinner with all of my Jewish aunties and grandmas. He's always looking to set me up with someone *nice*. A *nice girl*. I appreciate his effort, but nice girls despise me, as a rule.

"I'll go find her when we're done." It's getting stifling, sitting here, but I'll be damned if I look overeager to these guys.

Todd looks for our waitress. "I need a beer."

I shoot him a look, one that hopefully shuts his trap up. Andy is surrounded by us, and all we've talked about since we've gotten here is drinking. I feel for him.

The waitress is scarcely at our table for twenty seconds before Todd speaks up again. "What's on tap?"

"Jesus, Todd." There's a bite to my voice. Maybe I will punch his lights out on this trip.

He drops his chin. "Sorry. There's just a lot going on."

Andy, ever the counselor, probes. "What's up? You want to talk?"

Todd waves a hand, dismissing the subject.

Still the waitress stands, watching us. I point to Todd. "He'll have a Coors, and so will I." It's not often I'm the polite one. The waitress nods and leaves.

Todd looks at Andy. "Sorry."

Andy waves him off. "This is the real world. Hell, this is a cowboy bar in the middle of nowhere in the real world. I'm a big boy. You're allowed to drink in front of me. Jeremy here does it all the time."

I roll my eyes. "I try not to. At least I apologize about it."

Tucker interjects. "Most of the time."

"Yeah, most of the time." I agree with the biggest man in the room. It's a good habit to have.

The hostess comes back to check on us, and I suspect it's because she's taken a shine to Tucker. He chats with her, and we're all treated to a history of her husband's livestock and his ranch and how her whole family moved to the other end of the state when her brother got a job with a huge agribusiness company in Boise.

I'm about to count the number of times she touches his gigantic forearm when the waitress comes back for our order.

We all order steak. Andy orders his, and he waffles about the sides.

"Andrew, just get the baked potato. No one orders mixed vegetables. Please." Tucker razzes Andy about the carbs.

"Raise your hand if you have to stand in front of a camera in less than two weeks." Andy holds his hand high and keeps talking. "Just me? Guess I can order the mixed vegetables since I'm the only one who'll look like a whale if I don't." He nods at the waitress.

She shrugs her shoulders, makes sure we're all taken care of, and leaves the table to go put in our order. She must really think we're all crazy. She probably can't stand out-of-towners.

Tucker looks at me. "So, where is she now?"

"Who?" I try to sound nonchalant.

I know exactly who. Macy stands with her back to me. About a minute after the waitress came to get our order, she edged back into my line of sight. I caught her looking in my direction for one millisecond, but she looked away with a toss of her head. Since then she's purposely had her back to me.

"Fine. We'll all pretend along with you that you're not staring at her." Tucker can tease me, partly because he's not invested in the girl game at all and teases all in good fun, and partly because he's a pretty good sport when I tease him about being massive.

Andy's phone buzzes. He makes a move to get up, but Tucker tugs him back into his seat. "If it's Kelly, I want to say hi."

Andy hands the phone to Tucker. "Here. You're shameless."

Tucker smiles. "Kelly Jo! How're you?"

Andy turns to me. "I think I'm jealous."

A loud pop shocks all of us out of our conversations. Tucker puts the phone down, and I can see him scan the restaurant for threats.

My eyes land on Macy at the same time his do. She steps back from the bar, hands to the front of her outfit, drenched in beer. A glass is broken at her feet, and there's a guy in a ball cap, Wranglers, and boots trying to get a hold of her by the elbow.

"Hold up." It's out of my mouth, and I'm out of my seat before I really can think, and I cross the distance to the bar.

"I don't think—" I come up behind Macy.

And catch the back of her fist straight in the mouth.

"Damn!" I reel backwards. I taste blood.

The guy Macy was about to punch, before the wind-up of her fist connected with my face, looks at the two of us and backs up about five paces. "No harm done. It's just a little beer."

I point at him. "Back off. You don't put your hands on a woman. Time to leave."

Macy turns and glares at me. "I've got this, Mr. King," she hisses through clenched teeth.

The guy in the ball cap is on his way out of the place. I hear him mutter under his breath something about an uppity bitch.

"Excuse me?" Macy steps to go after him, and I put an arm up.

"Don't take his bait." I'm careful not to touch her. I don't want another fist to the mouth. The first one stung plenty, and that was just on the backswing.

She snorts. "You should stay out of a stranger's business. I told you I had it handled."

"I guess I ended up getting the short end of the fist, didn't I?" I smile at her.

She frowns. "Not finding you funny or charming right now." She grabs her purse off the bar and looks at the ruined front of her outfit. "This is just great."

I'm working up to some pithy line when she pushes past me.

"Good night, Mr. King. See you on the river in the morning." She walks out of the bar.

I stand there, stunned, rubbing my sore lip. Tucker comes up behind me.

"I guess you got told." He puts an arm on my shoulder.

I sigh. "Not how I thought that would play out."

He points to the waitress, bringing plates of food to the table. "C'mon, you can split your lip back open on your steak."

"I think my ego took the brunt of the blow." She's a puzzle, this girl.

Tucker nods in agreement. "Tomorrow's another day, Mr. King. For now, come eat with your brothers-in-arms."

We sit and have dinner, and I chew on how all of that went sideways.

Miss Macy Summerlin, fisherwoman, bare-knuckle brawler, and tangle of a mystery.

I'm starting to think that I'd like to try to unravel her.

We enjoy a big dinner and drive back to the lodge.

As we get out, I look around. I don't know what she's driving yet, so I don't know if she's here. Does she stay here? Do the employees have a bunk house? That sure would be convenient.

The thunderstorm has cleared, as Andy predicted. The air cools around us, and Andy strolls to our lodge. I hear him take in a deep breath.

"I wish Hunter and Beau were here. They would love this." He looks up at the deepening purplish sky, fishes out his phone to take a picture. "I've got to text them—it's so purple, they'll love it."

I look at him for a minute. I've never had that. Never. Never since maybe I was a kid—I remember missing my mom like crazy when I was at sleep away camp. But since then? I can't say there's been some-one I miss like that.

He looks at me. "You're staring at me because?"

I shake myself out of it. "I was just waiting for the next poetic thing out of your mouth. I might start taking notes."

He tilts his head, grins a little. "One day, J. The love thing, it'll catch you."

"Yeah, but the mushiness for the kids even? I don't know."

He catches me on the shoulder with a playful cuff. "I'll give you that. I don't know about you and small people. There's a reason Kelly doesn't like you to babysit Quincy."

I smile, happy to have moved on from the subject. "Q loves me. She's the exception to my rule."

We come through the front door.

Tucker's already clearing the centerpiece off of the dining table. "It's time for me to clean all of you out, gentlemen. Hope you brought your wallets!"

I crack my knuckles and clear my throat. This is an arena I do know a lot about—money. "Ante up, friends—Tucker's gonna lose his sizable wallet and his sizable shirt."

Todd even sits at the table, and I take the opportunity to snatch up his cell.

Todd throws his hands up in protest. "What the hell, Jeremy?"

"We're entering into the bro zone, and it's cell free. Whatever LA 'I'm-with-the-band' bullshit has got you distracted, leave it out of our evening of poker." I pull my cell phone out as a peace offering. "If I can set mine over on the top of the fridge, then you damn well can too."

I put both phones up on the fridge and come back to the table.

Tucker raises an eyebrow as he deals. "Bro zone's a little cheesy, Jeremy. You're not our camp counselor."

Andy laughs, and Todd does, too, even though he shoots me a pissed-off look.

I have to smile. "We're here to have fun, and I'm goal-oriented, damn it."

Tucker nods. "You heard the man. Time to ante up."

EVERY WHICH WAY BUT LOOSE

The morning light streams in through my windows, and I can see it even through my eyelids. Mornings here are so damn persistent.

I drag myself into the shower.

I'm not going to lie, I spend a minute contemplating being, you know, in the shower, and thinking about Macy. But then the water goes cold. Empty-water-heater cold.

"Jesus!" I can't help but yell—I'm mid-lather, and I'm going to have to suck it up and rinse off in the icy stream before I can retreat.

I manage to get clean at least, but I'm shivering when I get out.

Andy knocks on my bedroom door. "Did I hear a cry for help?"

I pull on my jeans and open the door. "Which asshat used up all the hot water?"

Andy purses his lips. I can tell he doesn't want to answer. "Four guys should be fine all taking showers. I don't know why you'd run out of hot water. I can say something to the manager."

"You didn't answer my question, which means it was Todd. I swear to God."

Andy shakes his head. "Listen, can you give the blatant loathing a rest? I know you're not a big fan of his, but can the whole trip not be about you versus him?"

I take a deep breath, pull a long sleeve shirt over my head. Andy doesn't ask much of me, he really doesn't. And he truly is the nice guy. He does care about his friends, and he wants all of us happy. All at the same time. I decide to hold my tongue about my real beef with Todd. I should let go of it, anyway, and I don't like reminding Andy about his tough days leading up to rehab.

I nod. "Fine. I'll stop being a dick. He just, I don't know Andy, he's just always rubbed me the wrong way."

"You don't say? I couldn't tell. You two, you're just different kind of people. But you're both my friends. I appreciate it, J." He checks his phone. "Tucker's making breakfast. We have time to eat something. Then you can spend the day wooing the fishing guide."

"Macy." I feel my mood lifting, just saying her name.

Andy points at my face. "The lip seems to be none the worse for wear."

I smile. "I'm a fast healer. That was quite the scene at the Double A."

"I don't think she's one to be trifled with." Andy gets his serious face on, looks me in the eyes. "Proceed with caution."

"Are you worried I'm going to be left broken-hearted?"

"I was thinking more along the lines of broken-nosed, but sure, that'll do."

I nod. "I've dealt with some tigresses before, you know." I point at the coat hook behind him. "Hand me my fleece."

He pulls it off the hook and tosses it to me. "You almost dated Amanda Walters. You have no sense about you." He shakes his head. "But I don't know, J. This girl, she's not from where we're from, you know?"

"Where is that exactly?"

"You know, middle-class, suburban, white-bread world. I'm a pretty good judge of people, and I think she's used to a tougher life than we are."

I can feel my jaw tighten a little. "You're calling me soft?"

"I'm calling both of us coddled. I just know from experience that some people see us, and they can smell the privilege coming off of our candy-assed hides, and it just—"

He leaves off. I know where he was going with this. "People resent that we've had a good turn of it. But we both worked damn hard, really damn hard."

"With some people it's not resentment, it's a swindle. Getting something from someone who's got more than you do."

"Wow. That's a lot to assume about someone you've traded maybe six words with."

"I know. I'm probably full of shit."

I smile and clap a hand on his shoulder. "You read people well, though. I'll keep it in mind. Macy could potentially be jealous or want to con me, and she's a woman who smells really good—"

"And has a nice ass, don't forget you said that about her."

"Yes, yes, I did. In her presence, no less."

"Let's go eat. And then you can stand next to her and sniff her all day."

We make our way down to breakfast. I wonder about Andy's intuition. Macy's tough, that's a fact. But the other stuff? Is she from some wrong-side-of-the-tracks situation? Maybe she's just a country girl. Andy is right, though, where she's from is definitely not where I'm from. Moose never swam around my neighborhood where I grew up.

I grew up in Cherry Hill, New Jersey, the son of a salesman for a sporting goods company and a bookkeeper. My dad is Jewish; my mom is a lapsed Catholic. I'm an only child. School was fine. I was really short until about the end of 9th grade, which wasn't great, but most of the time, I just floated along, kind of a middle-of-the-road, forgettable kid. I got middle-of-the-road grades. We weren't rich, but we weren't struggling, either. I played soccer, had a brief stint in Boy Scouts. Nothing memorable to report about that. I worked for what I wanted—I was so proud of my first car in high school, an old piece-of-crap Buick Skylark. When I went off to college, my parents helped to pay for school. My dad and mom got along fine, and I think they raised me pretty well. I was just like everybody else.

In my sophomore year of college, my dad got laid off. He and my mom sat me down, told me I'd have to take out more student loans. The look on my dad's face killed me. Killed me. He'd worked for those pricks for twenty-five years, and the best they could do was give him three months of severance when they "right-sized"? That's bullshit. That's when I decided I wasn't going to just sit back and be average. Average, good guys like my dad? He got screwed, royally. So I decided to chart a different course. Enough of being normal, middle-of-the-road, forgettable. Jeremy King was going to be a name no one would forget. I took a look around and asked myself what I wanted. And I decided I wanted it all.

When a young man's interested in conquering the world, Hollywood makes a lot of sense. I wanted to be noticed, respected, maybe even envied. Who said "attention must be paid"? Willy Loman in *Death of a Salesman*, I think? That's me, people. Except I'm not going to wrap my car around a tree as a forgotten, chewed-up, and spit-out husk of a man. Maybe I'll wrap my Tesla around a tree trunk, but at least it'll be on the PCH going a hundred miles an hour with my hair on fire. More James Dean than Willy Loman.

After breakfast we get to the river, and to say that things have changed overnight is an understatement.

"What in the hell?" Todd says this as soon as we round the corner of the house and face the river. He must've gotten the memo, because he stands on the opposite side of Tucker and Andy from me, avoiding my wrath and irritation.

"Flows are up." Tucker states it flatly.

The river is swollen, muddy, and running fast. Where we stood in the riffles and fished yesterday is under water.

"We're pushing 20,000 c.f.s. This is no kiddie pond, gentlemen." Macy isn't wearing waders today. She approaches us with several rods in hand.

Todd takes a step toward her, offers to carry the gear. I hate him. "C.f.s?"

She hands him one rod. "Cubic feet per second. I told you Palisades Dam was going to do a release. Pretty high water."

Andy takes the rest of the gear from her. "So drift boats today? Where do we put in?"

I'm not crazy about boats. "Boats?"

"Since there are four of you, we'll go two and two. Evan will man one, and I'll handle the second. You'll like it—it's an easier day, and we'll get more strikes, maybe even land more trout." A worried look flits across her face for a second. Maybe she thinks one of us is going to make a stink.

No way in hell am I going to be her pain-in-the-ass customer. "Sounds like it'll be epic."

Her face relaxes a bit. "It's safer, too. Evan's with the van—we'll put in upstream a couple miles."

We follow her to the van in the parking lot, and I fall back to Andy.

He looks at me, smiles. "We'll get you in that boat with her. I give you my word as a man."

"Just saying that proves you're an actor. Pretty sure that's the weakest promise I've ever heard."

"Pretty sure I said that in *Redcoats Rising*. Damn, I loved that script. The speech-making, the battles—"

"The scenery-chewing." I smile and size up Tucker and Todd. Tucker'll get it, and I won't even have to say anything to him. Todd? He's a dumb ass, and if he gets wind of what I want, he'll be sure the opposite happens. "Play it cool, Andy. I don't want her to think I'm desperate to be in her boat."

"I thought you were desperate to be in something else of hers." He laughs. "Ha! I'm good."

"No, you're not." I leave his side and take a couple casual strides to put myself directly behind Macy as she approaches the van.

She turns to see me and smiles. It seems like she's pleased to see me. I hope she's pleased to have me with her, in close proximity, for the entire day. I'm salivating at the thought.

"You're in my boat today, Mr. King," she says.

Damn, that was easy. I nod and go to introduce myself to Evan, the other guide. I can be friendly now that I know I don't have to hang out with him for the day.

"And you, too, Mr. Ford," Macy says.

Todd smiles. "Excellent."

Seriously? Is he going to try to edge in on Macy? Maybe he needs more than a good punch in the mouth. Flows are high—maybe a nice, hearty shove overboard would do the trick.

We all climb in the van and set out on the road, headed upstream.

Evan the other guy (seriously, my investment in him will not go much farther than this) explains that he and Macy will be the oarsmen on each of the boats. Our jobs are to not fall out of the boats and not put a fish hook into anybody on a cast.

I pay attention. I want to just watch the back of Macy's neck and think about nibbling it, but I want to look competent more than I want to fantasize right now.

Since college, I've worked hard to earn my place as an alpha, and I'll be damned if I'm not the alpha in that drift boat with Macy. Todd's sensitive musician thing might draw some women in, but I'll wager that if Macy's had it tough, she likes a man who knows who he is. Someone self-assured. Evan the other guy might tell me something useful, and I want to be useful.

Soon enough we pull into a dusty turn-out from the highway and park. The river rushes by us, high and angry-looking. The sun is hot in the bright blue sky. The guides are out of the van quickly, leaving us civilians to unload at a more leisurely pace.

Andy gives me an elbow. "You almost look like you're enjoying the day."

Tucker joins in. "This is the color the sky is supposed to be, Jeremy. Crazy, huh?"

"I don't know why everyone seems to think I've never left LA. I travel. I've been to the Maldives, let me remind you. I'm not an idiot."

Macy's down by the river. She waves the group over to the shore. "Time to put in. Mr. Pettigrew and Mr. Caldwell, you're first."

Evan and drift boat number one wait at the river's edge. Tucker and Andy spring into the boat and push off into the current. They make everything look easy. Damn them.

Todd looks at me, and I ignore him. I'm going to ghost him as much as I can. I exist; he does not. This is the plan for the day in the boat. I walk over to Macy. "Where'd the boats come from?"

Macy shakes her head. "They appeared on the river at your summoning, Mr. King."

"That's quite the salty tongue, Miss Summerlin." I consider giving her a nudge, but she's not really given me the "touch me" signal, and the last time I got too close, I got a split lip, so I keep my distance.

She looks like she's reconsidered the sass. "Kevin and Kramer came up with the trailers earlier. As soon as we got up this morning, I knew we were on the boats today."

"Kevin and Kramer?" I think about the river guide crew. I haven't sized all of them up. Is one of them a boyfriend?

She points to a truck and trailer rig, and I notice two guys sitting on the tail gate, killing time until we leave, apparently. With my eyes on Macy, I've been missing lots of other details of my surroundings.

I give them a little nod. One of them has a ridiculous beard and the other is freckly and beanpole-thin. I don't peg either them as competition. I'm not contending with them for Macy, I wager.

"Ladies first?" Todd offers Macy a hand.

"Guests in the boat first, but thanks." Macy holds the prow of the boat, steadying it against the insistent river current.

Todd shrugs and climbs in. He's not as agile as Andy and Tucker, but he manages.

I follow quickly and size up the seating arrangements. Macy'll be in between the two of us. I take the seat at the stern. I'd rather not have Todd behind me. I'll have a better handle on the situation, and maybe Macy won't be able to see me as well, but I can watch her.

She proves me wrong quickly. As she pushes the boat into the river and climbs aboard, she takes her position at the oars. She faces me and smiles, digs into the current and pulls the boat into the middle of the river with a nice backstroke. "Mr. King."

I watch her face, and the muscles in her shoulders under her t-shirt as she pulls the boat along under her power. "Nice view."

She actually ducks her head a bit. I like that. I think I made her shy, just for a split second.

Then she's back to business. "We're going to ride out the current for just a bit, but around this bend, the river opens up wide and it'll slow quite a bit. Then we'll do some side drifting and you all can get down to catching fish."

She points to her dry bag. "Mr. King, if you'd be so good as to dig in there for the fly boxes for today."

I do as I'm told and pull two boxes out. I hand one to her.

She nods. "You gents will be using wet flies today. Nymphs."

As much as I've tried to ignore Todd, there he is in the front of the boat, and damn it if he doesn't speak up. "Why wet?" Macy hands him the other box of flies. He still hasn't caught the clue about his invisibility, I guess.

She turns a bit, speaks to him over her shoulder as she continues to pull us through the current. "Sunken flies in high water. That's what the trout want today."

I pop open mine and work to be the first one ready to cast when we clear the bend.

Soon enough, the current slows, just like Macy said it would. We come to a wide, brown belt of water, and Macy's insistent rowing slows, narrowed to small, sculling movements that turn the boat and keep us in essentially one place.

I'm eager. I don't really care about the fishing. I do care about winning. "Are we all systems go?"

Macy sweeps a hand over the expanse of river in front of us. "It's all yours. Make sure you're steady on your feet and have at it."

I'm up and get the first cast out. My overhead cast sucks, really, but I don't put a hook in the ear of the guide I'm trying to impress, and my fly lands on the water and sinks just so.

"That was nice." Macy keeps scanning the river, upstream and down, adjusting our position with her work on the oars. I feel guilty. She's working. Really hard. Just so some rich jackass like me can be amused.

But then, *then*, she smiles. She closes her eyes and lifts her chin, lets the sun illuminate her smile, her cheekbones, play in the loose tendrils of hair around her ball cap.

And Todd calls out. "Hey! It's a strike! A fish, a fish!"

Damn him.

Macy pops to attention, swivels her chin to the prow of the boat. "You got him? Is he still on the line?"

In response to her question, Todd's rod bows under the weight of the sizable fish who'd rather not be hooked. "It's pulling hard!"

She maneuvers to give him the broad side of the boat. "Let him run, don't fight him now."

Todd lets the line run out through the guides of the rod.

"Okay, pull him in a bit, pull your rod to the side just a bit."

I watch her shoulders as she rows, steady and sure, keeping Todd and the trout in line with one another. I feel a sharp stab of jealousy.

"Mr. King, I think we're just about ready for the net." She tosses her head in the direction of the landing net stowed near Todd's spot.

I set my rod in its place and step carefully to Macy. She relaxes, lets the oars loose, and waves me by her. "After you."

I slip by her, close enough to brush her. I swear I feel sparks.

I can see the trout's spine arch in the sunlight, twisting and writhing against the hook set in its jaw. I reach for the net and come to the side of the boat, in between Todd and Macy.

"When the fish's within reach, gently net it. Then I'll help to get it in the boat."

Todd's still working line through his fingers and reel. "I'm ready for a little back up. This is exhausting."

I lean over and sweep the net low, catching the fighting fish.

Macy's right there, and I can smell her, feel her at my side. "That's right, just a big scoop. The net won't hurt him."

I lean back and the net and fish come up and into the boat much faster than I expect. I'm off balance, and put a hand out, looking for something to brace against. It's Todd, and he's not prepared to be the brace. So, instead of having something to right myself against, I've given my fishing mate a nice hearty shove.

Net, fish, Todd, fly rod, and almost me, all go loose in the bottom of the boat.

"Hey! Watch out, man! Jesus!" He's ass over tea kettle, and the fish leaps around the boat.

Macy scoops the net and fish up and gets all of it over the side of the boat in a swift, graceful motion. "Nothing to worry about. The fish can still pose pretty for its close-up."

But Todd and I aren't paying attention to the catch anymore. Todd's up off the bottom of the boat. "Dude. Next time you want to push me overboard give me a little notice."

Now I'm pissed. If I fumble something, give me room to save face. Don't call me out. I stand tall and take advantage of the maybe half inch I have over him. "If I wanted you overboard, you'd be overboard. I don't need your snarky bullshit." I lean into his face, gritting my teeth. I can feel the hot flush of embarrassment on my cheeks.

He backs down immediately, shuffles back a step. "God, Jeremy! It's not a pissing match. I know you didn't mean it."

Macy turns to us and stands up. "The fish is gone. Accidents happen, Mr. King. Sit down!"

I look at her face and immediately realize my mistake. Macy clearly does not appreciate my temper.

I curse under my breath and sit back at the stern. This is a royal fuck-up. She pointedly turns her position and rows with her back to me.

Todd knows me well enough to not poke an embarrassed and pissed-off bear. We spend a good two hours fishing in silence. And thank God neither Todd nor I land another trout so we can stay in the corners we've been put in by Macy.

It's painful. I want to apologize. I really do.

Listen, looking stupid in front of other people, I know I don't do it well. Call it my Achilles' heel.

The sun gets really hot, and the fish go to the deep, cool bottom, uninterested in taking any of our flies, sunken or not. We drift on the current, casting in silence. I can make out Andy and Tucker's boat ahead of us. Thankfully I don't think they were anywhere near us when we just about capsized. I can see the lodge and breathe a little easier. The sooner I can escape to my room and pretend like nothing happened, the better.

Macy edges the drift boat gracefully to the take out, where Kevin and Kramer stand in wait.

The beanpole speaks first. "How was it?"

Todd's out of the boat and out of my reach when he answers. "Clumsy?" He looks at me, teasing.

I could let it go. I could laugh it off.

Unfortunately, I'm Jeremy King. Tucker may have been right. I don't find much funny. "Fuck off, Todd." I sit back and let him get up the bank before I climb on to shore.

Kevin and Kramer wrangle the boat as I take the rods out of the boat and make my way up to the lodge. I ignore Todd and drop the rods with the other gear that the guides have collected from the boats.

It's not one of my finest moments.

"Mr. King? Can I talk to you for a minute?" It's Macy. She's behind me, but I don't turn around.

My wish here is that I can just escape to my room and cool off and hope that everyone else forgets that I was an ass. I keep walking.

She doesn't call my name again.

I make my way around our house and get up the steps. As I cross the threshold, I notice that Macy and Todd have come around to the front of the lodge, too. He walks close to her, elbows almost touching.

No way he's going to make a move on her now. No way.

They talk for a moment, out of my earshot. Then he gives her a wave and strolls off to the main building. He looks pleased with himself.

Macy turns on her heels.

I should let her go.

I don't.

"Hey!" I step out on our front porch.

She looks at me, comes to the bottom of the steps. "What?"

"Just 'what'? Is that the way you talk to the guests?" As soon as I say it, I know it sounds horrible. God, I'm an ass.

Her lips are pressed tightly together, and I suppose if I were a more thoughtful or observant man, I'd notice that people do this when they're trying not to scream at me. "Mr. King, I'll treat you like a guest when you behave like one."

"I was going to apologize to you. I'm sorry. I was embarrassed. I do stupid things sometimes. I wanted to impress you. I didn't like looking bad in front of you."

Now I've done it. She climbs the steps, and I'm pretty sure I can see the steam coming from her ears. When she's eye to eye with me, she speaks to me again. It's in a deathly quiet voice. That's a bad sign with women. "Oh, do not put this on me. You totally and completely own that dick behavior. Don't say you were acting that way to 'impress me.' That's not my fault at all. No, no, no. Nuh-uh." She shakes her head so vigorously, I wait for her neck to seize up.

"Nuh-uh? Are you two? A toddler?"

She grits her teeth. "Let me put this more plainly. No. Heck no. Naw. No way."

"Fine, you can stop now. I get the point."

Now she puts a hand up, as though she's considering pushing me, thinking about giving me a hearty shove, maybe. "No one—" she takes a breath, and I think she's trying to calm herself— "no one tells me to shut up." She turns around and takes five steps down the stairs. Then stops and turns back to me, and all of a sudden she's up in my face, so close I can feel her breath and almost taste the peppermint Chapstick on those plush lips of hers.

I try to hold my ground. "I didn't say 'shut up,' I said 'stop.'" Now I'm the one who sounds like a toddler.

"You. I swear, you—" She can't get the words out.

"You have something else to say to me?" I've never gotten in a fight with a girl, but that's almost what this feels like. Either we're going to throw down or have really intense sex.

I'm not dumb. She wants to kick my ass.

She narrows her eyes to slits. "Self-deprecating."

I take a step back. "What?"

"That's what sucks the most about you. You wouldn't even begin to know what that word means." She kicks at the doorjamb. "God! Why, why do some men have absolutely no sense of humor when it comes to themselves?"

I stuff my hands into my jeans pockets in the hopes that I look less arrogant, or stupid, or whatever it is that's pissing her off so badly. It's time to suck it up. "Now what are we talking about?"

"You have no sense of humor about you. I bet you've gotten in fights over shirts."

I have. A pink shirt I wore in college. Actually it had pink under the white collar; the body of the shirt was poplin blue. It was a Brooks Brothers, one of the first really nice pieces of clothes I ever could afford on my own. Some douche at a soccer house party said it was a Ken doll costume, and I chipped his tooth in reply. "So?"

"I want a guy who can laugh at himself. I do not want some guy hopped up on testosterone who's worried about being the biggest, baddest guy in the room. I'm so sick of alpha males I could spit."

"So you want a sensitive guy. Until you want someone to tear off your clothes and be an animal in bed; fight for your honor. You're so predictable."

She spits. Seriously, she's so mad she's spitting. "I call your bullshit. Men like you build up tons of walls because you're terrified. Well, I hope you drown and rot. Leave me alone."

She turns around this time for real and charges off.

I stand at the top of the stairs and watch her for a moment.

That went well.

I walk around the house for a minute and reflect.

I've cooled off, and what's left after the anger is me hoping I can do some damage control.

Andy, Tucker and Todd come back to our lodge twenty minutes later. It's obvious they all were briefed on my outburst. On the occasional times when I've lost my temper, Andy usually gives me time to cool down and then comes and lets me know what a douche I've been. Then he gives me a chance to apologize, and we're good.

In this case, I feel the need to up the apology, so I'm cooking dinner when they get back.

A peace offering. I'm a good cook, and I was stupid, and hopefully this will fix it with them.

Andy strolls in first, with Tucker as back up. "Something smells good."

I hand each of them a piece of warm bread. "Dinner's a little early, but I thought we might have a chance to fish when it cools off. From the bank, not a boat, but you know."

Todd walks in, avoids eye contact with me.

"Hey, man." I wave him over to the table. "I was a dick. I'm sorry. Come eat."

He nods. "No worries."

Tucker smiles. "Jeremy's learning. Just the other day we talked about how to laugh at yourself. Or laugh, in general."

I give Tucker a nod. "I'm working on it." I set the bread basket on the table, and Todd helps himself to another piece.

"I get it, though," he says.

"What?"

"She's someone you want to impress. I get that." Todd looks at Andy, not me, maybe worried that the eye contact will provoke me.

I sigh. "She hates me. She'd like me to drown and rot. And before you exchange money on the bets, yes, this may be the speed record for a girl threatening my life."

Tucker smiles. "There's a little humor at your own expense. That's good growth, Jeremy."

Andy pulls out a five-dollar bill. "Who do I owe?"

"Andy? Really?" I sound hurt. It might be a little true.

He shrugs. "I was rooting for you, really I was."

We eat dinner together. My stomach settles, knowing that at least the boys have forgiven me. Macy, she's another matter altogether.

DOUBLE JEOPARDY

The next day we're in the drift boats again, and it's a surprise to no one that I'm in Evan the other guy's boat with Andy. I feel stupid, and I hope at some point Macy will at least look in my direction so I can try to apologize again.

"Maybe you should make a sign. You know, you could hold it up when she faces our boat. It could say something like, 'I'm a douche, but I'm a lovable douche.'" Andy enjoys it when I royally screw things up. I tend to be the one in control, so when a situation goes sideways on me, he likes to be sure I'm aware of it.

"I just want to apologize. I get it that I behaved badly."

"Douche-y. Or like an ass. Ass-ish? Is that a word?"

Evan the other guy has yet to say a word during this entire exchange. He sculls the oars, turns the boat in neat little circles while Andy casts. I'm taking a time out on the casting so that Andy actually has a chance to catch something. My fishing today is so bad, I'm pretty sure the trout two states away are spooked.

Evan chooses now to speak up. "Ass-like. I think that's the word."

"Thanks, Evan, for chiming in."

He nods, continues to row. "Happy to help."

I reconsider Evan the other guy for a second. "You know, you might actually be able to help. You know Macy, right?"

His face doesn't change. I can't see his eyes behind his sunglasses, so I can't read his expression at all. "I know Macy. I work with her, as you may have noticed."

I think Andy might be stifling a laughing fit, but his back is to me, so I press on with Evan the other guy. "Tell me everything you know about Macy."

"Because why?"

"Because you will get the best tip from a guest who didn't even fish if you do. And because I'm trying to find a way to apologize to her."

He raises his chin a little, like he's trying to defy me or something. He doesn't know that Jeremy King is tenacious. You can't defy someone as relentless as me. "I'll tell you the little that I know about her, but only because you want to say sorry."

Andy chimes in. "J does have redeemable qualities. You're helping someone rehabilitate himself. Think of it as charity work."

"You're not helping, Andy." I consider giving up and just lying in the bottom of the boat to nap.

"She's really good at what she does. She's a way better fisherman, or fisherwoman, then I'll ever be. She can cast anywhere in any kind of conditions."

I urge him on. "Keep going."

Evan thinks a little. "She loves her dogs. And she's from around here. A lot of us come from other places, just for the summer. Macy grew up around here."

"Keep going."

He shrugs. "That's about it. Oh, her favorite place to fish besides here is Henry's Fork. It's considered one of the best trout streams anywhere. Not just Idaho."

I feel a migraine coming on. "I appreciate all the intel on her fishing habits, but what about boyfriends, favorite music, kind of coffee she drinks?"

"Macy talks about fishing, she talks about her dogs a little. That's all." Evan the other guy points out to the horizon. "We probably need to get off the river before too long. Looks like we might be in for an afternoon thunderstorm."

I reconsider his tip. Evan the other guy sucks.

Soon enough we're out of our boat, and I have a chance to at least come within a few feet of Macy. Both boats are beached as our guides decide if the storm is going to amount to enough to put us off the water for the rest of the day.

Todd and Tucker are sitting in the shade of a cottonwood tree. Andy chats with Evan about his roll cast. Evan loves him already, and I want to tell Andy he can stop being so perfectly friendly and likable.

Macy has made a point of working on some project with one of the rods as far away from the rest of us as possible.

I edge over to her. I feel a little like I'm sneaking up on an unsuspecting snow leopard or something.

"Hey." I stand close enough to her to be heard but not hit.

"Yes, Mr. King?" She doesn't lift her head to look at me. She's tying on leader to the line on one of the rods. I watch her deft fingers with the line for a minute.

"Sorry again. Hope there's a way I can make it up to you at some point."

"Start by saying, 'I'm sorry I was an ass and tried to pin it on you.' I'd like to hear that out of your mouth."

I don't hesitate. "I was an ass, and I'm sorry I tried to pin any of that behavior on you. I would very much like to find a way into your good graces so let me know what else I can do."

She smiles. "What about, 'Alpha douches are way over-rated.' Say that." She still isn't really looking at me, but I can see she's watching for my reaction in her peripheral.

"Alpha males are big, huge, over-compensating douches who probably need a good ass-kicking."

She laughs. She looks up at me and smiles for a second, and then her gaze goes stony again. "That'll do for now. I'm considering whether to speak to you ever again in the future."

"Sounds fair. Keep me posted."

"Will do. Now go away." She bows her head to her task again, but I can see a smile on her face.

This is progress? I think it's progress.

The rest of the afternoon is boring. I'm stuck in Evan the other guy's boat. He asks Andy a million questions about famous people. Andy is so patient I consider pushing Evan in the river to spare him the never-ending barrage of "what about her? Have you ever met her?" questions.

"What about Selena Gomez? What's she like?" Evan's more animated than he's been the whole day on the river.

Andy smiles. "She's cute. Way young, but cute. Pretty nice, too."

I cough. "When have you ever met her? You're full of shit."

Andy points an elbow at me, as he's too invested in his last cast to mess it up by releasing his rod. "You don't go to every event with me. She was at the last Red Nose Day thing."

"Fine. You're way too old to get with her, regardless."

Evan sits in awe.

Andy frowns. "I'm way too happily married with children. It is possible for a guy to have a conversation with a girl and not be trying to nail her, J. For crying out loud."

I feel bad for a second. I know Andy's way too smitten with Kelly to even look at another woman. Now I worry that our dumbass guide will get the wrong idea and say something stupid to someone in town. "I know, you're all Kelly all the time. I may have been jealous for a second. Or distracted by the idea of Selena Gomez in the flesh."

Evan nods. "That one video where she has that black wig on? Damn, son." He sighs, picturing it in his head. "It's so cool you've met all these people."

Andy shrugs. "People are people. Except Jack Nicholson. He is a walking and talking legend. Seriously."

I cut in before Evan goes off again. "What's tomorrow's fishing look like?"

Evan squints. "Flows will be lower. We'll probably be able to wade or use float tubes. Maybe fish from the bank."

I brighten. Maybe I'll be un-grounded and back in closer proximity to Macy. "All the group together again, then, huh?"

Andy knows why I care. "If you're off double secret probation."

"She spoke to me. She even smiled for a second. I'm close."

Evan butts in. I'm thinking Todd Ford has a competitor for "most irritable fishing companion" in the form of this dude. He shakes his head. "You know Macy's never gone out with a guest. Like never. And she especially hates rich dudes from California."

"Thank you Evan, your input is always appreciated." I give him a glare that I wish could melt the flesh off of his bones.

He puts his hands up, lets the oars go loose for a moment. "Just sayin', man."

"Tip, Evan—just think about your tip and stay quiet." I point at the bank and the fishing lodge. "And get us back to our home away from home so I can have a shower, a nice meal, and possibly a beer."

Andy laughs at me the rest of the way.

Later that evening, I've accomplished the shower, and the meal (Tucker's really a great cook, in all seriousness), and I check in with the rest of the guys.

"I'm thinking a cigar, a beer, and maybe put a line in and see if anything's biting." I pitch this to Todd, Tucker, and Andy, all of whom are crashed in the living room after dinner.

"You go on. I need to call Kelly. I'm missing my family. And my woman." Andy stretches and heads toward his room.

Tucker waves me on. "I got too much sun. I think if I had a beer right now I'd fall asleep standing up."

Now I don't want Todd to say yes, because the thought of the two of us trying to hang out alone together is painful. He must pick up on the vibe or feel the same way. "Jeremy, I'm hanging it up for the night. I've got to see if I can get a hold of a couple people in LA before it's too late anyway." He salutes me with his ever-present phone.

With no one taking me up on my offer to fish, I decide to take a walk outside to check out the water, see if the flows are down at all for tomorrow. I'd like an opportunity to be closer to Macy in the morning. I take my fishing rod in case the mood strikes. Maybe Andy will have sucked me completely into another one of his hobbies by the end of this trip.

I slip out the front door and make my way to the back of our lodge on the gravel path. The moon comes up over the foothills to the north east. In the distance the Tetons are tinged with pink and the sky is midnight blue, like the Crayola color. I swallow hard. In LA the moon is usually brownish from the smog.

Here the moon's bathed in a pearly haze. It's wider than I've ever seen, and quivers as it rises from the green gray hills. This place is coming damn close to taking my breath away.

"Beautiful."

"You talk to yourself a lot. Isn't that a sign of crazy?"

Macy's standing next to me all of a sudden.

"Jesus Christ. Where'd you come from?"

"I materialized out of thin air. Don't be a dumb ass. I came down from the main lodge."

She seems a lot less likely to punch me than the last time I saw her. "Watch the mouth."

She squinches her nose. "Dang. What is it about you that makes me want to cuss a blue streak? Oh, that's right. You're a pain." She lights up a long thin cigarillo. "Want one? I'm going down to the river bank. The big browns like to rise on a full moon evening. You're sure to score."

I want to score with her, and I don't want it to be catching a fucking trout. "I'll come with you. And I'm sorry again, by the way."

She side-eyes me. "Yes? For what, again?"

"Everything? My toddler temper-tantrum? My general demeanor? Existence as a hopped-up testosterone-addled stereotype?"

She shrugs. "Fine. I've already decided you're on probation."

I think I'm wearing her down. She's just invited me to fish with her. Not long ago she wanted me drowned and decomposing.

This is a huge improvement. Maybe I'll score yet.

Down at the river, we cast out and let the lines float slowly down the current. She pulls hers first with a deft flick of her wrist, waits for me to pull mine before she flicks the rod in the most graceful ten-to-two cast I've ever seen.

I'm not an expert fly-fisherman, but I know when I see an expert. Macy's gifted. For a split second, I might even be jealous. I know how to do things. I'm Jeremy King. I'm good at everything. That's my image, and I want to keep it that way. I'm doing a rotten job of it this week, but a man has to cling to some shred of dignity. "You're an amazing fisherman. We're lucky to have you as our guide."

She smiles. "Thanks."

I cast again. I stand a little behind her and to the left, watching the line of her neck. "How long are we going to do this?"

"We just put our lines in. Please don't tell me you're one of those idiots who expects a trout to strike a line in the first twenty minutes. There's a kiddie pond in West Yellowstone if you want to go do that."

"I was just wondering how long we were going to pretend like we annoyed each other before we started sleeping together."

She laughs. Like, a loud, head tilted back, open-mouthed guffaw. "Your mistake there is you think I'm pretending." She smiles a bit and shakes her head. "You are unbelievable."

"Yes, I've been told that. Which is why I asked the when are we getting together question."

"You would not even know where to start."

"I have a lot of ideas. That little spot where your hair curls right above the base of your neck. I could start there."

"I'm not some empty-headed, silicon-filled, implanted moron. I bet you have some weird Hollywood strain of STD that only movie types get."

"Are you kidding? Did your high school counselor just give you the scared straight abstinence talk?"

"Are we going to fish or are you going to continue to bark up the wrong tree? Go into town on the weekend, and I'm sure you'll be able to find some young Barbie girl from Darby who will wrap her legs around you for a story about Andy Pettigrew, in hopes of meeting him while banging you."

I have no come back. No woman's ever been that mean, just flat-out, straightforwardly mean to me.

She dips her head for a minute, looks up and down the river and casts again. "I'm sorry. That was out of line. You've been an arrogant pest, but you haven't been mean. That was just mean."

"Yeah, it was."

She turns to look at me, all the while gently reeling the line in, threading it through her delicate fingers, an action she does thoughtlessly and gracefully.

"I'll be nice to you, but this isn't going to be some dumb *Doc Hollywood* movie where the small town girl has stars in her eyes and falls for the cynical Hollywood producer."

"I'm an agent, not a producer. Plus, Michael J. Fox was a plastic surgeon. And it's nine hundred years old, that movie."

"Whatever. I'm not falling for you, that's the point of me referencing that movie."

"We'll start with civility. Fine by me." I stand still for a moment, then cast out. My fly sinks like a stone.

"You're doing it wrong." She smiles, slyly, keeps her on eyes on the river in front of us.

"You don't say." I pull the line slowly back, give it a jerk, and it skips messily across the surface to me.

"Unless you're trying to freak out every brown trout in a five-mile vicinity." She pulls her line in, sets her rod down next to her. "Here." She's next to me. "You need to false cast a couple times."

"And that is what?" I have the line under control again, but I hold the rod still, waiting to see what she's going to do.

She takes a step slightly behind me and reaches around, puts her hands on my forearms. It's a bold move. I like it. It's miles ahead of her punching me in the mouth, I can tell you that.

"You start with your basic overhead cast. Keep an eye on the back cast so you don't hook me in the eyeball, though. Do you know how to do that?"

I can feel her breath on the back of my neck. She's shorter than me, but she leans in close.

"Yes." I'm a little at a loss of words. "I promise not to sink the hook into any part of you."

"Do that now." She guides my hands as I back cast. At the pause, when the rod is at the top of its arc, she speaks again. "Power the rod forward but pull it right back."

Her hands are still on my arms, and she guides me through the motions.

"And I'm doing this because?"

She chuckles and releases me, steps back into my line of sight. "Your fly was water-logged. A false cast dries it out so it'll float again."

I'm disappointed that she's not next to me anymore. I do as I'm told, though; I cast out again and watch the fly as it settles like a feather on the surface. "Thanks."

She picks up her rod and casts out again. "My pleasure, Mr. King."

We fish, casting in silence, for another half an hour. I bite my tongue. Usually I'd be full of stories, or small talk, or something. But I think she might be wary, and she definitely didn't like when I was all "alpha," in her words. I decide to see what she'll do next. The dusk deepens, and now the inky night cools around us.

What comes next is unexpected, to be sure.

She grabs her gear, tucks her rod into the back of her vest, takes one last drag of her cigarillo. "I'm headed home for the night, I think." Then she casts a glance around us, back toward the lodge, and leans in and kisses me on the lips.

It's short, strong, tastes of peppermint and a hint of cigar smoke. Her lips are full and soft and the sensation of her on me charges adrenaline through my lungs, heart, guts, groin. She pushes her lips against my mouth and parts my lips. Her tongue teases mine, and now my blood is jet fuel.

Just as I make the move to drop my fishing rod and take her in my arms, she slips away and jogs up the path toward the parking lot. "Have a good night, Mr. King."

"And you, Miss Summerlin." I watch her disappear over the ridge.

I can hear the intake of air when I finally remember to take another breath.

I fish for a while longer. It's black now, and I strain to see the path as I come back around to the front of our lodge.

I have a passing thought about bears or other predators that might want to eat me, but then I see something across the parking lot that's a lot more intriguing.

Macy. She stands in front of a little black sedan with its hood popped. The driver's door is swung wide. She leans over the engine, then stands back up. I can't hear her, but I bet she's swearing, despite her best efforts.

I don't know about divine intervention, but I owe someone for this opportunity.

I leave my fishing gear at the bottom of our steps and stroll over. I call out to her well before I'm close. No sense in surprising her. "Problems?"

She turns around. "I swear, just once, I'd like things to go my way." She kicks the tire of the car, hard. "Just." Kicks the tire again. "Once." She takes hold of the car door and slams it with all she's got. The car trembles a little.

"But you're not cursing. That's impressive."

"Oh, no, I promise you, I'm thinking a blue streak. Like wash-my-mouth-out-with-a-bar-of-Ivory swearing."

"Grandmas would be blushing?"

She smiles. "Mothers weeping."

I wave her over. "Come to our place so I can get my keys. I'll give you a ride home."

She frowns. "I can't. I was just going to run home and let my dogs out. I've got to work the front desk tonight. I'm covering a shift."

"I can run you home. And I can take you back home after your shift."

"No."

"Why not? 'Cause you kissed me?" I wonder. I hope she's not having second thoughts.

"No. It's just too much." She drops the hood and notices the grime on her hands. "You don't need to drive me all over. That's more than I'd ask any friend to do for me." She wipes her hands and looks right at me. "And it's not because of kissing you. I liked that part."

"What's wrong with the car?"

"I think it's the starter. I replaced the battery not three months ago. I cannot deal with this."

I pull my phone out. "Let me drive you. I'm a guest, and this is what a guest wants."

She stands for a minute. I can tell she's trying to think of another option. The parking lot is empty except for us. The chance that some co-worker comes by to offer her a ride home (and back, for that matter) is slim.

"Come on, Macy. I can give you a ride." I try to sound as mellow as I can.

She sighs. "Fine. I mean, thank you. I just can't leave the dogs in for too long."

I nod. "Let me get the keys." I point to the Yukon, sitting in front of our lodge.

"Okay." She picks up all of her stuff and walks to the SUV.

I hustle and get the keys. Andy's on the couch. The other guys aren't downstairs.

Andy arches an eyebrow. "Something up?"

"I'm running Macy home. Her car won't start." I can't help it; I can feel the grin bloom on my face.

"Aw, good job Jeremy. Unless this a scheme to get you alone so she can drown you."

I shake my head. "I think I'm forgiven."

He turns his attention back to the TV. "Well, good. Now try to stay quiet so you don't say something that ruins it."

"You're lucky you're my best client. I don't take that kind of abuse from everybody."

He waves absently over his shoulder. "Go get her, Tiger."

I get outside and back to the car. Macy stands there, leaning up against the passenger side. "Ready?"

She nods. "Thanks for this."

We get in, and she directs me as I pull out of the lodge parking and on to the state highway.

"You don't drive like a lunatic, do you?" She pulls her feet up underneath her, almost perches on the seat next to me.

"I drive like a Californian, so the answer is relative. In Idaho terms, probably yes. In LA, I'm tame." I keep my eyes on the road just to prove it to her.

We drive for a while in silence. I try really hard to avoid saying something stupid. Then Macy sits forward a little and points into the distance and sagebrush ahead of us.

"My place is just up there. On the left. You can see the lights of the complex." She seems nervous, eager to get this little road trip over with. She worries at the lanyard with her house key on it, picking at the seams.

I pull into the parking lot of her apartment complex. It's nondescript, but not terrible. There's a dinky little playground off to one side of the big, low building. The whole place is tan, and the vinyl siding buckles in more than one place, but it's clean, and it reminds me a lot of college housing when I lived on campus.

She points out her front door, and we get out of the car.

As she walks to the door, she looks over her shoulder. "You don't have to come in."

"No, I don't have to." I hang back, give her the space she needs. I don't want to press. I haven't figured out exactly where she stands yet.

She gets her keys out. "I guess I don't mind if you come in."

"That's enthusiastic. I can wait here while you hide the bodies." I smile, trying to put her ease. She may be the most guarded woman I've ever dated (if that's what we're doing). And I've dated actresses who had a lot, *a whole lot*, to hide, believe me. She tops those ladies.

"Just give me a second to let the dogs out the back door. They have to go pee before you come in or they'll pee everywhere from excitement. I never have visitors."

The prospect of animal bodily fluids slows me down. "I'll wait here until you give me the all clear."

She disappears behind the door, and there are sounds of dog barks and whimpers. Then it's still. Then the door swings open.

"Mr. King." She has her head down as she steps back to let me by.

"What's with the shy stuff? And when are you ever going to call me Jeremy?"

"You're a guest. Never."

"I'm at your apartment. You kissed me. I think we're past the pleasantries."

There's a howl from the other side of the sliding glass door I can see at the back of her place.

"I have to let them in. They'll tear the screen off if I don't." She trots to the slider and opens it. Two dogs bullet through as soon as their bodies will fit through the crack and make straight for me. "They're nice. They won't bite."

I'm surrounded by dancing furry bodies and the sound of toenails tapping on the linoleum and whining.

"Sit. Pierre and Justin. Sit!" She uses a commanding voice, confident and stern.

The dogs sit quickly, tucking tails.

"Impressive. That's kind of hot." I smile at her, but she's holding the dogs' attention, her hand up in front of her.

"Stop. Don't tell me you're turned on by basic dog training. It's just too easy to insult you from there." She takes a step to the dogs and lowers her hand. Both of the dogs lie down, eyes still trained on their mistress.

"A French bulldog and a what, exactly?" I examine the dogs. The French bulldog is black with a fat little neck and wide-set eyes and ears.

The other dog is a mystery. Half-wiry, half-angora-fuzzy brown and white fur, one ear up, the other down, and an under bite that would put Muttley to shame. It looks as though it's been kicked one too many times and is still waiting for the loose rattle in its brain to settle out.

"He's a mutt. His name is Justin Trudeau."

"The prime minister?" I ask.

"He was named Rob Ford, after the mayor of Toronto who did crack and got fired. Both the mayor and my dog may have had some residual brain issues. Then the mayor passed away, and I felt bad, so his name's Justin Trudeau now."

"And this one's Pierre as in Pierre Trudeau?" Pierre and Justin are both statue still, waiting for Macy to put them at ease. I scratch the French bulldog's ear.

"Yes."

"What's with the Canadian leaders of government?"

"I kind of love Canada. Don't tease me about it."

This girl completely mystifies me. "Why? What's so special about it?" I take a breath, about to really give her a hard time, when a teeny, tiny light bulb goes off in my brain. A way in. I've been looking for a way in. Who in the hell would figure it was Canada?

"I don't know. It's not here. They've hosted the Olympics, which is cool. Justin Trudeau does yoga, which is cool for a world leader to do. Toronto seems like a cool city. Mostly, it's not remotely like Idaho. It's the anti-Idaho."

I try to seem disinterested. "Yeah. I see that. I have to say I like Vancouver the best, though."

She tries to seem disinterested, too, but I can see the last comment light in her eyes. "Why, exactly?"

"Weather's not as frigid. Better sushi, too." I go in for the kill. "Andy and I are headed to T.O. after this week, though. His next movie shoots there." I didn't even lie—that's the God's honest truth, we are shooting in Toronto. This is too easy.

"Really?" She bites her lip, holding herself back. She really, really doesn't want me to have the upper hand.

I think she was about to say, "That's so cool." She just couldn't bring herself to admit it. And here, here's where I drop in the bait. "You could visit if you wanted. I like you, you know. You could come see the set."

Her eyes widen, but then she drops her head and her attention back to her dogs. She nods her head to them, and they spring to their feet. I don't know what just happened, but I was very close for a second there, and now some shield's back up in position.

"No passport. But nice offer. Really. You can be nice, I see that. Thanks."

"I want to try to be more than just nice to you." I lower my shield, in response to hers going up. Maybe now's the time for a little honesty.

"What do you mean exactly?" She side-eyes me.

I sit down at her little kitchen table. The odd Justin Trudeau dog springs up into my lap. "I haven't met a girl like you before. I like you. A lot. As much shit as you give me, you make me smile. I want to make you happy. You seem like you're overdue for someone to make you happy."

She's considering. "I don't know about that." She points to the two dog beds in the corner of the room, by the couch. Both dogs immediately rush to the beds, the mutt springing from my lap, and curl up on the beds.

She sits next to me. "You want to make me happy? Right now I'm hungry. Feed me. Take the dogs on a walk with me. That might make me happy."

It's a start. "People get passports all the time, you know."

Instead of smiling, she flinches. Something big hides behind that shield. "I know they do. Change the subject."

I nod and get up from the table. "Let's drive back to the lodge. We've got loads of groceries. I'll feed you. We can walk the dogs down along the river after. Then you man the front desk, and I'll take you home when you're ready."

"It's gonna be really late when I need to come back home. You'd have to dog sit. And the dogs aren't really allowed on the property."

"If they're Andy Pettigrew's invited guests, they sure as hell are." I put out a hand.

She stands up, ignoring the hand. "Fine. You're going to get me fired, you know that? Is that your real mission with me?"

"Just the make-you-happy mission. I promise. Maybe make myself happy in the process. I'm always about the added benefits. Win-win's never a bad idea."

I pile the dogs into the giant SUV, and Macy climbs up on the passenger side.

"If it really is the starter, I'm screwed." She's texting somebody.

"Why?" Justin is on my lap, looking out the driver side window. I feel something wet and realize he's resting his tongue on my arm. Not licking, just resting it.

"Because a starter is like eight hundred bucks, and I don't have that kind of money right now."

"Put it on a card."

She snorts, "Yeah, of course. Sorry, Daddy Warbucks, I've maxed my cards out, oh, I don't know, last century."

"I'll pay for the fucking starter."

"Language! And I don't need your charity, Mr. King. I'm not a pity case."

She turns her attention to the phone again. "Yeah, see? I've got it all figured out."

"How?" I try to pay attention to her and to the road in front of me—all the sage brush and scrub looks exactly the same to me, and I'm sure as hell not going to get lost when driving a woman. Not a woman I want in my bed.

"Richard, the lodge owner. I offered to lead a couple extra trips in October if he fronts me the money for the starter now. An advance, you know. We're good."

"That's a long way out. You could just borrow the money from me and pay me back by the end of the summer."

"How? With what? No, you do not answer that, or I'll probably get really ticked at you for the dumb words falling out of your mouth." She pokes me on the arm.

I smile, a little because I was about to say something totally bad and a lot because she touched me. I want her hands all over me, to be honest.

The odd drooling under bite-y dog sleeps now, draped over one of my thighs and snoring. I hope that the guys decided on the going into town thing. I want the lodge to myself. I want Macy to myself.

We get back to the lodge, and I park in the lot next to Macy's dead car, on the side of the main lodge. There's one car besides hers.

"Damn, Richard's here tonight. That sucks." She picks the French bulldog up and tucks him under her arm like a handbag.

"Why? He just did you a solid, lending you the money."

"Yeah, but he really will be chapped if he sees my dogs on the property. Ernesto usually takes nights. Huh. Hope the twins aren't sick or anything."

"The twins?"

"Ernesto's the night watch guy after eleven weekday nights, when the restaurant closes. He's got a wife and twins. Little girls."

I'm about to open my door, but Justin the prime minister dog is still sacked out on my leg. "What am I doing with this guy here? Must have been quite a bender earlier."

"Just carry him. It's easier anyway. He likes to run off."

He's a sack of potatoes. I scoop him up and carry him football style, scooped into the crook of my arm. We get out of the car.

"Is he dead? He's not waking up."

Macy shrugs. "One of the other guides has a theory that Justin's narcoleptic."

"A narcoleptic dog. Interesting. Maybe you'd be doing him a favor if you put him down."

Macy's eyes narrow. "You better be joking. Them's fighting words."

We walk across the lot to the path to our house. "So you grew up where, exactly? I was going to say around here, but there is 'no around here' here."

She sets Pierre Trudeau down at the foot of our stairs. "I was born in Teton County. Grew up, went to all grades in the same school building, graduated from high school, made the big move to my own little apartment, which you've now seen, and started working here. That is my life."

I carry the weird dog, who is still asleep, up the stairs to the door of the lodge. The lights are off inside. I thank Andy and Tucker and maybe even Todd for not being around and push open the door.

This startles Justin Trudeau. He starts yipping and tries to climb up onto my head.

"Jesus! Macy, your dog!" I pluck him off of me by the scruff of his ugly little neck. I resist the urge to drop kick him outside.

"Justin! Sit. Sit!" She takes him and sets him down on the slate floor. He sits and then flops over, begging forgiveness.

"At least he minds. He's not going to pee all over the house, is he?" The other dog has already curled up in front of the fireplace.

Justin stays on his back, legs up in the air. Macy snaps her fingers and points to the other dog. Justin springs up and joins his pack mate on the hearth. He goes down into the stay pose and rests his head on his front paws.

"He'll be asleep in a minute." The dog already seems to fight to stay awake. Macy's shoulders loosen. She looks more at ease with the dogs settled.

"Do they need a fire? I could turn the fireplace on." When did I get so helpful? Plus, these jeans will have to be burned—Mr. Suave Justin Trudeau has left an odd smell on me. I have money, and right now not ever wearing these again is worth whatever money they cost me.

"That'd be nice. It'll relax them." Macy twists the bottom of her t-shirt in her fingers. She must be nervous. I like that. Maybe she'll be more honest if she's a little off-center.

I stroll over and turn on the gas fireplace. "Looks like ol' JT's done for." His slobbery under bite rests on the back of the other dog, who appears to tolerate him.

"What are you feeding me?" Macy walks around the kitchen island, finally releasing the hem of her t-shirt.

What am I feeding her? I get over to the fridge. "Let's see."

Now, I have to say, I'm a good cook. I love impressing a girl in the kitchen. And I can improvise, too. Nothing is cooler to a girl than a guy (me) pulling a meal together from whatever crazy stuff she's left in her fridge. I consider it *Chopped*, the seducing edition.

We have a ton of beer, we have one fresh-caught cutthroat trout (that Tucker will tear my head off if I use), a carton of eggs, and leftover steak. There's a crusty loaf of bread on the counter and a fresh tomato.

"Bird's nest. That's what we're having."

Macy arches an eyebrow and pulls up a stool at the kitchen island. "And that is?"

"You'll just have to see, won't you?" I pull out eggs, the steak. "Can you slice the tomato into wedges?"

"We'll see." She holds up the hand that was bandaged.

I look at the wide fresh scar on the palm. "And how did you do that again?"

Her face clouds over for a moment. Her brows knit together, the eyes go down to the counter, her lips press into a thin line. Then she looks up at me, transformed, a smile on her face and a shrug on her shoulders. "Stupidity." She tilts her head, waiting for me to tease her or laugh it off.

I don't. "No, Macy, really. How did that happen?"

"I already told you, I was helping a guest gut a fish and gutted my hand instead."

I lean closer to her. "Then how come every time I ask your face looks like somebody ran over JT over there?"

Her smile drops. "I do not."

I point the loaf of bread at her. "No, don't lie. I hate lies. Your face tells a different story, even if it's just for five seconds, until you paste the fake-girl smile on. Something bad happened."

I swear her eyes well with tears. Then she shakes her head no, tosses her hair, like she's shaking the memory to the edges of her mind, or clearing the etch-a-sketch of a horrible image. She's still for a moment.

"Lots of bad stuff happened. Life happened. This?" She holds the palm up. "This is nothing. I cut it gutting a fish. End of story."

It's clear from her tone, clear that she's not trying to lie. She's trying to get me on board with the approved story. Trying to protect herself by putting another witness in her court. Another witness to stand up for her.

If that's what she needs right now, so be it. "Fine. Don't tell me now. But don't lie. I fucking hate liars."

She seizes on an opportunity to change the subject. "Mouth! You, Mr. King, need a swear jar."

She jumps up and starts rifling through the cabinets. In the cabinet to the left of the oversized Subzero she succeeds. "Aha!"

She pulls out a mason jar and plunks it on the kitchen island. "Put a buck in there."

"What?" I've cracked an egg and use the shell to separate the white from the yolk.

"You owe the swear jar a buck. Out on the river, I'll keep track for you. At the end of the night, you come home and put your fine in the jar."

It hurts me to hear the strain in her voice. I answer, help her forget our earlier discussion. "Who gets the jar at the end of the week?" She's trying so hard to lighten things up, steer the conversation far away from her. Her wounds.

"Consider it an extra tip to your favorite river guide."

I point to the back pocket of my jeans. "Wallet's in there."

She smirks. "I don't think so. I'm not touching your butt."

I hold my hands up. "I'm covered in egg. Just grab the wallet."

She rolls her eyes and comes over to me. The weird scruffy dog lifts his head up, watches her. She stands behind me for a minute and lingers. I smell her and feel her warmth against my back. I take a breath in through my nose and try to exercise some restraint. "Fine." She quickly snatches the wallet out of my pocket and pulls a bill out.

It's a twenty. She frowns. "No, it's a buck for the jar." She pulls the billfold wider and thumbs through the bills.

"What?" I'm back to cooking. I don't look up. I know exactly what.

"There's nothing smaller than a twenty in here, Mr. King."

I keep my head down. "Guess a twenty will have to do."

She huffs and plucks one out, stuffs it in the new swear jar. "You are a piece of work."

"So I've been told. Why don't you crack open a bottle of wine for us?"

She shakes her head. "No thanks." She drifts over to the mantle, looks at the fire dancing in the hearth.

"We've got a ton of beer. They're in the blue cooler over by the door to the back deck." I wipe my hands on a dish towel and try to hustle up on the meal. She seems restless, and I wouldn't put it past her to run out of here on me. Of course, I'd have her two little dogs to hold as ransom, but even my instincts tell me that doesn't win many second dates.

She shakes her head again. "I can't. I have to work the desk after this, remember?"

"Yeah. Sorry. Not trying to get you into trouble, I promise." I put the pan with the bread "nests" and the egg white, steak, and tomato filling into the oven.

"We'll see about that." She kneels to give each a dog a scratch under the chin.

I set a timer. "We've got twenty minutes. You want to give them a quick walk?"

"Sure." She snaps her fingers. Both dogs bounce up and go to the door. They sit like little book ends.

"Again, impressive."

"Again, no comments. It's just too gross." She pulls leashes out of her purse and snaps them on.

I pull the door and hold it for her. "Ladies first."

She walks the dogs down the steps, and we make our way around our lodge to the path by the river.

"I have to say I'm hoping the river's down tomorrow." I chuckle.

She smiles. "Trying not to repeat the tantrum-throwing?"

"Now, I apologized. You're not being fair." I consider trying to defend myself more than that, but I know I don't have much of a case.

"Oh for the love of SpongeBob SquarePants." She grits her teeth and stops in her tracks, motions for the dogs to sit.

"What?" I can't imagine I said anything to anger her. We just got started.

"It's Richard. Coming this way. I'm dead." She puts her head down, waiting to be chewed out, I suppose.

"Gorgeous evening!" I stride up to the doughy-faced man. He wears a button-down shirt, puffy Patagonia vest, jeans, and expensive Salomon off-trail shoes that, by their lack of wear, clearly haven't been off trail. Lots of heart surgeons and accountants in LA dress like this—a cross between the prep they really are, and the Everest climber they think they are.

He reaches out and shakes my hand. "Richard Neeley. Nice to meet you."

"Jeremy King. Likewise."

"I see you've met Macy. And Macy's dogs."

I can hear the tone in his voice. It tells her she's in deep shit. But the difference this time is that Macy has Jeremy "Gets What He Wants" King here as her advocate. I jump in. "Her car broke down, and despite her best efforts to put me in my rightful place as a guest, darn it all if I wasn't the pushy Hollywood agent and insisted on driving her home to get her dogs. I miss mine like crazy. I figured I'd get my dog fix while she covered that shift someone else cancelled on you. Always accommodating, Macy."

His eyes go cold, and his lips settle into a thin line. "Macy knows her dogs aren't allowed on the property. And even insistent guests shouldn't be giving our team rides home."

He's not going down without a fight. I get a little whiff of my crabby grandpa who always gave me the passive-aggressive but polite dressing down about "LA corrupting my mind and my soul."

I smile. Andy calls it my sharky smile. "Richard, I appreciate that you run a first-class resort here, and order is what makes that work.

And I certainly know that you've had your share of entitled, wealthy dickwads—mouth, sorry Macy—try to intimidate you, or act above the rules of the outfit."

Richard nods, a tiny nod, in agreement. "True." He's about to say something else, but I don't give him a chance.

"But I also know that you're passionate about the preservation of trout habitat in Eastern Idaho, and I know that Andy Pettigrew shares your passion for that. He's loved his visits here. Enough to brave bringing me."

He turns his head slightly more to face me, taking his eyes off Macy and her statue-still dogs. "Uh-huh."

"So I could be awfully persuasive, gush about your forgiving nature when I broke all sorts of rules, how you knew Macy had nothing to do with my impulsive behavior. Andy loves stories like that. I'd remind him how the Silver Creek Conservation Fund was looking for its annual donations and looking into fisheries to fund. All that stuff that was in the brochure we got at check-in."

He lifts his head up, barely a half-nod. "I see you know you're in the wrong, Mr. King. Macy, I think it's about time to cover that shift. If Mr. King could take the dogs to his lodge for the duration. Then straight home for the night after your shift."

Macy speaks up. "Thanks, Richard. I told him it wasn't a good idea."

"I insisted. I'm insistent like that." I hate how scared of him she sounds.

Richard watches as she hands me the leashes. "And Macy, don't forget that I'm already bending over backwards on the starter thing. You're on a short leash already."

Leash. He just told her she's on a leash. Like she's his pet. I want to punch him in the mouth. "I'll see you after your shift, Macy."

She brushes past me, and her cheeks are flushed in shame. "Fine."

She's mad at me again. Great.

I take the dogs back to the lodge and stew for the remainder of the night. Pierre Trudeau sleeps by the fire, and Justin Trudeau sleeps with his weird, wet tongue resting on my lap. I try to watch Sports Center with Tucker and explain to Andy how I came to be a dog-sitter and how he and I both came to be donors for a new Silver Creek conservation project right here in Eastern Idaho.

Then, well after midnight, there's a knock at the door.

I open it to Macy. "I need a ride home." She snaps at the dogs, and they rush to her sides. I give her the leashes and her purse.

"You never got a chance to eat."

"I need a ride home, Mr. King." She looks at the dogs.

"I'm sorry. I didn't mean to get you into trouble."

"You don't mean to do a lot of things." She sighs. "I know you were being nice, but I got in trouble. This is the only job I've ever loved. I want to keep it. Next time I won't let you talk me into anything."

I walk her out to the car and give her and the little dogs a ride home.

She doesn't speak to me until I drop her at her door.

"Good night, Mr. King."

She shuts the door in my face.

None of this is involving the winning I am used to, and I don't like it one bit.

A RIVER RUNS THROUGH IT

I wake up the next morning with a brilliant idea. I went to bed and stared at the ceiling for a long, long time. I cursed Richard, with his insults and his passive-aggression and his financial sway on Macy's life. I plotted how I was going to take her away from all of his bullshit.

Then I got stuck on the part where she was mad at me, and for the millionth time in the very short time since I had met her, how I had made a mess of things between me and her.

At some point in the "Million Ways Jeremy King is an Ass" review in my brain, I fell asleep.

But the subconscious brain can be a miracle worker.

The idea I have now is brilliant in its simplicity. I will take her fishing.

No, I haven't lost my mind.

The Snake River is a monster of a river where it flows into the Columbia: wide, deep, charging hard toward the Pacific. But where we are, here close to the Tetons and the Snake's clear, cold headwaters, it actually begins as three separate branches, destined to flow into one another, but not quite yet: Henry's Fork to the north, the main Snake, and the South Fork.

We've been fishing the South Fork. I have money. I've decided I want to fish Henry's Fork, one of the most famous trout streams in the country, as Evan the other guy said.

Alone. With a guide. For the day.

You and I both know it's not about the trout. And I know exactly which guide I'd like to have for the day. One who may love to fish Henry's Fork.

I get out of the shower and get dressed and try not to congratulate myself for my brilliant idea. Actually, I spent most of the shower patting myself on the back, but now I need to put the plan into action.

I gear up and make my way to the kitchen. I inhale a piece of toast and some coffee while I call over to the guide shop and book Macy for a private day on Henry's Fork. Today. All day.

Andy comes in, the first guy up. Tucker is often up and out early, but Andy's been trying to get a run in before we hit the water.

"Jeremy's up and dressed and plotting something. And here I thought I was on vacation." Andy comes over to the stove and swipes the tea kettle, pours a fresh mug, and brings it to the kitchen island to sit next to me.

"Listen to this. Last night Macy was mad at me, right?"

"You got her in trouble. I'd be mad."

"We've covered that already. I think what I need is some time to make it up to her."

"Okay." He takes a big swig of tea. "I feel like this isn't headed in a good direction."

I stand up to appropriately make the big speech. "It's not a good direction, it's a brilliant direction. I just booked the whole day with Macy on Henry's Fork all by ourselves."

He drops his head, closes his eyes, and then peeks up at me with one eye open, teeth clenched in a grimace. "This is your good idea."

"This is my brilliant idea. Get on board with the vocabulary."

Andy sighs. "When you say, 'all by ourselves,' you mean you and Macy."

"Yep. And I just booked it. It's a done deal."

He stands up and stretches. "I'm going to go on a run. I want to say a lot of things, give you a lot of advice."

I take another piece of toast for the road. "And?"

Andy smiles. "I'm going to say, instead, remember that this is about getting to know a person, not winning. Enjoy the day and relax. Pay attention to her. Get to know her."

"So you just gave me advice."

"Yeah, but it was about a thousand times nicer than what I really wanted to say. But do me a favor and follow it. Seriously."

I nod. Andy is smart. He's smart about women. Kelly mostly hates me, at times just dislikes me, but she's a good woman, and Andy landed her, so I take him as a person who knows about women. "Done. Today will be about Macy, and getting to know her."

"Good. Enjoy. I'm going to go run and try not to get eaten by a grizzly." He pulls his hood up and leaves, pulling the door shut behind him.

Getting to know Macy. That's a plan I can get behind.

I stroll over to the main lodge dressed down and ready for a day of epic fishing. The guy I talked to on the phone, Kevin or Kramer, told me to bring waders. I don't care if I'm in a boat or on the shore or in waders, what matters here is that I have unfettered access to Macy so I can apologize (again) and get to know her better.

I make my way inside and cross through the lobby to the guide shop. Macy is at the desk with one of the guys. She chats and smiles and looks relaxed until she spots me. Then her back arches, and she hisses at me. Not really, of course, but if her body language were any more hostile, she would morph into a black cat and take a swipe at me.

"Mr. King."

"Miss Summerlin, beautiful day." I turn to the scrawny one. "Good to see you again, Kevin or Kramer."

His freckled face contorts into a frown. "It's Kevin."

"You bet." I turn to face Macy, shutting him out of the conversation. He walks away in defeat or disgust, but I'm all eyes on Macy, so his departure is no loss.

"You always so polite to people?" she asks.

"I can be polite. I will work on it for the next time I see Kramer. Kevin. Evan? One of the guys. That one that just left."

She shakes her head. "You can't tell any of them apart?"

I don't deny it. "You want me to be polite or honest?"

I can tell she's a tiny bit, the teeniest bit amused. "Tell me."

"I don't want to tell them apart. I want to pay attention to you. I want all of my attention on you. You are who I'm interested in, Macy."

She rolls her eyes. "What do you need, Mr. King?"

"I'm here to meet my guide for the day."

"And that is?"

"You, of course."

"I'm already your guide. What did you do?"

"You wouldn't speak to me, so you're my river guide, private, for the day."

"Private. Whatever. We're all still on the same river."

"Oh, I beg to differ, Miss Macy. You and I are fishing Henry's Fork. Hope you know it as well as the staff thinks you do."

She tilts her head and lets out the longest sigh I've ever heard. "You don't need to do this to apologize for last night."

"I need a chance to apologize, and the odds weren't good I'd get one."

"You're your own worst enemy on that front. You need to stop trying to control everything. You can't game all of it."

"All of what?" I watch her shift her weight from foot to foot. I make her, what, nervous? Do I literally throw her off balance a little? I'd like to think that's a good thing. Maybe I'm different than the guys she usually meets.

"You can't game life. Life will play you, to be sure, but you've got to know the second you think you've got it all under control, life'll smack you down. Especially when you're all hubris and big pronouncements and the like. That's when you catch the eye of fate and get pounded into the dirt."

I smile. "Glad to see you're an optimist. Should we get going?"

She grabs up a pile of gear on the counter and motions to a similar pile. "You're not a 'learn from someone else's mistakes' type, are you?"

"If anyone's going to get pounded into the dirt, it's going to be me. I want all of life or fate or the universe's undivided attention."

"Let's go fish and hope we can stay under destiny's radar."

I can't help it. "I've got it all under control. No worries."

She shakes her head again, but I spy a tiny upturn of the corners of her mouth. It might officially rate as a smile. It's a good start.

We get out to the parking lot with our gear as Kevin/Kramer pulls a truck to the curb. He hops out and hands Macy the keys.

"Our ride for the day? We could take our rental."

"I'd prefer to drive. I know where we're going. And I trust me. I don't know if I trust you to actually get us to the correct river."

We load in, and I sit back. Macy tries to talk to me about actual fishing details. I listen enough to say "uh-huh" at appropriate intervals. But really I'm waiting to get to know Macy.

She is quiet though, and we make most of the almost-hour drive to Henry's Fork in silence or in brief bouts of conversation about what's hatching and whether I can tell the difference between a caddisfly and a mayfly.

We finally pull off the main road. "Are we there yet?" I try for humor.

"Cardiac Canyon. This is a good stretch."

"Any reason it's called that?"

"If you're running it in a boat, there are two sets of falls about eight miles downstream. That would give anybody a heart attack."

"Let's not do that, then."

"You brought waders, right? We're wading."

I nod. "Hence, the waders."

She crinkles her eyebrows. "Don't say 'hence.' It's not your kind of word. Please."

"Fine." If this is how she's going to play it all day, I'm not going to make much progress in the getting-to-know-Macy plan or the apologize-and-win-her-with-my-charms plan. She needs to think I'm charming for that to work.

Maybe she can tell she's burst my bubble. "C'mon. This is one of my favorite stretches to fish. I don't bring everyone here. You have to pay attention, because with the water high we can't fish all of this. Some of it will be too much."

"Not for you."

"Even for me."

We come to the river. It's rocky, upstream and downstream. We seem to be in the one place where we can edge into the water without falling in. The river cuts a deep-v into the mountains surrounding us.

"Pretty."

"This is pocket water. And even in the middle of the busy season, we might have this stretch to ourselves today."

I follow her to the river's edge and get my waders on. I listen closely as she warns me about losing my footing, or disregarding all of her warnings and setting foot into a surprisingly deep pool. By the end of it, I don't feel much like fishing at all.

"Macy?"

"Yes, Mr. King?"

"You didn't bring me here to drown me, did you?"

She tilts her head to the sky and laughs, loud and long. When she's done, she looks at me over the sunglasses on the bridge of her nose, straight-faced. "No."

So I've got that going for me.

I work to be her star student for most of the morning. I creep slowly up on trout, I cast upstream, I even crouch down to avoid spooking the fish that I want to hook. I am a true protégé.

We take a break at lunch, but in the shadows of the canyon, it's clear we'll be able to fish into the afternoon. There's no sun bearing down, lulling the river into a warm afternoon siesta. It's still cold and wild.

She leads me to a bend in the river. She stands still for a minute, looks upstream and down, and I can see her stand a little taller.

I wonder if this is a favorite spot. I try to attend to what might be attractive to her about it.

A large rock slab with moss and ferns and trees growing out of it makes up the shore opposite us. We stand on a rare flat piece of shore, an emerald patch in a rocky quilt. Below us are rapids, and from the looks of it by my untrained eye, the rapids seem deep. They make up a short stretch of the river before it flattens and widens into shallow riffles. But here in front of us the river splits into two pools.

She points at the pool closest to us. "This one you can fish without even wading. If you cast upstream from the big boulder, you can keep most of your body hidden from the fish and still get a lot of good casts into the water."

I point to the other pool. "What about that pool? You'd have to wade halfway into the river to get to it."

She pulls off her ball cap for a minute. "But if I edge downstream, see how the bottom isn't too deep? I can get over there without getting in over my knees."

I don't like it. The river is so high, it roars. We actually have to raise our voices over the tumbling water. "You've fished this before. Have you fished it when the flows were this high?"

"Hundreds, heck, even thousands of times, probably."

"You sure it's a good idea?"

"It's a great idea."

"It's your favorite spot."

She blushes. "Maybe."

"Well, let's do it, then. Lame-ass Mr. King the newbie will fish the easy side. Am I allowed to put a toe in or will I ruin the whole river for you?"

"Swear jar." She smiles. "No, you can wade upstream after you've worked the pool from the rock. It's allowed. Just keep your eyes open."

I wave her off. "I know, I know. I heard the 'scared safe' river lecture."

I think it's probably a half hour, maybe forty-five minutes, when I give up on casting from the rock and edge upstream in my waders. It takes a while to get used to navigating the current in them. My legs feel bulky and slow.

Macy's in heaven. I'd call it hog heaven, but maybe there's some fishy term for it. Fly heaven? She makes big, beautiful loops of her line, and she lays it out across the other pool.

I stop and watch her.

She hooks one. The line bends, hard.

"It's a big one!" She turns and looks at me over her shoulder, and I can see what Macy must have looked like when she was little. The grin on her face is sheer innocence, pure joy. I wonder who taught her to fish. Where is that person now?

I give her a thumbs up and watch.

She's not kidding—the fish must be massive. The rod bows, almost a C, pulled by the fish she's hooked.

Maybe because she looked over her shoulder at me, maybe because it's a bigger fish than normal, but Macy loses her footing for a minute and has to step forward into the pool.

It's one step, but where she was in to her ankles, she's now in the water up to her thighs. And it rages around her, piling up in angry white eddies and waves around her legs. She tries to edge backwards, but she's just wading farther into the rapids.

"Macy! You okay?" I turn and start to make my way toward her, pull my line from the water and snap the hook on one of the guides on the rod.

She works her rod, but she's still struggling against the current and the strong fish, and she's in motion. Her feet aren't planted. I don't like it.

She's stubborn, damn it, and she still thinks she can land the fish. I can see her look down, in the water around her feet, looking for that footing that will help her get some leverage against the fish pulling so desperately in the other direction.

"Macy! The current's too strong! Just cut the line and let him run!"

She doesn't even look up. The water is too loud. I start to wade closer, and I notice that my heart pounds. Sweat chills on the back of my neck.

I don't know very much about rivers, or fishing, but I know people. I can read faces, and what I see, in the next split second on Macy Shea Summerlin's face, is the knowledge that she's gotten herself into trouble she can't get out of. Fear. Fear is in her eyes and finally, finally, she looks up, across the rushing river to where I am, waist deep in my fucking awkward-as-hell waders.

She needs help. She looks right at me as she lets go of the rod completely, off balance, and is knocked over by the current.

She's little, she's barely over five foot, and the river's too strong for her right here.

There's no way in hell, if she wasn't fishing with me, would she have taken that chance, put herself in a position where she was going to swim.

Her waders will fill in a moment, drag her to the bottom with the current, and drown her.

I push down current, let the river carry me a bit, and I can see the shallows coming up on my left. If I can get to her quickly enough, I'll be able to drag her to shin-deep water myself.

Her blonde head submerges fully now, and I'm three big strides away from her.

"Macy! Macy!" I scream, hoarse with panic.

Her hand comes up, fighting and clawing to find a hold, a way to pull herself up out of the current.

I throw my hands deep in the water, just below the spot where I last saw her hand, stick a foot out, hoping to block her progress downriver.

My knee bends backward, pushed and hyperextended by a body. Macy.

I grab and pull hard, and the force of the current fights me for her. My hands are numb, the ice of the water biting at them. I use my elbows and hook her under her armpits and pull up as hard as I can muster.

Finally, she comes loose, her body up out of the water, the current unable to trap her anymore.

"Macy!" I pull her into my arms, hold her out of the water as I try to figure my path out of the river.

She doesn't move, limp. I can't do anything for her here, in the middle of the river. I have to get to shore.

Five steps down river, the river shallows out and the bottom silts up, the slippery jagged river rocks giving way to firm pebble and sand.

I push hard, aware that my waders have taken on a lot of water. Macy's body feels cold and still.

The bottom changes, and I am only knee-deep now. I look up and down the river bank. There's got to be someone that can help us. I start yelling again, yelling for help this time.

No one. The storm clouds overhead have opened up, and now the rains come down.

At last I get her to shore and throw her up on the grassy bank. I scramble up next to her and get a straight look at her face. Her lips are blue, and I can see slivers of white between both pairs of eyelids. No pupils.

She looks dead.

I sit her up and give her five hard, rib-breaking back thrusts. Then I lay her gently back down and sweep two fingers to the back of her throat, clearing her tongue and anything else out of the way.

I give two rescue breaths and start chest compressions.

"Macy! Macy!" All I can do is scream her name while I count in my head, *and one, and two, and three,* as I press down with the knot I've made from my two fists.

It's probably forty seconds. It feels like an eternity. But suddenly, she gags, hard, and contracts into a ball, rolling on her side in the fetal position. She coughs, vomits up water, and cries, sobs, and I feel tears of relief streaming from my eyes. I strip off my coat, frantically searching the pockets for my phone.

"Macy, Macy." I lift her into my arms, looking for her eyes on mine.

"I'm here." She shakes in my arms, violently shuddering.

"I can't get reception here. I'll drive us. Are you all right?"

She can only nod. I run with her in my arms to the truck. Her body still wracked with cold and adrenaline, I can hear her teeth clacking together in between her coughs and sobs.

I get us into the cab and start the truck with her on my lap. I turn the heat on high and turn up the seat warmers. I strip off my wet shirt and wrap my arm around her, rubbing her back briskly with one hand. The feeling's finally coming back into my fingers.

"Macy, breathe for me. We've got to get you warm. You need to breathe." I pull her so close to me, hoping to still the shudders of her body.

Her tiny blonde head, and the way her arms are folded up in mine, I have a vision of her as a bird, feathers wet, unable to fly, tremble-fragile and terribly vulnerable.

I hold her on my lap as I drive back to civilization, terrified. I have no idea what to do beyond getting her breathing and warming her up. What comes next is beyond me. And I don't know where help is. The only place I know is the lodge, so I drive in that direction.

I don't know how long it takes. I speed the whole way, as fast as the turns of the highway will let me. The cabin of the truck is sweltering to me when she finally stills, curled tightly against my chest.

"Macy?" I stroke her curls, not sure how responsive she is. I've yet to get any signal on my phone. The highway all looks the same to me, scrub and sage and a river on one side of us.

"I'm here."

"That's the second time you've said that. You have to tell me— where's the fire station? The EMTs? You have to have a rural district around here somewhere with paramedics. Please think."

"I don't need—I just need to get warm."

"You drowned. You were blue."

"I'm here." She moves her arms, wraps them around my torso, presses her hands against my back, wraps herself more closely against me. Her face turns, and I can feel her cold cheek against my chest.

"This is bullshit. Bullshit." I have no options here. I drive to the lodge.

When I get to the lodge, I carry her up the steps at a full run. "Andy! Get your phone! Andy!"

The rain's stopped finally, in the deepening dusk, and the doorway is a gold rectangle when he opens it. "What the hell's going on?" He pulls me inside, and I start barking orders.

"Get Tucker. He's trained. He needs to look at her. We need to call for an ambulance."

"Don't." Macy speaks, weakly, as I try to pull all of her sopping layers off of her. The thermal shirt she wears is still ice cold, despite the full-blast heat of the truck.

Tucker is above me. "What happened?"

"What's hypothermia look like? She wasn't breathing when I pulled her out. On my count it was two sets of rescue breaths and maybe thirty chest compressions before she started breathing."

Todd stands behind Andy. "I didn't think you were supposed to do rescue breathing anymore. Was he supposed to do that?"

"You really, *really* need to shut up, Todd." I would punch him in the mouth if he were closer.

Andy speaks up. "There's a cardiologist staying in the main lodge. Todd and I'll go get him. Tucker, does she need an ambulance?"

He stands tall over me and Macy. "I can't tell. I'd feel better if the doctor looked her over. Her vitals are okay. The pulse's a little thready for my taste."

"She's still so cold. What about hypothermia?"

"Just get me warm, for Jesus' sake." Macy croaks.

I look down at her. Her face is still too grey. "You don't speak. Your bullshit tough girl act almost got you drowned over a fucking fish. No talking."

She smiles. A tiny, tiny smile. "I'm grounded?"

I feel better. She's giving me attitude, she can't be too close to death's door, right? "Yes, you're definitely grounded. Don't talk."

I drive her back to her apartment. She lets me pull her close, keep her held next to me with one arm. Every so often her whole body shudders, and I hear her teeth clack together violently. I look down each time, and she smiles faintly. I see her shoulders square as she wills herself to stop trembling.

"I wish you would've just stayed. I could've put a cot in front of the fire. You need to stay warm."

She shakes her head. "It's June. I'm fine. I'll be fine."

We pull into her parking lot, and I help her into her apartment.

"Thanks for the ride." She stands in the middle of her living room, waiting for me to leave.

"I'm not leaving yet. I'm going to wait while you take a hot shower, and then once you're settled, I'll go."

She frowns. "Since when are you the boss?"

"Since you almost died. You're grounded, remember? Stubbornness has its consequences."

She sighs. "Fine."

She drifts into the bathroom, and I hear the light click on. I stand close, in the hallway, listening to make sure everything's fine. She's right—since when did I get so bossy? Protective, actually. When did this girl make me want to protect her? I feel the weight of that on my shoulders as I remember the weight of her body, cold in the water.

"Jesus." In the bathroom, she sucks air in through her teeth.

I take two long strides and push the door open. "Macy? What is it?"

The fluorescent light flickers a little. She stands in front of the bathroom counter in sweats and a bra.

"Geez." She raises her left arm.

"Damn." I look where she's now gingerly poking with the tip of one small finger.

Her whole side, from armpit to waist, is black, blue, purplish-red. Bruised like a side of meat.

"Dang. No wonder it hurts so bad to take a breath."

I turn on my heels. "Put your shirt back on. We're going to the hospital, like I said we should from the start."

"What hospital? I don't want to drive to Idaho Falls. All the doc in the boxes are closed. There's nothing, Mr. Bossy Pants. Nowhere to go." She pulls the shirt back on.

"Fine. Are you going to shower then?"

She comes close to me. "You know what? Will you help me get settled, like you promised?"

"Sure."

She leads the way down the hall, calls to the dogs. "I usually kennel them up, but I like the idea of them sleeping at the bottom of the bed tonight."

She swings the bedroom door open.

This is a weird moment for me. I try to think of another occasion when I've been in a woman's bedroom, a woman who I want, without a doubt, when I've had no desire to knock her down and make mad, passionate love to her.

But I don't. First of all, the whole bedroom is pink. The walls she must have painted herself in wide, dark rose and light pink stripes. It's atrocious. Not a love den, as far as I'm concerned. Plus, there is a ridiculous, huge flag of Canada pinned to the ceiling.

"Oh, Canada, that is a big ol' flag."

She snorts. "You are not allowed to make fun of my flag. Not when I can't beat you to a pulp for teasing me."

She crawls so carefully under the pink covers, I wince. She must be in an insane amount of pain.

"Let me help." I hold a hand out, and to my surprise, she takes it, presses hard against it for leverage as she swings her legs up on the bed and gingerly scoots down under the covers.

"Good night, Mr. King." She lies on her back, holding still, hands resting on either side of her body. She looks like she's afraid to move, she's so banged up. The two little dogs jump up on the bed and curl up together at the end of the bed.

"I'm not leaving. I'll crash out on the couch in the living room. Try to get some sleep." I get up and snap off the light, walk out the door.

"Um, hey. Hey, can you come here?" Her voice squeaks.

I come back to the doorway. "Macy?"

"I leave a light on. Can you come turn on the dresser lamp?"

I turn the overhead light on again, go to the dresser and switch on the little pink and white gingham lamp, shut off the overhead light. "Macy?"

"Uh-huh?" She's pulled the covers up to her chin.

"I can stay in here if you want."

"I'd still leave the lights on. You aren't some big knight in shining armor."

"What are you afraid of? This isn't about almost drowning today, is it?"

"I've just always slept with the lights on, that's all. And thanks for the unnecessary 'you almost died' memo. I don't need it—I'm too sore to turn over, remember?"

I sit on the other side of the bed. "You didn't say no."

"About what?"

"Do you want me to stay in here? I'll sleep on top of the covers, if you want. No hidden agenda. Just company for you."

She closes her eyes. It feels like she's testing out the darkness behind her lids, testing to see if she's strong enough to stay in the darkness. "You could stay in here. There's an extra blanket on that chair by the closet. And don't get your toes too close to Justin Trudeau. He's a toe-biter."

I walk over to the chair and pluck off the fluffy pink blanket. "What's with all the pink?"

"I like pink. Shut up and lie down."

I slip off my shoes, lie down next to her, cover up with the blanket.

I prop myself up a bit and slip my phone out of my pocket, scroll through the e-mails I've ignored for two days now. I never ignore e-mails.

"You can't do that. It's bad for your brain. You won't be able to sleep."

I look over at her. Her eyelids droop, and her voice sounds faint, wispy almost.

"Fine." I set the phone down on the bedside table and turn to face her, propped on an elbow. Her eyes are closed now.

"Thanks."

"My pleasure, Macy."

She falls asleep hard, her lips parting, a rough sound at every inhale. I worry. Is that damage? Water in her lungs? I lie there, grind my teeth in frustration. No one listened to me. The girl should've gone to the hospital. I don't care what Mr. Cardiologist says.

Macy tries to roll over and cries out in pain.

My hand shoots out and touches her shoulder. "You're okay. Just stay still."

She takes my hand and wraps both her hands around my arm, pulling me close. "It hurts."

"Shh. Sleep." Now my face is dangerously close to hers. But she's out. I just lie still and feel the warm, ragged air on my skin as she exhales.

I watch her sleep for most of the night before I have the nerve to untangle my arm and close my eyes. I don't let go of her hand, though.

It's a nice last thing to see before you fall asleep at night. You know, a delicate, soft hand, clasped in your hand.

That's not some mushy bullshit, it's just true.

THE GETAWAY

I finally wake up the next morning to look into warm, brown eyes.

The warm, brown eyes of JT, wonder dog extraordinaire. Whose underbite is agape, with tongue lolling, and he's very, very close to my face.

He's wedged himself between Macy and me, and the alleged toe-biter is either about to tongue-kiss me or bite my face off.

"Good morning." I say it to him in as sweet a voice as I can muster.

Macy sighs. "Good morning."

I wonder if she remembers that if she moves, she's gonna hurt. What was a black purple reddish battle ground over her ribs has probably turned for the worse.

I close my eyes, mostly to shut out the moist dog breath on my face, but when I do, I see her lips, blue, and her eyes, white without pupil. I feel her cold, wet body limp against mine.

I give her hand a squeeze. "How do you feel?"

Justin Trudeau suddenly wags all over. The movement may have started in his tail, but his whole spazzy little body is now shaking and quivering.

We're awake, and his dumb doggie brain has registered it, and damn, he's one excited little dog.

Macy squeezes my hand back. "I think I'm just a giant bruise. I hurt."

Justin whimpers.

"Does he need to go out?"

I've apparently said the magic words. Justin Trudeau is no longer in between Macy and me. He's shot down the bed, on to the floor, and out into the living room. I can hear his toenails tipping and tapping on the linoleum floor in the kitchen.

I can see Macy now. She still has her eyes closed. Her long, dark lashes fan out over her pale cheeks. She's not got her color back.

In front of her sweet face, her hands are entwined with mine. Her fingers lace between mine, and her fingertips sparkle pink.

She opens her eyes. They are blue-green, flecked with gold. I've never been this close to them indoors. They're exquisite.

"He needs to go out, definitely. That's the potty dance he's doing, and in a second, he'll pee on the living room carpet. And then I'll lose my pet deposit." Her brow furrows in worry.

She makes a move to turn over, and it's clear that it's not a good move. She sucks in her breath. "Oh, ow, ow that hurts. Oh!"

"Hey, I got this. Stay put." I spring off the bed and shoot into the living room, looking for the little dog's leash.

By now, though, Justin has alerted the rest of the Canadian delegation, Pierre Trudeau the French-Canadian bulldog, and so I'm greeted with two eager dogs doing the potty dance.

"Keep a lid on it, mutts. Show me where your leashes are." I try to locate both of my shoes and the leashes all at once.

By some miracle the dogs have honed in on what I need and bounce under the breakfast bar. I spy the leashes in a bowl above them and grab them.

"Sit! Sit? Sit, for Chrissakes!" I bark at the dogs.

"You don't need to be a jerk!" I hear Macy call from the bedroom.

"Handled! It's all good! Not being mean in the slightest!" I have JT's leash on, and the more peaceable bulldog sits like an angel as I circle his chubby neck with his leash.

Then we're out the front door. I half-have my shoes on—I'm ruining a very expensive pair of Gurkha boots by stepping into them without unlacing them.

It's biting cold and blazingly bright. "Jesus!" I can't help it. In LA the temperature is a steady 64 degrees, whether six am or six pm or high noon or midnight. Kind of tepid bath water twenty-four seven.

In Idaho, in June, it's chilly. Then it's blazing hot. Then it hails, then it's frosty. If you take two steps down the river, the temperature in the shade suddenly drops ten degrees.

The cool air sinks into the bed of the river, and until the sun arcs over the high foothills, the freezing river and the cool air chills.

Which is the temperature situation right now, and I'm wearing jeans, a t-shirt, no socks, and sort of shoes—I'm wearing them like scuffs.

The dogs tug and bounce.

I follow them down the sidewalk in front of Macy's apartment to a little patch of grass at the end of the townhouses.

"Okay gents, time to do your business." I stand and feel my neck and nipples freeze solid while the dogs contemplate the mysteries of life to be found in the blades of grass and that one gum wrapper they've found on the scrap of lawn.

"Mornin'." A deep, smoke-scraped voice speaks up behind me.

I spin around. The bulldog barks, and it's not a friendly hello.

In front of me is a bigger guy, thick forearms, wide nose, sandy blonde curly hair, with a shark tooth necklace and a gray sweat shirt. He smokes.

"Can I help you?" I try to sound confident. Not beat-up-able.

"You Macy's friend?" He takes a pull on the cigarette, pulls a piece of tobacco from between his lips, flicks it away between his rough fingers.

I size the guy up. "Who wants to know?" The dogs are done and crouch at my feet. Maybe they're my reinforcements.

"Tell Macy that Troy came by. She knows what it's about," he says.

"Any reason you need to see her at seven in the morning?"

He sneers. "I've got five-hundred reasons. Remind her there's a deadline and there's interest."

"Call her if you need to give her a message. Not my job."

He smiles, slow, flicks the lit cigarette at the dog closest to him. Pierre jumps sideways to avoid being singed. "Will do. Keep an eye on your pets, mister. The girl included. They get themselves in trouble a lot."

He turns and ambles away across the parking lot. He climbs into an old burgundy pick-up, still idling. I pull the dogs down the sidewalk as the truck screeches out of the parking lot, leaving burnt rubber on the pavement and the smell of it in the air.

"Fucker."

Justin Trudeau agrees with my assessment of Troy. He barks loud, once, calling after the departed truck.

I bring Macy some toast and a glass of water. There wasn't much in her fridge.

"Can you give me a boost out of bed? I need to go to the bathroom, too." She hasn't made it very far. She is turned over on her side, facing the edge of the bed.

"Are you doing the potty dance?" I grin. It is a feeling beyond relief to see her awake and functional. Yesterday's scare at the river still has a grip on my nervous system.

She reaches out for my hand and pulls on it. I hear her suck in her breath. Then she's out of the bed.

She wears what I put her in last night—sweats and a t-shirt from one of the guys' suitcase. I can't remember who ran to get dry clothes when we were waiting for the cardiologist to finish checking her out.

She shuffles into the bathroom and I hear it—a rasp, almost a rattle, when she breathes in. Then she speaks up. "Can you go feed the dogs? I have a shy bladder."

"Fine." I go tend to the pups.

The toilet flushes, and then I hear her coughing. It sounds terrible, like a loose penny at the bottom of a Coke can.

I fish my phone out of my shirt pocket. Dialing, I can feel my heart pounding faster and faster as I think. *Something's wrong. She's not supposed to cough like that.* My brain chews on the thought, turns it over and over, to the point that I think I'm short of breath by the time the phone is answered on the other end of the line.

"Hello?"

"Hey, Tessa, it's Jeremy. Jeremy King, Andy's friend?"

I think I hear a snort. "You mean Andrew. What's going on? Is everyone all right?"

"Everyone's fine. Well, not everyone, but everyone you know. Listen, can you put Dr. Joe on the line? He's not left for work yet, has he?"

A loud exhale. "No. He's here. This better be good. You're sure you didn't do anything stupid to Andrew? Kelly'll tie your balls in a knot if something happens to him."

"I told you he's fine. Tessa, please." I hear my voice crack, just a tiny, tiny bit, but it's clear. "Please."

"Wow. Okay, Jeremy. I'll get him." I can hear her muffle the phone. There's a long pause.

"Hello?" It's Joe, Tessa's husband, and the Pettigrew/Reynolds family doctor. It's not my family, but it's the closest I have to a family, so right now I'm claiming him as my family doctor, too.

"Joe, it's Jeremy. Listen, I appreciate your time. I'll make it quick. So there's this woman—"

"I don't want to know about your sex life, please," he interrupts.

"Jesus, it's not anything like that. I have plenty of LA doctors for stupid stuff like that. This girl, she almost drowned in the river yesterday, well, actually she did, I gave her CPR, she was blue, she was unconscious for at least, I don't know, maybe 90 seconds, a cardiologist checked her out, but now this morning her lungs sound rotten—"

Joe breaks in again. "This a friend of yours?"

"Yes. Well, she's our fishing guide. The cough. It's terrible. I'm worried, Joe."

He takes a deep breath. "You are a man with a lot of money and connections. You want to make sure she's completely okay, take her to a real hospital. She might have aspirated water into her lungs or she could develop pneumonia. Wouldn't hurt her to give her a thorough check."

"Where?"

"You could bring her to Boise."

"If I have to get a jet, I could take her pretty much anywhere. Where would you take her?"

"Seattle, then. You can't go wrong with Virginia Mason. They've got a top rate pulmonary clinic. More than likely she just needs to rest. She's young, I take it."

"I don't know how old she is, but yeah."

"She's twenty-one at least, right?" Sounds like Joe is judging by the rise in his tone.

"Of course." God, what kind of impression do I make on people? Jesus. "C'mon, Joe. This isn't easy for me, asking for your advice."

"Fine, I'm sorry. Okay, I have to go. Andrew okay? Tucker good?"

"Everyone's fine. Thanks, Joe. I know it's not standard. I appreciate it."

He chuckles. "Hope she's worth the plane ride."

"Definitely. She definitely is worth it."

It surprises me to hear, but I said it and I believe it.

I hang up and walk back into the bedroom. Macy's back in bed, trying to pull pillows behind her to prop herself up. Each movement she makes is tiny.

"I'll do that." I get her tucked in, settle her in on the pillows.

"Thanks." She picks up the toast and nibbles.

"Now that I have you right where I want you…"

"Helpless and injured?" She smiles.

"That's how I like my women. No, really."

"No, really." She takes my hand. "I do want to say thank you. Completely. You saved my life. I drowned." She holds my hand in both of hers and looks down at it, avoiding my eyes.

"I'm glad I was there. But now you do something for me."

She frowns. "What?"

"Come to Seattle with me." I pick up my phone again.

"What? Why?" Her head tilts, confused. Then she leans back suspiciously.

"Humor me. I don't like how you sound when you breathe. It's not right."

"That's ridiculous. You're being ridiculous."

"I'm being cautious. No one even let me take you to the emergency room."

"No." She crosses her arms over her chest.

"No, you don't get to say no. No one else saw you when I pulled you up out of the water. No one gets it."

She looks doubtful. "I'd miss work."

"You can't guide all banged up. And ten bucks says you're on light duty until a doctor gives you release anyway. That's how getting hurt on the job works."

She chews on her lip. "Worker's comp is no good. I have to work. That looks bad if you take worker's comp."

"It's there to take care of the employee and the employer when someone gets hurt during work. This is exactly how it's supposed to work. You let me take you to Seattle, the doc there will clear you to return to work after a couple days tops, and I can show you around Seattle while you rest up."

That last thing makes her think. She raises an eyebrow. "You know good places for seafood there?"

"Of course. And we'll stay somewhere really nice, so you can sleep on soft sheets and heal up a little."

"If we go, I'd want to go to the Space Needle."

"Done." I don't tell her that I think the Space Needle is cheesy tourist crap, because I can see a little of her twinkle coming back into her eyes.

"All right. What about the dogs?"

I smile. "They can come with."

"They'll be scared on the plane," she worries.

"They can sit on your lap."

She questions this. "No, they can't. They don't let you do that on a flight, do they?"

"They do if you're on a private plane."

Her eyes go wide. "What?"

"Macy Shea Summerlin. I am a Hollywood agent. I am loaded. You need to be a better listener."

"Okay. You have a ton of money. I just assumed you were full of crap."

"I am about a lot of things, but that one's the truth."

"It's a deal then." She puts out her hand.

I take it in mine and kiss it, Prince Charming-style. Then I turn it over and kiss the tender bright pink scar on her palm. "Thanks. It'll set my mind at ease."

Maybe I can be the man in the white hat this time. She needs it; I can just feel it in my bones.

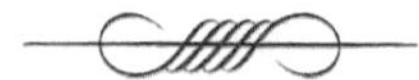

I don't even want to say anything to the guys. We're supposed to leave in three days. I ignore that part and start planning our trip to Seattle. I go out front of Macy's place and begin making calls.

It actually feels good. This is what I do. I call the office, put my best assistant on getting the plane to Idaho Falls, and I call in all my doctor friend chips that I have in LA.

Twenty-five minutes later, Macy Shea Summerlin has a private room on the fourth floor of Virginia Mason Hospital in Seattle waiting for her. The pulmonologist will be waiting to consult this evening. The plane should be in Idaho Falls by the time I get her and her little dogs out of this place and convince Andy to drive us all to the airport.

And so now I have to call him. He texted to say they were headed out on to the river and should they wait for me. I told him no.

He knows me. He knows none of what is going on is normal. He didn't even ask about the rental car in the text.

I call him.

"Jeremy?" He answers before it even rings.

"Andy."

"Is she okay? Is everything okay? Kelly called and wanted to know what the hell you were doing calling Joe at home. She's worried sick, and she hasn't even met Macy."

"Joe told me to go get her checked out. Said it could be bad. When she breathes, it doesn't sound right."

"So you're taking her into town?" I can hear his gear rattling. Maybe he waited for me to call. It sounds like he's walking down to the river.

I swallow hard. "I'm taking her to Seattle."

"What?"

"Joe told me that's the best. I Googled near-drowning. She could deteriorate rapidly. That's what it said."

Andy covers the phone, and I can hear him calling out to somebody. Then he's back on the line. "Come here and pick me up. I'll take the two of you to Idaho Falls in the Yukon."

God love him. "Thank you, Andy. I really owe you one."

"No, you don't. I trust Joe, and I trust your gut. Your instinct has never steered us wrong before. Take care of her." He breathes in deep.

He almost lost Kelly. Maybe the way I feel right now, maybe that's how he felt then. Kelly was in danger, and he would have moved mountains for her.

Maybe that's how I feel right now. "I'll get everyone loaded up and get over there. Thanks, buddy. And Andy?"

"Yeah?"

"Can you keep a lid on this to the guys? I don't need a lot of grief. I just want to make sure Macy's okay. She doesn't have anybody else to do that for her."

"I will. I promise to punch Todd in the face if he so much as makes one snarky comment."

I end the call and slip back in the front door. "Okay, troops, let's get moving."

Macy shuffles out of the bedroom. "What?"

"We're on the move. Do the dogs have carriers?"

She opens her eyes wide. "Like, now?"

I nod. "Plane's leaving in fifty minutes. Let's hop to it."

She stands frozen. "I don't know where to start. I need to pack, I need to call Richard and tell him I'm not going to be in town, I can't go right now."

I put leashes on both the dogs, who've come to sit at my feet. They may be crazy, but they can hear the "we're leaving" sound in my voice. I turn to Macy. "I will buy you anything you need when we get there. You can make calls from the car. Bring your purse and the charger for your phone, and you're golden."

She shakes her head. "You're unbelievable. I don't need this. I'm fine."

On cue, she coughs, and there's that loose penny rattle again.

"Not fine enough for my liking." I take the dogs by the leashes and lead them out the door. "I'll be back to help you to the car in a minute," I call over my shoulder.

"Fine!" She calls after me.

Andy waits on the front steps of our lodge when we pull up, and he doesn't hesitate to hop in the SUV. I don't even have to turn off the engine.

He slides in the back seat, and immediately little dogs besiege him. "Hi, kids. I hear you're going on a trip."

Macy dips her head. "Your friend here is crazy."

Andy arranges the dogs, one on each side of him, pats their heads. "He's saner than usual. And it never hurts to play it safe in the major organs area."

I nod and look Macy in the eye. "You kind of have to breathe. It's not optional. Even Andy knows that."

She sighs and sits back gingerly against the passenger seat. "Fine. You win."

We chat aimlessly for a while after that, mostly about the Toronto shoot that looms in the near future for Andy. I'm supposed to go with him to location next week. It's the first time since we've been here that I've thought about it. And it makes my gut clench. There's not enough time. I need more time before we go do that.

Then we're at the terminal, and I get out, and Andy helps me with the dogs and the one bag Macy crammed full of who knows what, and then I help Macy out of the car. I can hear the plane powering up, and I make a mental note that I'll owe quite a few favors when I get back to LA.

Macy and the dogs are slowly walking toward the tarmac. I turn to Andy, grateful for a minute to talk with him out of Macy's earshot.

"I can't thank you enough." I shake his hand, turn over the car keys.

"J, I know how this is. When someone you love needs help, you do whatever it takes."

"Love. I don't know about that." I cough uncomfortably.

He shrugs. "You've never behaved this way in the eleven years I've known you. If this is just how you treat river guides, I've been working at the wrong job."

He claps me on the back and gets in the car, waves as he pulls off the curb.

I jog to catch up.

Love.

There's no time to think like that. It's ridiculous. I've known this person five days.

This person who I am flying to Seattle.

I shake it off and help her up the steps of the plane.

"Wheels up in ten, Mr. King." The pilot and the flight attendant stand at the front of the aisle.

"Thanks. And thanks for being so responsive."

The pilot shakes my hand. "Our pleasure. Trisha here will get you settled and comfortable."

The dogs cry and whine at first, but Macy pulls out two new chew bones for them, and they curl up on either side of her legs and settle in for a good long chew.

I sit next to her, and our shoulders touch.

We take off without incident.

The flight attendant takes a seat in the galley when she's certain there's nothing else she can do for us. I'm glad to have Macy to myself.

"So?" I touch her gently on the hand.

"So, what?" She looks at me, straight in the eyes. She hasn't done that since she agreed to come with me to Seattle.

"Is this going to be okay, me taking you to Seattle? You aren't going to freak out and tell me to go drown and rot, are you?"

"I was cruel once, and now you aren't going to let me live it down." She smiles. And she turns her hand over so that she's holding my hand.

"I promise I'll leave you alone once I know that you're okay." I give her hand a little squeeze.

"I hope not." She yawns. "I think I'm just going to close my eyes."

"Okay."

She adjusts her seat a bit. "I guess now is when I tell you I've never been on a plane before."

I can't believe this girl. "I've spoiled you for good. This isn't the usual experience. Flying commercial isn't at all like this—think Greyhound bus with wings."

"M-hm." Her eyes are shut. She coughs a little bit, and my pulse revs up with worry.

Then her head drifts to the side, and suddenly, she's resting on my shoulder.

And holding my hand.

And I'm getting pretty damned used to it.

SLEEPLESS IN SEATTLE

We make quite a crew. The dogs are in absolute orbit until the excitement overtakes Justin Trudeau, and he passes out in the town car on the way to the hotel.

"How is this going to work? I'm staying here at the hotel?" Macy pets the little French bulldog and looks at the passing city blocks.

"You stay where the doctors say. Right now we're dropping the dogs off and driving to the hospital."

"They can't be in a hotel room by themselves. They'll tear it apart. You don't want that kind of a bill on your hands, even if you are rich like you say."

She's unbelievable. "You still don't believe me. You think the plane was an elaborate con?" I think for a second and pull my sleeve up. "Look at my watch."

She takes my wrist in her hand, which I love the feel of, and examines the watch. "So?"

"That's a Rolex Cosmograph Daytona in 18 karat gold. It runs about twenty-nine grand."

"Wow." She looks at it again for a minute. "That'd be a new car for me."

"I'm not saying it to impress you. I'm saying it so that you believe that I'm being straight with you. I like honesty. I'm honest with you."

She nods. "I get it. Mr. King is an honest man. A rich man, but an honest man." She looks back out the window. Something has her quiet.

"The dogs'll be fine. I asked the concierge to get a dog walker to come play with them while we go to the hospital. We're five blocks apart. Everyone will be fine."

She looks back at me. "Really?"

"Here's another thing about me—I handle details. I am all over the little stuff. My job demands that I do." All this talk about me would usually give me a hard-on. I love when the topic of discussion is me. Except it just doesn't feel right with Macy. Like we don't need to talk so much. Or I don't need to prove myself like I usually do. I don't know. "Look at all the stuff you've learned about the mysterious world of Hollywood agents. You could come with me to LA tomorrow."

She raises an eyebrow. "If you weren't so overprotective, you mean."

"Well, yeah."

We pull up in front of the W hotel, and Macy oohs and aahs.

"Never been to Seattle, I take it." I take her by the elbow, help her out of the car.

"Never been out of Idaho. No, scratch that, I've been to Wyoming and Utah. Just over the state line fishing in Yellowstone for Wyoming, and to Bear Lake once camping in Utah. Also just over the border."

I wrap an arm around her. "I haven't been to either of those places, so there you go. We both have more exploring to do."

She likes that I evened things out, I can tell—her shoulders straighten up a little. So much of the time she's looking at the ground or rounding her shoulders in. She almost cowers. Like the little dogs, like she's been hurt before. Physically hurt.

How anyone could harm this girl, I don't know…I drop that train of thought before it enrages me.

We make our way into the hotel lobby.

Macy looks all around, wandering into the bar and lounge area, as the concierge waits on me.

It's clear she's still hurting, but she has a big broad smile on her face as she shuffles back over to me. "Have you seen all the hot pink chandeliers? This is my kind of place."

We meet the dog handler, and the concierge falls all over himself to get the dogs settled in the suite.

"We'll be back." I call over my shoulder to him as I guide Macy back out the doors.

"You're in a hurry." She seems reluctant to leave.

"I'm in a hurry. The pulmonologist is waiting." I pull the door of the waiting cab open for her and help tuck her inside.

Inside, she shifts, trying to settle in comfortably. "Maybe your doctors can help me feel less sore."

"Did you take anything?" I think of Andy, when he was clipped by a car two years ago—he didn't take pain meds, and the pain showed on his face. Macy looks like that now. My friends seem to get put through the ringer. Maybe it's hanging out with me.

Macy shrugs. "I don't like that kind of stuff. I've seen too many people wrecked by it."

We're at the front doors of the hospital, and they're expecting us. An orderly, a big guy in scrubs, waits with a wheelchair as we pull into the turnaround.

"Here we go." I jump out and pay the cabbie, get around to the other side so I can help Macy into the chair.

She eases into it, and I see her shoulders relax as she sits back. "Fun times."

Upstairs we wait in a very gray and very antiseptic lounge area. A nurse has given Macy pages and pages of paperwork to fill out. Macy scribbles for a while, and at the last page of forms, she starts to squirm and chew on the cap of the pen.

Macy snaps the pen down on the clipboard. "We should just go."

"What?"

"It's asking about insurance. I don't have health insurance. We should go." She tries to stand up, and I put a hand on her arm, pull her back into the chair gently.

"Hold up. One, it's worker's comp. You're covered, insurance or no. Two, I'd cover you, and you could pay me back if it weren't. Finish filling them out."

She gnaws through the pen cap by the time she finishes it. "Fine. Done."

"What's with the pissy attitude? You're covered."

"I don't like all the personal questions. It's just invasive. Too much." Her hands cross her chest.

The nurse comes back to usher her back to a room. "We're ready for you, Miss Summerlin."

She stands up and takes a few steps, and then she turns back to me.

"Well?"

"What?" I don't know what she needs.

"You're coming in with me. Come on."

I'm surprised. "You sure?"

"You're Mr. Details. I won't remember everything they say, and then I'll come out, and you'll be all like 'what did they say?' and then I'll feel dumb. And I want the rest of this trip to be fun. So come on."

I hop up and follow. "Good thought. I'll take notes on my phone."

"Good job, Sherlock. Way to be thorough."

In the exam room, I turn my back for Macy to slip on one of those disposable exam gowns. She's still got on her black yoga pants. Her hair is pulled back, like she wears it when she's fishing. She's not wearing make-up, not that I can tell.

She looks down at the gown and picks at the hem of it, tearing little notches into its paper.

She's gorgeous.

The doctor strides in, puts out a hand, all smiles. She's got bright blonde hair all pulled up on the top of her head, and she's got curves. A knock-out pulmonologist.

"Dr. Kathleen Kirkland. Macy?" She shakes Macy's hand.

Macy points at me. "This is my friend Mr. King. He's the scribe. He's also supposed to ask the good questions. Doctors make me nervous."

Dr. Kirkland smiles. "Big job. Nice to meet you." She shakes and pulls a chart, points at my phone. "It's going to be a minute before we go there, but I'll give you the sign."

Twenty minutes later, Macy's been wheeled down a long, white hall, off to imaging and labs for work-ups. After a long listen to Macy's lungs with her stethoscope, Dr. Kirkland seems mostly satisfied with what she hears, but she also pays me the favor of humoring my first person account of what Macy looked like fresh out of the water, and how she's sounded since.

I pace in the waiting room. I take a minute to look through work e-mails, and it takes all of two e-mails about the latest contract wrangling with Amanda the crazy movie star to convince me to shut off my phone.

Usually that's the kind of contract fight that gets my blood up, but right now, it feels like so much petty bullshit.

Here, where I am right now, we're talking life and death, and we're talking about taking care of each other. I like the way that feels.

Dr. Kirkland comes back down the hall. In any other situation, this would be a woman whose number I would get. Successful doctor with a body like that? I'd be all over her, literally and figuratively.

Right now, though, I want info on Macy.

"Macy said it's okay if I fill you in, as long as you pay good attention." She smiles.

"She's kind of bossy. I'm just doing what I'm told." I pull out my phone and prepare to be attentive.

"Seems like that's a role reversal for you." She raises an eyebrow. Of course she probably knows who I am. I called in a very big favor from a very big name in LA to get her to consult on Macy's case. We're in a hospital at four in the afternoon on a Friday. Not usual doctor territory.

"Everything about this situation is upside down, I'm not gonna lie."

Dr. Kirkland looks at the chart. "So here's the long and short of it. No aspiration damage. It's definitely possible that she did take some water into her lungs. The length of time her brain was without oxygen, that can be a concern, but the water temperature induces a shock state that probably inhibited that response. So pneumonia is your main concern, and if she takes it easy for a few days, she should be in the clear."

"What do you prescribe?"

"I'd watch her, keep her in Seattle, nearby, maybe overnight, maybe two days. You could go back on Sunday. I'm on call for the weekend."

"She wants to see the Space Needle," I say.

"Let her. Don't let her do a lot of walking. She got pretty banged up, and I wrote a scrip for an anti-inflammatory and an antibiotic, the first one to help work all that swelling and hematoma out of her system and the other in case she did take bacteria into her lungs with the water."

"Thanks, Dr. Kirkland. I owe you."

"Not to worry. This is what I do. She's a lucky girl."

I nod. "Yeah, it could've been bad."

"She's lucky for that, and for your vigilance. Never hurts to have someone watching out for you." She smiles and shakes my hand, and just like that, I'm free to take Macy to the hotel.

To. The. Hotel.

And so my mind gets to thinking, but I remind that side of me that she's bruised and beat up, remind myself to knock it off.

So I do. Which is not easy.

At the hotel, we get in the elevator with keys in hand and a full report from the dog handler, who met us in the lobby with the dogs. The dogs seem happy but tired. Little JT's tongue hangs almost to the floor.

Macy leans into me a little as I push the button for our floor.

"What button'd you push?" She says drowsily. It's been a long day. From her apartment doorstep to now, I'd count about eight hours. Pretty tough on someone who almost drowned a day ago.

"Top floor, of course." I slip an arm around her shoulders.

Now this is the part where I usually kick it into high gear. Remember what I told you about my dates? Create an experience for the girl, casually knock her socks off with displays of thoughtfulness paired with conspicuous consumption.

But tonight, I've just got a really nice hotel room. I don't even have a plan. I have a small-town, hell, no-town girl in the big city, the old country mouse story, and I don't have a wooing agenda.

The elevator arrives at the top floor, and I guide Macy and the bouncing dogs down the hall. The dogs know the way—they've already become accustomed to the lifestyle of suite living.

I take the key and let us in.

"Wow." Macy takes in the floor to ceiling window views of Seattle. Everything sparkles.

"Appropriate word choice. This is the 'extreme wow' suite."

She's over by the wet bar. "Look! Come look at this!"

I stroll over to her. She's freaking out over food and water bowls with placemats for the dogs.

"That is so cool. Look Justin and Pierre, you've got your own placemats!"

"You better go check out the bedroom." I smile.

"What?"

"Just go look."

She walks in as fast as her sore body can carry her. "Aww, they each have their own bed! And there's a treat on the little doggie pillow!"

"Turndown treat." I walk in the bedroom and stuff my hands in my pockets. I'm afraid if I see Macy—see the big fluffy bed, think the thoughts I've been thinking about her since I realized I'd be alone in a hotel room with her—well, let's just say that hands in my pockets means hands to myself. Macy needs me to be the knight in shining armor, not some horn dog.

"This is beautiful. Damn." She stands there, turns a full circle, taking in the room and the view.

"That's one for the swear jar. I like the W hotel in Barcelona the best, but this one is cool."

She sits down on the bed. "Mr. King. I'm suitably impressed. You don't have to keep dropping the 'I'm good at everything' hints."

"Long, bad habit." I sit on the bed next to her. "Can I be honest with you?"

"You say you always are." She's sitting awfully close to me.

"I think it's pretty important to me that people are impressed by me."

"Huh. That's honest of you. What do you think makes you feel like that?"

I take a deep breath, try to think about that. Jeremy King doesn't do introspection. Self-reflection doesn't win deals. "It feels good. I like to feel good at things. I'm good at things. I want people to know it."

That's all I've got. Navel-gazing moment over.

She ponders this, purses her lips. "Seems fair. So. There's only one bed." She looks at me and licks her bottom lip. I think nervously. I don't think she's trying to be hot. She is hot, smokingly so, but I don't see seduction in her eyes. I see worry.

"No, there's a spacious sofa out in the living room. That's mine." I sound nonchalant. I'm proud, because that's the most lying I've done to Macy. It kills me, *kills* me to not sleep in the bed with her.

Her eyes lighten, the crinkles around them relax. "Oh, okay. Not that you couldn't sleep here, too, but I'm so sore, and…"

"The point is for you to heal. Me tossing and turning won't help." Look at me, being all man in the white hat.

She points out at the Seattle night. "What should we do? We should go out."

I shake my head. "I'm pretty beat. This was a big day. Dr. Kirkland wants you to stay in town 'til Sunday. Tomorrow night we can go out. Deal?"

She looks relieved. "Deal." She puts her hand out for a shake.

I lean in and kiss her on the cheek instead. "How about room service?"

"Let's order a ton of stuff. Do you mind?" She gets up and walks into the living room.

"Of course not. I like to take two bites off of everything. We can even drink tiny stupidly overpriced bottles of liquor out of the minibar." I go to it and open it up.

Her face falls. "No can do. Antibiotics, remember?"

I have an Andy déjà vu moment. I can't drink with anybody, I swear. Maybe someone's trying to send me a message. "No worries. It's a dry weekend. No point in ruining your liver when we just saved the rest of you, right?" I pull a smartwater for both of us out of the fridge instead.

We spend the evening ordering room service, feeding the dogs tiny bites of pepperoni pizza and pulled pork for dancing on their hind legs, and cleaning up Justin Trudeau's puke in the bathroom (too much pulled pork for him, apparently).

Then it's close to eleven, and Macy's done for. We're sitting on her bed, watching TV. She tries to keep her eyes open, but her chin dips and her mouth goes slack.

"Macy." I reach out and touch her cheek.

Her head pops up, and her eyes are wide. "I'm awake."

"Get under the covers." I stand up and lift the creamy duvet. She slides under, and her eyes are drooping already.

"'Night." She's out. The dogs snore from their beds at the foot of the bed.

I pace.

I stare out the window.

I do suck it up and go through my work e-mail. It's all bullshit stuff. I forward most of it to junior agents, offloading all the politicking and maneuvering.

I pace some more.

I consider taking a shower and taking care of my needs. I ditch this idea. I think "my needs" will only get worse if I deliberate on what I want to do to Macy. Oh, what I could do to her.

Except when I cruise past the bedroom door (open) and look in on her (light on, per her request), I don't want to jump her bones. Shocking, I know.

I want to hold her. I want to kiss her. I want to keep her with me, next to me.

I want to love her.

Then I go in the other room and consider slamming my hand in the minibar door for fun.

I'm fucked.

At some point, I decide to have a drink out of the minibar in hopes of relaxing enough to get to bed, and I find the local paper.

I strip down to my t-shirt and boxers and pull an extra blanket and pillow from the closet. I crash on the couch and fall asleep reading about Seattle traffic and the Seahawks.

I should have known. I wake in the cold of the early morning, dissatisfied and aching. I have had the most tantalizing dream about Macy. Intimate, scorching hot, and teeth-grindingly frustrating.

I lie there for a minute when a blood curdling scream rips through the room.

"Macy!" I can't even conjure what would cause such a shriek. I cover the distance to her bed in three panicked galloping strides.

She sits up, her body pulled in tightly, her arms wrapped around her knees. Her eyes are wide open, and she cries, howls.

"Macy!" She doesn't respond. She looks right through me. At something that terrifies her.

I sit there. I reach out to touch her arm, and my touch sets off a new round of cries.

"It's okay, Macy. It's okay." I sit close to her. I don't know what to do. The light's already on.

She cries and whimpers and stays pulled into that tight little curled position for about ten more minutes.

I'm about to get on the phone and call Dr. Joe again when her eyes close. She slowly releases herself, stretches her legs out and eases down under the covers.

"Macy?" I say her name one more time.

"Please." She puts a hand out of the nest of covers.

I take it, and she pulls me close to her, with a strength I'm surprised by.

"Macy, it's okay."

"Please." She has her head on my chest, and her arms are looped around mine. My body shields hers.

From what, I don't know. I wish I knew.

The next morning, I wake up feeling like I stayed out all night tying one on. My head pounds, and my tongue is cotton.

And there are dogs on top of me. The little brown eyes of crazy dog number one peer over the top of the duvet.

I'm still in my t-shirt and boxers. However, the girl who had woven herself next to me is nowhere in the pile of covers and pillows.

I hear the shower.

I have to go get dressed *now*, because if she comes into this room in a towel, and she's wet, and she smells good, I'm going to die of a coronary.

I go into the other room to pull on my jeans.

"Morning!" Macy's behind me.

I turn to look at her. She has clothes on, thank God. Her hair's loose, and wet, and yes, she does smell positively edible.

Help me.

"Good morning. How are you?" I wait to hear how poorly she slept, the terrible nightmare she had.

"I'm great. I feel nine hundred times better. I don't know if it's the meds or just the night in a nice bed. I feel so much better."

I try to puzzle this one out. "You don't remember anything? No bad dream?"

She crinkles her brow, thinking. "No. Is that why you were in bed with me this morning? Must've been a night terror."

"What's that?"

"I've had them since I was a kid. Used to scare the daylights out of my mom. Eyes wide open, howling like a banshee. I never remember a thing."

"Your mom? Where's she now?" I've never heard her mention family at all.

"Gone." She walks right past me and picks up my laptop. That talk of family was short. She continues, ignoring any more talk on the subject. "I have some ideas about what we're gonna do today. I took the liberty of Googling a bunch of stuff while you were asleep."

"And?" I tuck my t-shirt in and wonder if I'm going to get a chance to brush my teeth.

"First stop is the original Starbucks. And I found an awesome place to sip our coffees. You have five minutes to get ready."

I'm usually the ring master, but she looks excited. I hustle, get ready in the bathroom, and grab a coat.

We walk a block to the light rail, and I drag Macy on, even though she insists she's fine. The dogs have stayed behind with their favorite Seattle dog babysitter (the treats might have something to do with their enthusiasm).

We stand in a ridiculous line (my opinion) to grab a coffee at the original Starbucks, and Macy pulls out her phone.

"Now we'll take our coffees and go drink them somewhere cool." She pulls me along back the way we came, hops on the Link again, headed back toward the hotel.

"Where is this cool place?" I fight the urge to take the reins. She's lost. We're headed nowhere.

"Just wait. It's gonna be cool. I asked the concierge about it before you got up, too, so it's not just me and Google that thinks so."

We walk a short block in the opposite direction of the hotel, past the gleaming steel and glass public library, which Macy takes several pictures of as we walk.

We cross the street, and she walks up to the front doors of a grey stone modern office building.

"What?" I feel a little unsettled. I'm the one who does the surprising.

"Trust me." She takes my hand and pulls me in through the revolving doors.

We get on the elevator, and she presses the button for the seventh floor.

"Okay." I stand next to her, but I'm concentrating mostly on the way it feels to have her hand on mine. I think about her lips on mine, her hips against mine…

And then she coughs. It's two, quick coughs, but there's that rattle again.

And my mind's back on the business of keeping her well, keeping her safe.

We get off the elevator. She looks like a kid with a great secret. "Just wait. This is so cool."

"You haven't been here, how do you know?"

"Don't be a crank. Nobody likes the stick in the mud."

"Fine."

She pulls me through another set of chrome and glass doors.

And yeah, she's right. It's pretty cool.

So apparently Macy from Teton County, Idaho, has discovered the rooftop park hidden in the middle of downtown Seattle. And it's gorgeous. She hands me my coffee and walks over to the railing. The sun is out, and the water and the waterfront is laid out in front of us.

"There's the Space Needle! We're going there later today. After dinner."

I laugh. "Are you at least going to let me pick a spot for dinner?"

"Do you want to?" She doesn't look like she wants me to.

"There's a great place I know, and it's a short walk from the hotel."

"Fine." She takes a sip from her coffee and looks out over the view.

I kiss her on the cheek again. "Don't sulk."

She turns and kisses me full-on, on the lips, for the briefest possible moment, before pulling away and facing out to the view again. "I'm not." I taste mint and feel sparks down to the base of my spine.

Then she smiles the slyest, crookedest grin I've seen. I haven't seen her smile like that.

And I grin back.

We go back to the hotel for a while after that, and then I'm swept along to Purple Café and Wine Bar for lunch.

She is a cruise director on steroids. On antibiotics and anti-inflammatories, to be exact.

After we eat, she strolls along, satiated and proud. "That was amazing. I was going to have us have drinks there before dinner, but since I can't drink, I thought lunch would work."

"I thought I was going to play tour guide. You need to slow down, sister."

"Let's go look in fancy shops and pretend we can afford something."

"I can afford something. What do you want?"

She frowns. "I don't know. Nothing. That takes the sport out of it."

"I could get you a little something. You don't want anything?"

"Not like that. If a guy buys me something, all I'm going to think of right now is how many months of rent it could have paid for instead. When I'm successful, then buy me something."

"I tried to buy you a car part. You turned me down flat."

She pokes me on the arm. "You're missing the point. I don't want stuff from you. I don't want your charity." Now her face clouds over.

"It's not charity. It's a gift. People give those to people who they care about."

"Huh. Whatever."

"So are we going to go look in fancy shops or no?"

"No. Let's go watch them throw fish at Pike Place instead."

We finish the tourist stuff and ride the Link back to get ready for an early dinner. Macy wants to go see the Space Needle when it's dark out, so I humor her with old man dinner reservations for five-thirty. Who this woman has turned me into, I don't know.

In the hotel room, I finally get to take a hot shower. I shave, and it feels great to be clean.

I come out into the living room.

Macy's on the couch in tears. My brain seizes up. What could've transpired in the twenty minutes it took me to get cleaned up?

"What is it?" I sit next to her, put a hand on her back.

"I'm terrible." She turns into my shoulder, pulls me to her.

"I think you're pretty un-terrible. What happened?"

She sits back and picks up her purse, a little backpack thing she's been wearing all day. She reaches into the front pocket and fishes out my watch.

My watch.

"I've carried it all day. You didn't notice it was gone. I was gonna blame it on the maids if you missed it before we left tomorrow. I took it." She presses her lips together and takes a huge breath in, suppressing more tears.

"What?"

"I stole it. I wasn't gonna give it back, either. I stole it."

I look into her blue-green eyes, rimmed red and streaked with runny mascara. "Why give it back, then?"

"I listened to you in the shower, and I thought about you saving me. And how it feels when I wake up, and you're next to me."

"Why'd you take it? What do you need money for?" I think back to Troy, the cigarette-flicking thug outside her apartment. "There was a guy yesterday morning, outside the apartment, didn't look like a friend. Is it about that?"

She shakes her head, her blonde-brown curls falling out of her messy ponytail around her shoulders. "No, it's not. Sure, it's an ungodly amount of money. I really could buy a new car with it. But really? I just take stuff. I have for as long as I can remember. Mrs. Reber in first grade caught me taking the snacks out of other kids' lunches. I don't know. I get this feeling. It's like if I was a smoker, and I wanted a cigarette. I think it's like that. I don't know."

She closes her eyes and drops her chin to her chest. I can see tears landing in plops on her sweats.

"Well, this time you gave it back. Have you ever done that before?" I'm reaching here. This feels like something serious, something dark, and I don't know how to approach it.

To be honest, in the past, if I came up against a flaw in a woman, she'd be gone. Or I'd be gone. I don't have time for weakness. I don't like messes. I definitely don't date messes.

She looks up at me and kisses me on the mouth, puts her hands on either side of my face, pulls me to her.

Then she gets up and goes into the bedroom. I can hear her crying.

I follow. "What are you doing?"

"Packing. I'll get a cab. I might need to borrow money to get back home, but I swear to God I'll pay you back. I don't know what Troy told you about me, but the money I owe him, I've been saving up to pay it back to him. That's why I had to get an advance from Richard for the starter for my car. I couldn't spend that other money—it has to go to Troy."

I should let her go.

She packs all her random stuff, and I sit there and watch her. Then she calls the dogs and leashes them.

"Stop." I say it.

"What?"

"I can't figure this out, except that you told me the truth, and you didn't take it."

"But I did take it. I took it for a whole day. You just didn't notice."

I stand up and go kneel with the dogs. I let them off leash. Justin Trudeau tries to bite my nose off, he's so excited.

"What are you doing?" She stands very still.

"The dogs aren't invited to dinner with us."

"We're still—"

"You don't have a dress for dinner though. What're we going to do about that? We only have half an hour before we have to leave."

"Please, I don't know…"

I put a hand up. "Let me work my brain around this. Right now, first instinct, I still want to take you to dinner. I don't know what to think, but someone told me yesterday to trust my gut. My gut says we're going to dinner, okay?"

"Okay."

"Let's table the compulsive thief discussion until after dinner. Deal?"

"Okay."

"Right now, I'm taking you to buy a dress. No arguments."

"Okay."

I stand up and take her by the hand. I lean in and kiss her firmly, pull her close.

And then I lead her down the hall, to the elevator. And down the street, to Gucci. I buy a blue patterned dress that has a black beaded yoke and belt. It's halter-style, shows Macy's shoulders. She doesn't say a word, but she nods when I ask her to try it on, and it fits her beautifully.

She wears it out of the store. I watch her carefully as she pulls her hair up into a ponytail, then twists it and tucks it into a bun.

"You look great. Thank you for letting me get that for you."

"It's beautiful." She takes a little breath. "Where are we eating?" Her voice is changed. Quiet. Shamed. It hurts, pinches in my throat, to hear her cowed.

"The Brooklyn. Steaks and seafood."

"Okay."

I stop her, take her hand. "I'm here. I want you here with me. We'll talk more about it later, but we're here. Got it?"

"Okay."

I snort. "One more 'okay', and you're gonna drive me nuts. Smile. Please."

She closes her eyes for a moment, and then she opens them, and a broad smile spreads on her lips. "You're getting all alpha. You know how I feel about that."

There's a little sass. Good. "No spitting in Seattle. I don't care what kind of mess we get into; we aren't hocking any lugies."

We walk a short way to the restaurant. When she turns to go in the door that I hold for her, I notice that the bruise from her river accident peeks out over the dress in the back, creeps up to her smooth shoulder. Great. Someone will probably think I beat her up. But God, it hurts to look at it. Nothing, no harm should come to someone so delicate.

As she stands, all tucked in, hands clasped in front of her and shoulders rounded in, I think about little girl Macy. Stealing food in first grade.

Food. Kids I knew in school who stole food stole it because they were hungry.

And she wouldn't talk about her mom.

"Gone," that's all she said.

I don't like any of this.

We get seated in the back room in a quiet booth.

"It's nice back here. No one's here." She's loosening up, looks around the restaurant while she smooths the napkin out in her lap.

"No one's here because we're eating at senior citizen buffet time. Since Miss Bossy wants to go see the Space Needle."

She tilts her head. "You'll still go do that?"

"Yes, why wouldn't I?" I look at her eyes. Her lashes are a mile long. And the gold flecks in her eyes, they glitter in the waning light.

"Because I stole from you."

"Is it after dinner?"

"No."

"We aren't discussing this until after dinner. But I'm not mad."

"You're not?"

"No. Now I'm going to teach you about flights of oysters. These might be the best in the country."

"Flights?"

"Pay attention." I nod to a waiter.

Now I might be just a little bit in Jeremy-impresses-the-girl-mode. Just a little. My insides are all upside down and screwed over with the whole watch business, but for whatever reason, now I want to seal the deal with this woman. I might be moving out of protector mode. I might be moving into seduction mode.

The waiter comes over. "Sir?"

"We're not drinking tonight, but we are indulging. Bring us a baker's dozen of oysters."

Macy thins her lips out. "I haven't had oysters. I don't know about thirteen of them."

"You're not going to eat them all alone." I look up at the waiter. "Do you have Wildcat Cove oysters tonight?"

He nods. "We do. And can I get something to drink for the lady? Tea or coffee?"

Macy nods. "I want a Roy Rogers. It's Coke and grenadine syrup. Can you do that?"

I raise an eyebrow. "Really?"

"Why not? It's celebratory, and it's not alcoholic, so it fits."

The waiter looks at me. "For the gentleman?"

"Pellegrino with a lemon."

He slips off and returns with Macy's drink and my water.

Macy pulls the cherry out of the drink. "Watch this. One of my few talents." She pops the cherry in her mouth, stem and all.

"What—"

She pulls the stem back out of her mouth.

It's tied in a knot.

God help me. Looks like I'm not the only one kicking it up a notch. If I think about the transferable areas for that skill, I might pass out. "Very impressive."

"I can wiggle my ears, too. That's the extent of my bar tricks."

She seems to be relaxed for the time being. I don't know what's going to happen after dinner. I don't know what to say to her about stealing the watch.

It's not normal. It's not okay. But she told me. She didn't actually take it. Really, I don't know how to respond.

I put it aside. I can stretch dinner out, I can think about the knot tied in the cherry stem, and I can avoid dealing with whatever dysfunction is under this girl's surface.

Troy. The deep gouge on her hand. The comment about her mom. The way she cowers like she's been hurt.

I want to peel all of this away and find what's at the bottom of it. But this is not standard. I've never bothered to dig in with a woman before. I don't know what to do if what's at the bottom is more than I can handle. Maybe it's more than Macy can handle.

I wish I had a drink in my hand. It wouldn't solve anything, but it sure as hell would take the edge off.

The waiter brings the oysters to the table. "Enjoy."

I pick one up, and as I do, Macy puts up a hand.

"Stop right there." She turns her head away from me, grimaces as though I'm about to do something distasteful.

"What?"

"I'm just saving you from some stupid comment about aphrodisiacs." She looks at me now, a sly smile on her face.

"I'm not a cheeseball. Give me a little credit." I take the oyster and suck it down. It's delicate to the taste and just a bit salty. This really is the best restaurant for them.

And yeah, I was maybe going to make the aphrodisiac comment. So shoot me (no, don't).

She points to them. "Which one is the Wildcat Cove?"

I touch the shell. "This one. They're my favorite."

She picks it up and tosses it back, like a shot of whiskey.

"Well?"

She shrugs. "That's actually pretty good. I wouldn't chew it, but it tastes way better than I would guess."

"You've never had one before."

"You should know by now that my scope is pretty narrow. But I bet you haven't had a Rocky Mountain oyster, and I've had one of those."

I should have known. "No, I haven't. I know what they are, though. Are they really good?"

"Anything deep fried, even testicles, tastes kinda like chicken, to be honest." She eyes the other oysters and picks a different shell, downs this one more slowly. "These are really good. I think I like oysters."

"I'm glad."

We finish the flight and order dinner. Both of us have steaks. As we wrap up the course, Macy starts fidgeting. Her left foot taps in a little nervous dance.

"Macy." I call her out as the waiter is clearing our dinner.

"What?" She bites the inside of her cheek.

"We're not in a hurry. Slow it down."

She plops her napkin down. "I'm anxious. I don't want to talk about this afternoon."

"What do you want to do?"

"Just go see the butterflies and the Space Needle and be with you."

"Then let's do that." I touch her hand.

"Really?" She tilts her head, a question in her posture. She doesn't look like she believes me.

"Look. Dinner's over. Let's talk about this and be done with it and then we can go do our thing and hang out."

"I don't know what to tell you."

"You told me the truth, right?"

"Yeah."

"You take stuff without thinking. You want it, or you want to take it, like you have to take it."

"A compulsion. I feel like I have to. Like eating the last piece of chocolate cake that your grandma was saving for your little brother. I don't want it until I can't have it, then it's all I can think about. I just want it, whatever the thing is, want it in my pocket. When I take it, the feeling's over. Then mostly I just feel like shit. Shoot. Swear jar."

"How come you carried it around all day? How come you didn't come clean sooner?"

She stares at the floor. "I figured you'd put me on the next flight home, and I liked being with you, so I didn't want it to end."

"Is there a way you can control the stealing?"

"The less I think about it, the better I am. When I'm on the river, I'm happy and peaceful, and I don't need or want for anything. I have everything I need. I've never taken anything from anyone when I'm out on the river."

I chew on that for a minute. "When you were little, were you always taken care of?" I don't know if she'll let me probe, but I want to know.

Her eyes fill up with tears. "I don't want to talk about it."

I wrap both my hands around hers. "I'm not going to push."

She doesn't say anything, just nods.

I sit up a little taller as the waiter comes over with the check. I send it back with a card before I say anything to Macy.

"I think we're done for now. But I can't say that it feels good to have someone steal from me. It feels like I don't know if I can trust you. I don't know how to get to know you, the real you."

She takes in a deep breath, swallows hard. "I swear to you, I'm trying. I've never met anyone like you. The other guys I know, they've known me since I was little, or they're bottom feeders. I want to get to know you. I want to let you see me. There's just so much. I promise you right now, if I get the urge again, I'll just come right out and say something."

I consider. "Let's just see how it plays out. You lie to me again, though, I can't abide by it."

She looks hurt. "I didn't lie to you. I told you the truth."

"Taking something of mine, that's a lie of omission. Taking without telling is lying. That's the part that doesn't sit right with me. You know I like honest."

She answers in a quiet voice, eyes down. "I know. I like honest, too. I just don't seem like I do. I'm sorry."

I stand up and put out my hand, ready to be done with the uncomfortable feeling in my gut. "Let's go ride up an elevator."

She puts her hand in mine. "Let's."

The elevator ride proves to be fun. Macy stands close to me, and her hand brushes against the side of my thigh. She's looking up at the floor display, pretending not to notice, but each time she grazes me, I feel it all over. I look over at her shoulder, examine the place where her collarbone slopes toward her neck, the hollow there, and think about how it would feel to brush my lips against that soft skin.

I'd attack her right now, but I don't know. I can still see her favoring her bruised side, protecting it when she sits, so she must still be hurting. I haven't heard the cough since before dinner, but I'm cautious.

Plus, we've kissed, but there's some barrier up still between us. Hand-holding and conditional kissing, but I haven't felt the permission come across, the "knock me down right here, right now" green light.

I don't want to hurt her, and I don't want to scare her. And if my instincts are right, men haven't been gentle with her before.

But that doesn't stop me from thinking about running my hand up under the hem of the dress she's wearing, thinking how it would feel, as the elevator climbs the Space Needle.

The observation deck comes too soon.

The Space Needle is a tourist trap. On the observation deck, a large family with too many kids to corral chases them all over, and I mentally figure on which kid's going to end up in the ER by the end of their visit to Seattle.

"Hey! There's the Great Wheel! It's blue at night. I like that." Macy takes long strides to the edge of the deck, taking it all in.

"Next time we're here we'll ride that." I come up behind her and wrap my arms around her waist, gently.

She shivers. I don't know if it's me, or if it's the wind that licks its way around the Needle. Either way, those soft shoulders are covered in goose bumps.

I slip off my suit jacket. "Should've gotten you a sweater when we were out shopping."

"I guess Seattle's not LA."

LA. I've not had a single thought of my hometown in days. At some point I have to go back to real life. Hell, before that I have a movie shoot in Toronto to go to.

"You should come to Toronto with me." I whisper it into her ear.

She turns away from the view to face me. I enjoy the feel of her frame so close to mine. "No passport, remember?" And trouble crosses over her face.

"Well, next time, then."

She's distant, turns her back to me. "Yeah, maybe next time."

She shivers again, even in my jacket.

"We should go. Where are you taking me next?"

She takes my hand. "Back down the elevator to the Science Center. Butterfly time."

I endure another agonizing ride in the elevator. This time I study the black beading on the neck of her dress and try not to think about unzipping the dress.

We wander into the Science Center, and she takes me to the butterfly house.

It's humid, and I can feel the moisture in the air.

Macy pulls her hair down and shakes it out. I make sure my mouth is closed. She's absent-minded, not realizing what she's doing is driving me crazy. She turns in a circle, looking at all the tropical trees and plants, and pulls her hair back up, twisting it back into a bun.

I step closer to her. I'm going to say something. I need her.

Now.

A butterfly lands on her bare shoulder, and she hops sideways away from me. "Oh, that feels so weird." She cranes her neck to see the butterfly.

It sits on her and spreads its wings. It's brownish, moth-like on the outside, but as its wings come open, cobalt blue flashes out.

"Wow." I hate insects, bugs, plants, flowers, pretty much anything nature, but the butterfly is cool.

She puts a finger close to it, and it flits up and then lands on her finger. She's Snow White of the butterflies, apparently. "Look at this!" She turns to me, a relaxed smile on her face. "Thanks for being worried about my lungs."

"What?"

"It was a good reason for a trip. This has been amazing."

And my moment of need passes as I watch her wonder over the jewel-colored butterflies.

We catch a cab back to the hotel. I hope for a chance to be close to her, but the cabbie chats to her for the five-minute ride about his daughter and the butterflies.

Then we're at the hotel.

She takes my hand as we catch the elevator to the top floor.

"Well?" She looks at my hand, weaves her fingers in and out of mine.

"Well, what?"

"Did you have fun?" She looks up at me.

"Tonight? Sure. Of course I did."

She smiles. "I make a good tour guide."

"You make a better fishing guide, but yeah, you've done a good job ushering me around Seattle."

"For someone's who's never been, especially good, huh?" She takes a step closer to me.

I lean in and touch her on the shoulder. "Yes, especially." Then I kiss her on the spot I just touched.

She turns to me and tips my chin up. She kisses me.

At first it's soft, and she brushes my lips tentatively.

Then she opens her mouth to me and pulls me by the arm, closer to her.

And the elevator arrives at our floor.

She takes an abrupt step back.

"We're here." She walks off in front of me.

I consider screaming out loud in frustration.

We get down the hall to the suite. I'm dying to touch her, to have her. She's quiet as we open the door.

Who is not quiet are the dogs who greet us on the other side of the door.

Damn dogs.

Justin Trudeau dances around my feet, for some reason, and Pierre cries and whines until Macy picks him up. She finds a note from the dog babysitter. "They just went out not five minutes ago. She just left."

"Then don't feel guilty. They're just happy to see you." Justin Trudeau is resting his tongue on the toe of my five hundred dollar Prada driving shoe.

Dog slobber will ruin the mood any day. This I promise you.

"Okay pups, let's put you in your beds." Macy scoops both of them up and carries them into the bedroom.

I trail behind, hands in pockets, as usual.

I don't feel like being the man in the white hat. I want to do black hat things to this girl.

She tucks both the dogs into their beds and gives them the down stay command.

Then she turns her attention to me.

"Can you help me unzip this?" She comes closer to me.

"Of course." I take the zipper and start it, and the dress slips down her shoulders.

And there it is.

The bruise is green and blue and purple. It's atrocious.

"God, Macy, your side still looks awful. The bruising's spread all the way up one side of your back." I skim my fingers over it, and she winces faintly.

"It's gonna look worse before it looks better." She turns around, holding the dress to her. "Can I tell you something?" She turns her toes in, looks bashful.

"Always."

"I really want to kiss you more." She smiles.

"That's good, because I want to kiss you more."

"But I need to ask a favor." She's keeping her distance.

"Again, always." My hands are back in my pockets.

She sits back on the bed. "I need to go at my pace. I don't really want to go into a lot of reasons why, but can you believe me that I want you?"

"Yes." I breathe in through my nose, trying to calm my pulse. I want her so badly I can't see straight.

"Okay, so if I get into yoga pants, and we watch TV for a while, and we sit on the couch together, you've gotta know that we'll get around to where we both want to be eventually tonight."

I laugh. I can't help it. "We'll get around to it. Sounds fair. Not very sexy, but fair."

She looks hurt. Her eyes glisten up. "I've been seriously trashed on, Mr. King. You have no idea. I want to believe that you're not that kind of guy, but I have to put this out there, protect myself."

I step to her. "Hey, hey. I'm not trying to make fun of you. I just love how you are, Macy Shea Summerlin."

"How I am?"

"You put your own stamp on everything. And tonight, you know what?"

"What?"

"I don't care what we get around to. I want whatever you want, when you want it. It's important to me that I am absolutely one hundred percent nothing remotely like those other guys whatsoever. Am I clear?"

"You don't want to be like the other guys. Clear."

"So I'm going to go raid the mini-bar for a beer if you don't mind watching me drink, and I'll find American Pickers on the TV, and you get on those yoga pants." I lean over and kiss her.

"I love you for this. Thank you." Then her eyes go wide for a split second, I think when she realizes that she just said she loved me.

"I'll be out here waiting for you."

She comes out ten minutes later, her hair in braids, yoga pants on, make up off, brushing her teeth. "Did you find the show you wanted to watch?"

I'm sitting on the couch with the remote and a beer. Suddenly I feel positively domestic. We could be an old married couple. "Come sit. I even made you a drink." I hold it up.

"You know I can't drink." She goes to the wet bar and spits, rinses her toothbrush.

"It's a Roy Rogers. I took the liberty of having the concierge bring some grenadine up while we were out tonight. And some maraschino cherries. After you showed me your 'talent' at dinner, I couldn't help it."

"You want a re-enactment?" She sits down on the couch next to me and pulls her knees up under her.

I hand her the drink. "Tonight's your night. Let's watch TV."

But I won't lie that I'm not thinking about that cherry stem in her mouth.

We watch a couple episodes and chat. I'm just trying to make a connection. She keeps pushing the conversation back to movies I've been involved with, actors I know, places I've been. She avoids personal questions and makes jokes to cover her tracks.

It's getting late when I switch off the TV.

"Okay, Macy. Time to answer some questions." I turn to face her on the couch.

"Fire away." She scoots towards me.

"Why is your favorite color pink?" I ask.

She leans forward and kisses me on the lips. "It's pretty. I like it."

I shake my head. "Why are you afraid of the dark?"

She puts her arms around my neck and pulls me in for another kiss, this one long and lingering. "It's complicated."

I think I'm seeing stars. "Who cut your hand?"

She crawls on to my lap and starts to unbutton my shirt. "Another long story."

She kisses me and runs her hands all over my chest, wrapping herself around me.

"Jesus, Macy. This isn't fair. You're just trying to avoid this discussion."

She kisses me again and stands up. She points to the bedroom. "I am not. I'm just working my way around to what we both want. Are you coming?"

She walks in to the bedroom.

"Yes."

Thank God for question-dodging.

The next morning, I'm up before Macy and before the dogs. I call down to the desk. We've got to go back this morning, catch back up to our fishing party.

Last night was tender and passionate and amazing all wrapped up into one. I was careful with Macy, yes, because her body was still bruised, but also because it became more and more clear that she's got bruises I can't see.

There were moments where I watched her almost open up to me, but then she would close herself back off. She'd be wrapped up in a moment of pleasure, vulnerable, and I could see the switch flick off, and she'd turn her attentions to me, to my pleasure, a way to regain control and deflect.

The attention was mind-blowing, by the way. The cherry stem thing? *Definitely* a transferable skill. Still, her guard never came completely down.

Now I pack our few things, and I can't help but feel my shield going up, too.

This whole thing has an expiration date.

I'm due back in the real world, by way of Toronto, in two days.

I pick up my cell and dial Tucker.

"Tucker Caldwell." He's on the river, fishing, and he still sounds like the man that could snap my neck.

"It's Jeremy."

"The AWOL fisher in love! How's the patient?"

"She's got the all clear to come home. How's the crew?"

I can hear voices in the background. "The natives are restless. Andrew misses Kelly and the kids. Todd's been weird the whole time. I need you back here to balance everyone out."

I chuckle, but then I clear my throat. "Tucker, I need a favor. And if you don't mind, I need you to not tell Andy about it."

"Tell me what it is, and we'll see about it." Tucker's number one loyalty is to Andy. I'd never ask him to compromise that, but he doesn't know that, and he won't expose himself to the risk.

"I need a background check on Macy."

"What?"

"I need a deep check on her. She's got secrets, and I'm worried about her."

I can hear him breathe out in disapproval. Almost a sigh of judgment. "You could ask her."

"I have. She won't talk."

There's a beat. "Fine. Give me her details. For the record—"

"It's a bad idea, I know. I need to know."

"All right. Text me her stuff, and I'll put somebody back in LA on it."

"I owe you, Tucker. Thank you."

"I just want to say that I'm only doing this because Andrew thinks this Macy may actually have proof that you do, in fact, have a human heart beating somewhere in that ribcage of yours."

"I get it. I want to help her. This'll help me help her."

"Whatever you say. We'll see you back tonight?"

"See you then." I hang up.

The details will come. Not from Macy, unfortunately, but at least I'll know more.

Macy comes out from the bedroom, showered and dressed. "Morning, sunshine."

Now, before anything else can happen, I want her to know that last night was the right thing, not a mistake. We may both have lives to go back to, but I don't regret it for a minute.

So I walk up to her and pull her into my arms. I kiss her hard and deep and weave my fingers through her wet hair.

Then I pull away and look at her. "Good morning."

She smiles, traces a finger over my lips. "I could get used to that."

"Thank you for last night."

"No, thank you." She unwinds herself out of my arms. She kisses me again. "It was exactly the opposite of the usual jerk encounters I have. I can't even tell you how much that means to me."

"Mission accomplished, then. I wish the rest of my life was this easy—just be the opposite of what sucks. Easy enough."

She sits on the couch, and the dogs jump up on either side of her. "I wish life was that easy, too." She pulls her knees up to her chest and looks like she's defending herself from whatever in real life she's thinking of right now.

"We'll all packed. Breakfast and then the airport, yes?"

"Yes." She fiddles with Pierre's collar. Without looking up, she asks, "When do you leave the river?"

"Tuesday first thing. Off to Toronto." I can feel a lump forming in my throat.

"That sucks." She doesn't look up.

"Yes, it does." I don't have anything else. It just sucks.

"You could come back for Fourth of July. It's a huge party. You'd like it." Her voice brightens with this idea.

"I could do that. The production takes two days off for it."

"We're making that our plan, then. This feels less dismal that way."

I have to admit, she and I think alike. "Good plan." I grab our stuff and lean in for a quick kiss.

She chats to another cabbie on the way to the airport, and she chats with the pilot on the plane. He's a dog lover, damn it, so he fusses over the dogs, and Macy loves every second of it.

I hate it, because I have no chance for a re-enactment of last night.

We take off, and Macy dozes off, with the little Canadian dog-sausages (they were already so fat, and I think the Seattle pet sitter fed them treats non-stop) piled around her.

All too soon we're on the ground in Idaho Falls. I help Macy gather dogs and her bag and wince a little as I watch her gingerly descend the private jet's stairs to the tarmac.

"Still hurting?" I set both dogs on the ground and leash them up.

"It's been a big weekend. Maybe I should've taken it a little slower." She takes the dogs and takes my arm.

Just a little move like that, the way she circles her arm through the crook of mine, it makes my chest feel warm and wide and full. "Am I presuming too much if I say I'd like to spend this night, my second-to-last in Idaho, in your arms?"

Her eyes go wide. "That's extravagantly romantic of you, Mr. King."

I resist the urge to respond with sarcasm. "You make me capable of all kinds of extravagant gestures."

She pulls me closer to her. "I'd like to be in your arms tonight too. It's a deal."

We return to her apartment, and Macy frets and worries. I bring all of her things inside, the dogs sniff every inch of the apartment for interlopers, and she checks and re-checks her phone.

"What are you worried about?" I fight back all the thoughts I have about responsibilities I've blown off for the whole week, things which should be demanding my attention.

"I texted Richard. He says I'll be on light duty tomorrow."

"Makes sense. You need to heal."

"I need to work. I make tips on the river, and I make peanuts at the front desk."

"You'd just be fishing with Team Andy if you were on the river, and we're going to tip you anyway."

She shakes her head. "Oh no, Mr. King. You're not allowed to tip me at all."

"Why not?"

"Um, for what? Services rendered? Thank you very not."

"I see your point. But I can have Andy tip you extra. Stop worrying."

She frowns at her phone again. "I just don't want Richard mad at me again. He intimidates me when he's mad."

As she says this, I can feel my blood pressure rising. "You don't mean physically intimidates you?"

She backs off immediately. "Slow the roll, alpha boy. He'll say he's 'disappointed in me,' and I cower. This is about me. He's not an abuser. Trust me."

I let out a tense breath. "No one should do anything to intimidate you, period."

"Fine. I promise, I'll rat them out if they do." She sets her phone down and goes to the fridge. "I think we should have some lunch. Then we could hang out."

"What kind of hanging out are we going to do?" I can think of the kind I'm interested in.

She smiles, and then stretches and yawns, her fingers tentatively poking at her immense bruise. "I'd love to be all suggestive, but I think the hanging out where you watch me sleep for most of the afternoon."

"I'm completely in support of that." I walk up behind her and slip my arms around her waist.

And Justin Trudeau growls at me.

"Justin! Sit!" Macy snaps a finger, and the little dog rolls over on his belly.

"Now he's protective. He didn't seem to care in Seattle when he was slobbering all over my shoes."

She untangles herself out of my arms and goes and sits on the couch. "Home turf. Don't mess with his stuff."

"Including you."

"Yep."

I sigh and make lunch for Macy, eyed suspiciously the whole time by her Canadian security detail.

Macy called the details of our afternoon. I relax and watch TV. Macy sleeps, sometimes curled up against me, and sometimes stretched out on the couch in the opposite direction.

Jeremy King, super-agent, über power magnate, watching Judge Judy in a dinky little apartment in the middle of nowhere.

And I couldn't be happier.

Okay, that night, when Macy wakes up and feels better and wants to "hang out" with me in an entirely different way?

That makes me happier.

ALL QUIET ON THE WESTERN FRONT

We wake up the next day together.

Okay, the dogs and I do. When I open my eyes, trying to remember why I'm not sleeping in my Hästens Vividus bed in LA, I hear Macy in the shower. Justin and Pierre have taken this opportunity to sleep tucked under either of my arms. I'm pinned down like Gulliver by the fat little pups.

I extract myself from the covers and the dogs' best wrestling moves and go make coffee in Macy's shitty plastic coffee maker.

"I'm getting you a new coffee maker. Heck, I'm getting you an espresso machine. This is crap." I call to her in the bathroom, where she's brushing her teeth.

"Hold up, cowboy. You're not buying me anything."

"Why not?"

"I don't do that. Same territory as the tip. It's creepy."

I feel my frustration crawling up from my stomach, kind of a rumbling in my belly paired with a migraine. "No, no, I'm allowed to get you a gift once in a while. People do that for one another. It's standard. It's not creepy unless you decide it is."

"Fine. You're capped at forty bucks."

"What?" Now I can feel the aggravation settling in the muscles of my back. I understand why Bruce Banner tears off all those t-shirts when he goes Hulk.

"You can't buy me anything worth more than forty dollars. End of discussion."

I take a deep cleansing breath in through my nose, out through my mouth. "New discussion, then. Are you driving to the lodge? And can I get a ride?"

We took the Teton County shuttle from the airport, and though I hated every second of it, it didn't make any sense to have yet another rental car at the lodge. And Macy knew the shuttle driver from her church, so we couldn't turn down her ride, according to Macy.

This is what I've been transformed into—a guy who takes public transportation from a woman with gray hair and a pink Cabela's trucker hat.

But right now, I'm also a guy asking a girl for a ride back to his place.

Another thing Jeremy King has never, ever, had to do in recent memory.

On the drive, I listen to her make 4th of July plans with my whole social circle.

"And I don't even want to tell you about the afternoon stuff. You'll just make fun of us."

"Because?"

"Because there's a slippery pig contest, and I don't need to hear from you about mutton busting."

"I don't even know what that is to make fun of you for it."

"Good. I'm not telling you, then."

We pull into the parking lot of the lodge.

"Okay. I'm on front desk duty." She slides out of the car, and I watch her favor her bruised side. Someone who didn't know what happened to her last Thursday probably wouldn't even notice. I notice.

"I'm going to go check in with the pack. It's the last day. They might even already be out on the river."

"You better go catch up. I can meet you back at your lodge—I'm not even supposed to work a full shift today." She takes my hand for a minute and holds it, squeezes it. "I need more time with you before I have to say good bye. I suck at good byes."

"No worries. I'll see you later." I try to sound as casual as I can, but I know that I'm not even prepared to say good bye. I've never cared enough to say it to a woman before, not in a way that didn't signal "nice knowing you, now take a walk."

I take my things from the Seattle trip into the house, and I hear a noise from the bathroom.

Everyone's supposed to be out on the river.

"Hello?" I wonder if I should be worried.

"Hey." Todd Ford comes out from the bathroom. He looks like shit.

"You look like shit. What's up?"

"I'm sick. Tucker and Andrew are out on the river. They said to tell you to catch up. They're fishing near the lodge all day."

"You're not sick." I examine him. "Is this drugs? Is that why you've been so distracted and dick-ish all week? 'Cause that's such a cliché."

"Fuck you. It's none of your business."

"It is my business. You're tangentially associated with Andy Pettigrew, rehabilitated alcoholic. You're not to come within a hundred yards of him if you're into that stuff. And I think he'd say that himself if he knew you were messing around with drugs."

"It's not that, okay?"

"Bullshit. What is it, then?"

"Death in the family, and if you press me for more information, I swear to God I'll set you on fire." Todd looks at me, eyes brimming with tears.

"Jesus. I didn't even think. Does Andy know?"

"No, and I'll tell him when I'm ready, so I'd appreciate it if you didn't tell him, and if you left me alone now."

"Fair enough." I go dump my bag and gear up to fish.

Who knew Todd Ford cared about someone beside himself. Of course, here I am, wrapped around Macy's little finger, and I can name roughly a dozen business colleagues in LA who would testify under oath that I don't have a heart.

I guess things can change.

I fish with the guys, I even hook a healthy Yellowstone cutthroat, but I can't get off the river quickly enough. The whole afternoon feels like the last day of college before graduation—you can practically feel the time slipping through your fingers.

After a long day on the river, we all sit in the living room.

There's a knock at the door. I jump up to get it, and in the process show my hand to my colleagues. I'm toast, and they know it.

She stands on the door step when I open the door.

"Miss Macy. How was the day?"

"Okay. And yours?"

"Long. Longer without you."

"Stop. You're too extravagant." She smiles, and it makes me feel better already. "Are you all going to do dinner here?"

"We thought so. Tucker caught too many fish. We've got to eat some of them."

"Do you mind if I beg out?"

I can see the fatigue in her eyes. "Not at all." I don't push it. Yes, it's our last night together, but she's human. "Can I come see you later?"

"I might be asleep, but I'd like that." She leans in briefly and brushes my lips with a quick kiss. I notice she glances around the parking lot. She's afraid of Richard, still, doesn't want to get in trouble for messing with the guests.

I let her go and watch her drive away. The bottom of my stomach lurches.

I don't like her leaving me. What am I going to do tomorrow morning?

I plop down on the couch in the lodge and watch the light purple up over the foothills outside. The river turns darker and darker blue.

Tucker strolls in. "What say you and I smoke the last of the Cohibas out on the deck?"

I nod. "Last chance to poison the fresh mountain air."

I go grab two from my bag. I can hear Andy in the next room. Sounds like he's on the phone with Quincy, 'cause the discussion seems to center around doggies. Todd, as usual, is nowhere to be found.

Tucker's out at the rail, looking over the river. "Thank you for indulging my vice."

"The least I can do for the one who keeps us all alive."

We light up and savor the cigars for a moment in silence.

Tucker looks at me. "I got the background check on Macy."

My heart clenches. "You did."

"Do you really want to see?" His face is totally neutral.

"Yeah, I do." I take another pull on the cigar, try to steady myself.

He hands me a jump drive. "You want me to short cut any of it for you?"

"I don't know." All of this is wrong. I feel like I just took Macy's little dogs to the vet to be put down, for Christ's sake.

"Go sit and look at it. I'll be right here." He calls over his shoulder, "Be careful what you ask for. The need to know is dangerous poison."

I walk in and sit at the desk in my room, slip the jump drive into my laptop, and swallow hard.

There, on the screen, is Macy Shea Summerlin in all the gory detail I was afraid of.

Mother surrendered her to foster care four different times, the first time in kindergarten, and the last time, for good, when Macy was thirteen. Mother's whereabouts are unknown.

Macy was with a family for a while. The family accused her of stealing from them, so at fourteen and a half she went to live in a group home. The rest of the group home residents were pregnant or parenting teens. No one else was like Macy.

She has a sealed juvenile record.

She was arrested for shoplifting when she was nineteen. She was on probation for a year and a half.

She was hospitalized twice when she was twenty. The first time a man, who is in jail currently, put her through a sliding glass door at the local Baptist church. The second time she was the passenger in a roll-over accident. The man driving was arrested for driving under the influence. She was granted a restraining order against him until he was put in jail.

Richard, Mr. passive-aggressive owner of the fly-fishing lodge, co-signed with her to get her apartment. The local newspaper ran a feature on Macy, and Richard is quoted as calling Macy "the most gifted fly-fisherman I've ever known."

She receives a small benefits payment every month because her father was killed in action in Afghanistan.

Her credit score is in the tank. She's got three different accounts in collections, one with the local hospital, one with a furniture store, and one with a check-cashing place. She owned a car, co-signed with some other guy, and it was repossessed.

Finally, nine days ago, the police came to her apartment. They took Macy to the hospital with a concussion and a sliced-up hand. She wouldn't file charges against anyone.

I stand up and consider whether I need to throw up in the sink in the bathroom or not. I rally and go outside instead.

"Well?" Tucker looks at me.

"Most of it I kind of expected." I stand with him and hold the jump drive between my fingers.

"How so?"

"She already told me about the stealing. And the way she acts, I could guess about the guys, the abuse."

"There's a lot there." He reveals nothing in his tone.

"Yep." I roll the jump drive between two fingers, bite my cigar between my teeth. Try to breathe.

"And now, what do you do?"

"What I would've done anyway. I go to Toronto; she keeps working here."

"And that's it."

"You tell me what to do, Tucker. Take her away from here? She loves guiding. She's good at it. Where do I take her? To LA? To hang out with the crowd that runs there? That sure is a good influence on someone young and messed up."

"You do what you want to do, Jeremy. I don't have any answers for you." Tucker smokes the Cuban, stands tall and still next to me.

"I guess I just need some time to think." I think my hands might be shaking.

Fuck this.

"Well, right now we have two steelhead and steaks to eat. Maybe you just let it sit for a while. Maybe you'll know what you want if you sleep on it."

"Maybe." I look at the jump drive in my hand.

Tucker stubs out his cigar and walks back inside.

I wind up and throw the drive as far out as I can. It lands with a plop in the river.

I go to sit at the table when it occurs to me—the man who sliced up Macy's hand, who gave her a concussion. He's still out there. I know who he is, and he came by for a visit, that day I was with her, a visit to finish business.

Troy.

Tonight is the first time she's been by herself since that day.

"I have to go." I get up as Andy walks into the dining room.

"Did I miss something?" He watches as I take the keys off the kitchen island.

Tucker stands up. "I think we better go with you."

Now, most white hat guys in movies might say something like, "I've got this," and keep charging out the door, but you know what? Tucker is a professional.

And I'd like to destroy this Troy person.

So I'll bring back up with me, thank you very much. I will bury Troy, and if it takes me and an army to keep Macy safe, then fine. I'm not too much of a man to do it.

"Fine. Come with me then."

Tucker nods. "Let's go."

We pile in the Yukon. As usual, Todd is nowhere. We leave him.

I drive fast, faster than I should, but I can bet how this guy operates. He was there that morning, keeping an eye on her apartment. Surprised that I was there so early in the morning. Counting on her to take the dogs out.

She'll have to take the dogs out tonight, after it's dark, one more time before bed.

She's in danger.

"Can someone please give me a clue what's going on here?" Andy's supportive, but Andy doesn't know.

Tucker looks at him. "Macy's hand. It was a guy."

"She owes him money. He gave her a concussion. He was there the morning we left." I don't look over at him.

I don't think he'll judge, but if I were in his shoes, the first question I'd ask would be, *why would a girl borrow money from a guy like that?*

Because every decision she's made in her life has been out of self-preservation, and sometimes jumping from frying pan into fire makes sense at the time.

The stealing. First grade, she was stealing because she was hungry.

I don't know. The depth of this is way, *way* out of my league.

We're coming up on Macy's place. Tucker points past the turn off. "Pull in behind the complex; we can come in on foot in the alley."

This is why I invited the bad-ass special ops guy. I guide the car in behind her place, kill the engine and drift in to park in the empty lot behind.

Andy gets out and looks at me. "What are we getting into here?"

"I don't know." I think clearly for a second. "We need to get her and the dogs. If he's got a knife, he's got other stuff, probably."

We come even with a space between apartments where we can slip through to the front.

"Macy's is over to our left when we come out front."

Tucker puts a finger to his lips. We walk casually, but what are we doing? None of us has a gun.

Out front, I hear voices.

Macy's. A man's. Macy sounds scared.

We come around the building, and I see her.

Macy stands on the sidewalk by a parking space.

Troy has her by the wrist.

I cover the ground between us at a run and deliver a swift, hard fist to his nose.

He goes down, probably more in surprise than anything else.

"Macy, go with Andy to get the dogs. You're coming with us." I've never barked a command so convincingly before now.

She turns on her heels and runs into the apartment, followed by Andy.

I stand over Troy. "Stay down and listen, cowboy."

He looks up at me. "Who the fuck are you? She's no damn angel; she owes me money. This is none of your business."

Tucker looms behind me. I wonder for a moment if Troy has a gun. If he does, I am a nice, juicy target right now.

"How much?" I stand firm.

"I told you, five hundred."

I pull my billfold out and drop five bills on his chest.

"I want you to be clear. I don't care why she made the mistake of borrowing the money from you. You're paid now. You're done. You have no reason to come back here. Are we clear?"

Tucker steps to the side of me. "I know two ex-Seals who live within twenty minutes of here. You mess with her, we'll get wind of it. And my friends will, too. And they know how to dispense of problems."

Tucker's a huge man. A huge man who I've never heard say a menacing thing. Ever. I'm freaked out by his demeanor right now, and it's not even directed at me.

Troy gets to his feet. I've bloodied his nose. I'm proud of that.

He sneers at us. "I could press charges. This is assault, and you've made threats against me. I could get your ass thrown in jail."

Tucker snorts. "I know the Teton County sheriff. He's really interested to know what thug put Macy in the ER with a concussion. And the town of Driggs already knows you. Whose story is going to fly, yours or ours?"

Troy flips us off and walks to his car, gets in. He leans on the horn once for good measure, and then he's gone.

"What if he comes back?" I feel like that wasn't as satisfying as I thought it could be. "I don't like thinking he might hurt Macy to get back at us. There's no reason why he won't come back."

Tucker shakes his head. He texts someone. "I'm not lying that I know Zeke. He's wanted to toss Troy's ass in jail for a while. When I shared what you knew about him from the other morning, paired with what we found out in the background check, he was curious to follow up. Now I'm telling him we saw him with his hands on Macy."

"Background check?" Macy stands behind me, with Justin in her arms.

Tucker takes the dog from her. "We'll wait in the car." Andy follows him back to our car, Pierre Trudeau in tow.

I stand in front of her, the truth out between us.

"You ran a background check on me?" Her eyes fill up with tears.

"I wanted to know what I was getting myself into."

Her hands go to her hips. "I was just something you were 'getting yourself into'? That sounds awesome."

"That's not how I meant it. I mean, I wanted to help you, and you wouldn't tell me anything."

She's crying now, tears streaming down her cheeks. "Maybe because I didn't want you to know. God, you know how liberating it was for you not to know the whole mess of my life? I could just be Macy. I didn't have to be 'screwed-up Macy' or 'abused Macy' or 'white trash Macy' or 'abandoned Macy' or 'Macy the thief'. I was just Macy with you. I liked a clean slate."

"It doesn't change anything between us."

"Whatever. You could've asked."

"I did. Over and over. You wouldn't tell me."

"Maybe I don't like to rehash my stupid decisions over and over. Maybe I'm not super proud of the choices I've made."

"No one is proud of everything they've done. We all screw up."

She kicks at the bumper of the car in front of us. "Mr. Honest. That's a load of crap. You sure did screw up this time, Mr. King."

She turns to go back in her apartment.

"Macy, wait." I step towards her.

She waves me off. "No, we're done. I don't need to be the girl you save. Tell the guys to bring the dogs back."

"You're coming with us."

"Why? Tucker just said Troy's probably going to get arrested."

"'Cause I want you to be safe."

"You want to boss poor pitiful Macy around. You want to save me."

"Maybe I do."

"Well, there's nothing to save me from. You can't save me from my own bad decisions. They're mine to make and learn from. And it's getting better. I'm digging myself out of my own hole. I want to do that, damn it. I want to save myself."

I stand there. That stings a little. It must be true. Me wanting to be all white hat, wanting to save her. Except she's not interested. "You know, you're right."

She pauses. "What?"

"You're right. It's your mess to fix. And I'm headed to Toronto tomorrow. And LA after that. I guess this is where we part ways, anyway."

"I guess." She turns and goes in the front door of her place without another look in my direction.

The guys take the dogs back to her, and we drive back to the lodge without a word.

And that, my friends, is how love fucks with your life.

AN AFFAIR TO REMEMBER

I will skip giving you the details of the next day. We packed, I got drunk, we flew to Toronto, I holed up in a hotel room and contemplated never emerging.

It wasn't pretty.

Andy has his first meeting today for the reason we're here, the movie he's shooting.

I'm hung over. I'm heartbroken.

I don't know what to do, so I'm going to do what I know how to do: be Jeremy King, super-agent.

I wake up at five, shower, and take as many Advil as I think my liver or kidneys can bear.

I look at myself in the mirror for a long, long time.

The guys were actually understanding. Quiet, but understanding. Tucker never once said, "I told you so."

He *so* should have. I walked right into that one. I waltzed into it. He told me not to do the background check.

I screwed it all up. My need to know ruined it.

What's "it"?

I don't know.

I think I love Macy. I stare at myself in the mirror and think about her, back in Idaho, waking up to go guide. With those damn little dogs.

I feel like maybe I'm about to cry, so I smack myself, hard, on the side of the face.

Enough.

I made a nice, big, cozy bed for myself, and now I'm going to lie in it, roll around, suck it up, and get on with life.

I shave, I dress, and I feel stronger.

Jeremy King will not be brought to bear, be bowed, by something as petty as a pretty face.

She's more than that, idiot. You know it.

I pick up my phone, my wallet, a bottle of water out of the minifridge, and prepare to suck it up for four to six weeks while we shoot and I commute back and forth from LA to Toronto.

I will be busy. Busy is good.

I ride in the town car by myself. I need space. I need so much space, this town can't probably provide the expanse I'm after, but I can at least ride alone to set.

Tucker and Andy. They'll be gentle. They won't even mention her, probably.

Where in the hell Todd ended up, who knows. When we got back to the lodge, he was casually interested, and he must have been able to tell that I would have loved to beat him senseless. He got quiet real quick and stayed out of my way when I got into the tequila.

He went his way at the Idaho Falls airport, taking a flight to LA for some bullshit meeting with his record label.

He's the only one I don't trust to keep his mouth shut.

In LA, no one will even know the truth about what happened. Sure, I put a couple of my people on the case when I got Macy to Seattle, but as far as they know, I was just being a kind, benevolent guest, taking care with a guide who didn't have the means herself.

Or they'll assume I was screwing her, and given my reputation, they'll assume it was purely recreational. The Jeremy King adventure, the way I always romance the ladies.

And that will be that.

The car pulls up to the plain grey office building where we're meeting today.

I get out and get inside. Toronto is humid and stagnant in the summer. I feel a hot blast of air and then the chill of air conditioning as I duck through the big glass revolving door.

My cell rings. "King."

"Hey, brother." It's Andy.

"Good morning." I clear my throat.

"How are you? Where are you?" He sounds tentative.

"I'm fine. I'm in the lobby. You here already?"

"I'm upstairs, but Kelly's here. Quincy's got croup, and she might have to go to the emergency room. Can you come up so we can check in on this?"

"I'm there." I hang up.

Someone else's troubles. I can do this. I'm a fixer. This is what I do well—I attend to the details and the messes of every other person. I clean up in a clinical way.

I get off the elevator to see Andy standing with his arms wrapped around Kelly.

My heart pinches for a second. They, of course, remind me of Macy. What a pathetic sappy mess I am.

I come up to them. "Where's Q?"

Kelly turns to me. "She's headed to the ER with my mom."

Andy has his arm around her, and Kelly leans into him. Andy turns his cell over and over with his free hand. "Maybe I can persuade Tennyson to start table reads this afternoon or tomorrow morning. We can go to the hospital together."

Kelly pats his arm. "Hunter had croup a couple different times. I'm not super worried, but she's so congested and her ears are still clogged from the plane ride. I can just tell how miserable she is."

I step in. "Who are you calling?"

Andy nods at the phone. "First Tennyson, then Dr. Joe in Boise."

I wave him off. "Let me handle Tennyson. You do the daddy thing."

Andy's shoulders soften. "Thanks, J. Tell him this afternoon I'm his man."

"No problem."

He turns with Kelly and walks down the hall, on the phone with the family doctor. Calling about his little girl.

I want to go back to the hotel and get plastered again. There's a hole opening up inside of me, and it's this kind of bullshit about love that I never wanted to endure.

I get Tennyson to push rehearsals back to tomorrow morning, which he's relieved by, because the permits for two of his locations are screwed up, and now he can spend the day with his crew getting them straightened out.

My phone lights up with another call. For five seconds my heart leaps. It's a 208 number. Idaho.

Macy.

I answer it. "This is Jeremy."

"Jeremy, it's Joe. Tessa's husband."

I steady my voice. Not who I wanted to speak to, not by a long shot. "Joe. What can I do for you?"

"I just spoke to Andy. No big deal with Quincy, but can you make some calls for me? It'd be great if she could get into Toronto General with Dr. Drake. He's a terrific pediatrician, and then I'd feel like we were doing our due diligence."

"I can call around. I'm happy to."

"How's the girl?"

"What?" I don't follow him.

"The one you fished out of the river. How is she?"

I swear to God I'm just going to save myself the pain and rip my heart out of my own chest right now. "She's doing fine. Thanks for your help on that one, Joe. I owe you."

"You're helping me and Andy out now, so no worries. Talk to you soon."

"I'm on it. Bye, Joe."

So if Macy's going to come up in half-hour intervals every day for the next who knows how many weeks of my life, I might as well go wander into traffic right now.

I want to be busy and forget her. If everyone will get on board with that, I'd appreciate it.

By the time Andy texts me for the name of the pediatrician, I've gotten the name and arranged for an appointment within the next forty-five minutes. Health care is my new area of expertise, apparently.

I've also summoned a town car to take me back to the hotel. If Andy's not working, I'm going to get drunk again and crawl under the covers for a good long pass out.

Until I come up with a better option. I'm going to call her.

This idea springs to life as I watch the line of traffic we're snarled in, sitting four lanes across.

Well, partly it comes to mind because I know Andy won't abide by me drinking away my sorrows. One night's bender hurt a lot anyway. And I'm a man that likes control. And mastery.

But I could just call her.

"Hello?" She answers. She actually answers.

"Macy. It's—"

"I know who it is. What's up?"

"I wanted to check on you."

"I'm fine. I don't need to be checked on."

"I wanted to apologize."

"Apology accepted. Anything else?" She's frosty. Clipped short words.

I shouldn't have called. "I miss you." Jesus. Why'd I say that? I hang up.

She doesn't call back.

When I get back to the hotel, I change into shorts and go for a very, very long run.

It's humid, smoggy, miserable. I feel better. I can smell last night's alcohol sweating out of my pores. The older I get, the more I pay for a night of drinking. I make a mental note to never, never, let a woman get under my skin again.

Then I set to worrying about Macy. She's got a lot of enemies, she's been hurt by men before, she's by herself there. Who will take care of her?

She says she wants to dig herself out. But the money thing. I could use the background check to at least clear some of her accounts. She'd hate me, but it'd make things easier on her. I could pay Richard back the money she borrowed for the starter, so she wasn't working to clear an advance.

Then my phone rings. I stop running to answer it. "King."

"Mr. King." It's Macy. She doesn't say anything else.

I'm already breathing hard from running. When I answer her, I sound like a complete creeper, breathing heavy and voice low. "Yes? Are you all right?"

"I'm sorry, too. Take care of yourself."

"You take care of yourself, you hear me? What do you need?"

"I'm fine. Take care." She hangs up.

Now my head spins. What the hell was that? She apologized. She spoke to me.

I can feel everything in my heart winding back up, and I know how truly, completely, and desperately ruined I really am.

I don't know how to come back from something like this because honestly, I've never been this far gone over a woman.

The next morning, I get up impossibly early, go lift in the hotel gym, and I push it so hard I'll either have a heart attack or tear a hamstring. It's satisfying. It feels good to hurt in some other way than the crushing vise around my ribcage.

I shower and shave and dress and get to the set in time to see Andy heading into makeup.

His eyes are still closed, mostly. He's unshaven.

"Morning, glory. Another tough night?" I hand him a hot tea.

"I wanted Kelly to get some sleep, so I got up with Quincy and sat with her in the bathroom."

"For what?"

"I ran the shower really hot, and then I lay there on the bath mat with Quincy on my chest. The humidity of the shower makes it easier for her to sleep. And then I propped her up in the car seat, and she finally slept a little."

"So you're saying you slept on the bathroom floor last night." I look at him again, and I can see the fatigue in the slope of his shoulders.

"Yeah, who would've thought it? I give up raising hell and drinking and I still get to spend the night on the bathroom tile." He rubs his face, trying to wake up a bit. "But Kelly got some rest, so it's all good. And I think Q feels better this morning."

"Before you know it she'll sleep through the night. Then she'll be a teenager and sleep all day long." I sit in the make-up chair next to him.

"Let's not think about it. Hunter and Beau, I worry about them enough, and they aren't being chased around by a pack of teenage boys. I don't know if I'll be able to deal with Quincy when she starts to date."

"Hunter and Beau aren't being chased around by a pack of teenage boys as far as you know, but girls are just as scary. There could be a little mini-Amanda Walters out there."

Andy shakes his head. "No. Not even funny."

"Sorry. But speaking of her, do you think Quincy's over the worst part of the croup?"

Andy nods. "No ER or hospital I think. Her appetite's back. Always a good sign."

"I may have to go to LA to stitch up a contract for Amanda. You'd be fine if I did that?"

He waves a hand. "You do your thing, J. It might do you good to go crack some heads. Sharks gotta swim."

I feel less enthusiastic about it. "Something like that."

That night, Andy and Kelly invite me to their temporary place in Toronto for dinner. I'm the sympathy guest now, I guess.

When I get there, Kelly's at work in the kitchen, little Quincy in the playpen in the breakfast nook. Andy comes in from their bedroom, the stroller in one hand, dragging it across the foyer. "I swear to God I'm going to set this thing on fire. If the wheels jam one more time, I'm doing it."

Kelly picks Quincy up out of the playpen, walks over to him, hands him Quincy. "Please don't set it aflame with my child in it, though."

"Safety first, flames second." He plucks Quincy out of Kelly's arms and snuggles her into the stroller. "Jeremy, light that barbecue for Kelly. I'll do the steaks when I get back."

"Because I'm not capable of grilling?" I stand up and look for the tongs.

"And I'm not capable of lighting?" Kelly defends herself.

"Kelly, you don't usually like lighting the grill. You always tell the story of your uncle and his singed eyebrows. And Jeremy, you usually don't like to contribute. You're more of a taker, remember?" He grins at me.

Kelly pats me on the arm. "Jeremy can do it. I think it's a nice gesture."

"Now you're all just patronizing me. Stop." I feel the back of my neck getting hot.

Andy rolls the stroller out the door. "We'll be back. Don't burn the steaks."

Kelly pulls the meat out of the fridge and follows me out on the deck. As she pulls the door shut, she guides me to the grill. "Let's grill and chill, as they do in the Applebee's commercials."

I shake my head. "I think it's Dairy Queen. And this isn't like Netflix and chill, is it? Because Andy will set me on fire instead of the stroller. I'm afraid of him."

She sets the steaks on the table as I light the grill. "I find you lovable but mildly disgusting because of your general lack of moral compass, so no worries." She reaches into the cooler and pulls out a water. "But I do want to talk, in all seriousness."

I don't look up from scouring the grill with the steel brush. "Talk away." I don't want to talk.

"You don't want to talk, but you should. So tell me about Macy."

"What's there to say? I tried to do something nice, and she kicked me in the balls for it."

Kelly's face lights up in surprise. "Really? Andy didn't say anything about that. Damn."

"No, not really. Proverbially. Metaphorically."

"Oh." She's quiet.

Screw it. "Kelly?"

"Yeah?"

"I don't like how lonely I feel. Usually I like being alone. I like myself."

"You like yourself too much as a general rule."

"Very funny. I'm not kidding."

"Talk to me."

"Normally I'm content. I may not be happy, but 90% of the time happiness is bullshit anyway. It's something people chase obsessively and make themselves miserable in the process. Usually, usually I'm content. I like my life. Usually."

"And now?"

"Right now I don't feel right."

"You feel lonely."

"Yeah, and it sucks."

"Do something about it."

"You mean see somebody else?"

"Not in the slightest. We have an open invitation for the 4th of July, Andrew told me. We could all go down there, and you could see Macy again. Make things right."

"You might be invited. I'm not."

"You are. Stop it."

The steaks pop and sizzle on the grill. I consider. "I don't know."

"I know you well enough to know that this is as deep as we will explore the psyche of one Jeremy King, but consider this: you may have found a person who can go toe to toe with you. You're a big personality and a bigger pain in the ass, and from the sound of things, this woman has seen you, the real you, in spite of all of that. She's a contender. Contend with your feelings for her, because I think you're lonely now because you've decided to end your love affair with your-self and reach out. This is big for you, Jeremy."

"You talk too much."

"Let me shortcut it for you. Don't be a self-centered asshole; come back to Swan Valley with us. Come make it right with Macy."

"Go get a clean plate. Andy wants his steak rare."

BREAKING AWAY

I figured out a long time ago that I'm sometimes a guy who other people hate. At first, maybe when I was in school, it hurt my feelings. Yes, I had it in my head that I wanted people to like me.

Then I figured out that a lot of people are shit. They're hateful, greedy, self-centered, negative pricks. And after getting kicked in the teeth enough times, I decided to play hard ball. I was smart, I was good at figuring people out, and I was tired of being the nice one.

Which is about when I found my calling in Hollywood. If you've gone Team Hobbes instead of Team Locke, Hollywood is a great place to work. The way human beings behave in LA goes a long way to cementing Hobbes' theory that life is nasty, brutish, and short, and so are most people.

How I've found a decent person like Andy to rep, I don't know, but he is the opposite of a lot of my clients.

Take the reason I'm currently flying away from everything I care about right now: away from Andy's project in Toronto, away from the mess and the woman in Idaho I can't stop thinking about. The reason is Amanda Walters, movie star, huge diva, and general pain in the ass.

I'm in a town car at LAX, and my cell rings. I jump. Toronto was relatively quiet—the junior agents in the office know that I take a morning conference call when I'm on location with Andy, and I've trained them up to leave me alone for the rest of the day unless there's a crisis.

Now I'm back in the city of angels, so I'm fair game, and since I turned my phone on when we put wheels down on the tarmac, the texts and calls have been lighting my phone up.

"King." I know who it is.

"Jeremy, I hate making my own calls, but here I am, on the phone to you." It's Amanda's thick British accent. I can even hear the toss of those red curls, the attitude, through the tone of her voice.

"Amanda. Lovely to hear your voice. I'm on the way in to the office. You're there already?"

"Of course not. I had acrobatic yoga; just finished up. You want me to show my face around town after sweating? I don't think so."

"So you'll be in when?"

Her voice rises. "When I'm damn well ready. Calm yourself."

I breathe in, slowly. I close my eyes and think of cold water and casting and watching the riffles for the glint of a trout. "Sounds good. I'll see you when I see you." I end the call.

I watch the road and slip in headphones, trying to center myself. I don't know what the point of anything is right now.

And that is a problem. Winning is usually the point. Which is why I'm the very best at what I do.

A governor from a two-bit state tried to get me to run his presidential campaign once. I won't name drop—you wouldn't even recognize him—but it was damn tempting, until he told me what he could pay me. Because the gamesmanship of LA is probably only topped by the ridiculous Machiavellian nonsense of national politics.

I said no, because I enjoy what I do. I feel at home here. I fit.

Usually. Before now.

What in the actual fuck is happening.

The car pulls into the garage of my offices. I ride the elevator up and greet the office crew. The junior agents, they're harmless. The assistants are generally too hip, too hairy, and too young to give a shit about. I tend to call them all "bro" or "Miss" and wait for the day when one of them makes a power play and tries to take agency from me.

"Mr. King. Good to see you. It's been a while." My assistant Esther hands me a very large white mug. "Your bulletproof coffee."

"Is that still a thing? I thought everyone was moving on from Paleo."

"Everyone but you, Mr. King. Remember you like to buck the trends. And you like coconut."

"And you remind me what I like. Interesting, isn't it?" I take it from her and take a sip, and yeah, it doesn't taste horrible. If it keeps me from ballooning into an overgrown lump of lard, then fine.

She looks me up and down. "Toronto been good to you?" She squints a little from behind cat eye glasses. She's my favorite in the office, and she gives as good as she gets. And she's a lesbian, so we don't have to ever go through any awkward sexual harassment and ensuing lawsuits on either of our parts. Plus, she's gotten a haircut like that hot girl Ruby Rose from the chicks in prison show, and so sometimes I indulge in thinking about what she and her cute girlfriend get up to at night.

But right now, I try to give her no ammunition for questions or a lecture.

"Toronto was fine."

"You didn't check in much. You barely checked in at all from the fishing trip. Andy okay? His family all fine?" She's still eyeballing me.

"Quincy had croup for a while. She's still not sleeping. Other than that, everybody's peachy." I take another big swallow of the coffee. "Really."

She rolls her eyes. "Then you won't mind if I barrage with twenty details from the contract re-up?"

"Which one?"

"Seriously?" She takes a pen out from behind her ear.

"No, I know what you're talking about. The one with Cineaste. For Jessica Rabid Rabbit." I'm tossing Esther a bone here. She and I delight in nicknaming our pain in the ass clients as ridiculous cartoon characters. For Amanda, the more I think about Jessica Rabbit, the similarities are startling. One time she broke into Andy's trailer on set and decorated it, stripped down to her undies, threw herself at him. When he was already married to Kelly.

Amanda is crazy, but she's able to keep her shit together on set, and lord, people love her in movies, so she gets jobs and I get paid.

"Esther? You know what I need?" I soften my voice; she has to take a step in to be a considerate listener.

"Yes?"

"I want a Danish. A fritter. A carb for breakfast. Is there anywhere in LA you can get that for me?"

She follows me into my office. "I will get you a gluten-laden sugar bomb if you promise to get things wrapped up with Amanda today, okay?"

I sit and nod. Sometimes Esther reminds me of Sister Agnes Katherine, the nun who lived down the street from me when I first moved out to LA. She took it upon herself to be my Jewish mom in absentia. My own actual mom was a lapsed Catholic, but given that she was married to a Jew, she nagged in earnest. Mom may have hired Sister Agnes, for all I know. I always found her nagging ironic but kind of sweet. Esther is kind of like that, except in a hot lesbian nerdy way.

"I'll comply. I really want a doughnut or something, so you've got me over the barrel."

"I'm bringing in the last revision of the contract they messengered over last night, and you look at everything I've highlighted, and then you work your slimy Jeremy King charm on Brunhilda and get her to sign off on it so we can be rid of her for 60 to 180 days assuming they can put together the financing package."

"Yes, Ma'am."

"That's Miss Smartypants-who-held-the-office-together-while-you-were-off-having-a-midlife-crisis-or-something to you."

"Fair enough. Could you write it on an index card so I can properly address you?" I shoot a rubber band at her ankles.

"You know I can take you. Back off, King."

"And I think I take offense to the mid-life crack. I'm thirty-four. You want me dead by sixty-eight?"

"I'd like you dead by six-thirty tonight, sir. But we can't always get what we want."

"Fine. Buy me that Cronut, and I'll be one step closer to the grave."

"On it. Now look that contract over. Amanda's assistant called. They're on the way over."

"Maybe they'd pick up the carbs for me."

She leaves my office and pulls my door closed behind her.

And that's when the ennui sets in.

I love my job.

I like Esther, and I love our witty banter.

But today it all feels blah.

Empty.

Stupid.

Forced?

So I sit and look out the window at my view, which is mostly a view of smog and more buildings and sometimes the occasional sunset that's red from the gunk in the air.

Work is a great distraction, unless you're distracted already.

I force myself to attend to the contract. For no other reason than trying to expedite this meeting with Amanda.

A few minutes later, Esther pokes her head in. "She's brought Stephenson. You want me to cancel?"

Stephenson is Amanda's entertainment lawyer. He's a pain in the ass that takes another bite out of Amanda's checks. He's pompous for no good reason. He has weird hair. I don't like him. His ears are uneven.

"No, I want this to be done. I'll tolerate him."

Esther nods and brings them in.

Amanda's still in her yoga pants, but with heels. And legwarmers. And a torn-up plaid shirt. There's so much to look at, I don't know where to start with the insults.

"Amanda. Lovely as ever." I give her a kiss on both cheeks.

Stephenson puts out a hand. "Jeremy. You've got a little color. Heard you were out in the field. Good stuff going on, I'm sure?"

"Toronto. Another client's shooting up there for a couple more weeks."

Amanda plops down in the chair across from mine. "Andy. You can say his name. I don't give a crap about him."

I know better than to take that bait. "Uh-huh. Let's talk about this contract."

"Did you look at all the revisions?" Stephenson shifts in his chair, nervously. That's a tell if I ever saw one.

"What's the part you think I'll have a cow over? I thought Cineaste was pretty decent in the terms." I look at Amanda instead of Stephenson. He's just her lapdog.

"I'm the one who should have a cow. My cut of the backend is pathetic. Don't they know who I am?" Amanda twirls a red tendril of hair. God, I hate her.

"They do." I tilt my head, weighing my options. I go there. "You're a terrific actor, Amanda. But you're a huge pain in the ass. You wear people out. And you're terrific, but not wear-people-out terrific." I say this, and I'm amazed, because my voice sounds, I don't know, sympathetic? Tired? Actually not annoyed? Helpful?

She looks straight at me. I hold her gaze. "You think I'm terrific?"

"Yes. No lie. But a huge, huge jerk to work with." I don't know. Right now I think she could profit from a little honesty.

Stephenson holds his hand up, one finger extended, as though he's frozen. I think he was going to say something about the contract, but his eyes dart from me to Amanda.

She sits for a minute, and then her eyes drop to the contract in her lap. "Fine. I'll do it." She gets up and walks out the door.

Stephenson's still frozen.

"Good to see you, Stephenson. Your client's headed to the car, I think."

He shakes out of it, stands up and stuffs the paperwork in his briefcase. "That was unexpected. But we're done. I'll scan and send you signed copies when I deliver them to Cineaste."

"You aren't messengering them?"

He looks at me like I'm crazy. "I want this in their hands before she changes her mind." He shakes my hand and scurries out of my office.

Esther comes in, carrying a white box. "What magic did you do in here? I barely had time to find a maple bar."

I shrug my shoulders. "I was different. Honest like always."

"But different how?" She's intrigued.

"I don't know. I wasn't so fired up. Maybe I didn't maneuver as much."

"It worked, so whatever it was, good work. Now eat your heart attack of a pastry." She plops the box on my desk. I open it, and the maple bar has chocolate icing piped on it that reads, "Happy mid-life crisis!"

Esther cackles at her desk. "Eat that!"

"I am!" I take a huge bite and chew on what's become of me.

That night the drive home makes me somewhat happy. My Tesla and I are reunited—Esther sent one of the less hirsute assistants to fetch it so I could drive home in it. Usually someone else, especially some hipster in Toms, behind the wheel would put me into a panic, but today I didn't care.

It's nice to listen to my own stereo and push the car fast around the curves up the canyon roads. I consider having a soak in the spa and enjoying a cigar when I get home.

I pull into the driveway, and I get a text from Andrew.

When you coming back to T.O.?

I answer. *Deal done. I've set a record with PITA diva. So tomorrow night prolly.*

I consider just calling him, but I don't know if he wants to talk about my screwed-up life, and I'm not in the mood.

His next text: *We're going to Idaho for 4th of July. You're coming with. Swan Valley.*

This is why I didn't call him.

I'll pass.

Someone texted and asked for us to come. Someone you like. Who must not hate you.

She didn't say me, she said you.

My phone rings. I speak first. "She'd be happy to see you. I'm definitely dis-invited."

Andy laughs. "That's what Kelly said you'd say. Which is why she said I had to call and 'stop texting like a teenage girl,' to quote her."

"Your wife makes fun of us a lot. I don't know how we should feel about it. But really, I'll pass on the trip."

"Now I'm quoting from the text I received today: 'I'd like it if Mr. King would come. Please tell him that.'"

My heart skips down the street, little wicker basket in hand. My mental picture of my heart looks like Dorothy from *Wizard of Oz* if you're wondering. "Why didn't she just text me herself?"

Andy covers the phone; I hear muffled talk. "Kelly says get back to Toronto so we can wrap the hell up for the long weekend and go to Idaho for crying out loud. She's dying to meet Macy."

"I don't know."

"She texted me instead of you because she's stubborn. Just like you."

I consider this. "We can talk more of my mess of a life that you all love to meddle in when I get back to Toronto. I need to come back regardless of where I spend my 4th of July."

"Excellent. Catch a flight tomorrow, and Tucker'll pick you up."

He hangs up, and I pull into the driveway of my house.

She wants me to come back to Idaho.

There's hope for me yet.

I take myself up on the offer for a soak under the stars, and I smoke that cigar, and for good measure, I have a couple drinks, too.

And consider calling her.

Or texting. I could text her.

I close my eyes for a minute and the sensation of her lips on mine, the feel of her skin on mine, that night in Seattle, it all comes back to me.

Maybe this is a bad idea. I want all of this too badly.

I call her number.

It rings, and rings, and she doesn't answer.

Then I start to the obsessive worrying.

Then I text her.

Just checking in. Hope you're well.

I wait.

I smoke the cigar, sit in the spa until I'm a waterlogged prune.

No text.

I finally give up and go inside. I knock back another drink in hopes of falling asleep.

And then I go to bed.

It's humid, and all the windows are open, but there's no breeze. I can smell some sweet flower from outside, and I try to take in slow, even breaths and relax. I watch the shadows on the ceiling.

I finally fall asleep with the phone beside me, but Macy never calls.

So I will go back to Toronto and get on with the business of getting over her.

COMING HOME

The flight attendant is lovely. She wears her black hair in loose curls. She has huge eyes and big eyelashes and sports two beauty marks on her porcelain skin, one on her cheek and one just above her red lips. She reminds me of a storybook character, maybe like Snow White or Rose Red or something.

She's wearing the navy shirtdress all the attendants wear. She's cinched a belt tight, just below her chest, and I notice the effect.

Quincy could not care less. I've stopped the constant bouncing in my distraction, and she lets loose with a piercing shriek in protest. I'm about to stand up and go give Quincy back to Kelly when Rose Red, the flight attendant, comes over.

"What's wrong little bugaboo, huh?" She holds her arms out for the toddler, smiles big and broad for me.

"It's fine; Kelly's right over"— I look back, and Kelly and Andrew are both zonked out, fast asleep. The croup drama in Toronto must've sucked the life out of them.

Rose Red raises her eyebrows. "I'm not a patient woman. Hand the sweet pumpkin over."

I comply, and she holds Quincy up over her head, almost brushing the absurd bow on Quincy's little blonde head on the roof of the plane's cabin.

She coos at her and blows raspberries. "Who's cranky? Who is?" Then she brings her back into orbit and flips her around to face me, holding her with one arm under Quincy's armpits and one under her bottom.

Quincy looks surprised, her wet little mouth agape.

But Rose Red starts to sway, twisting back and forth at the waist, and Quincy seems to relax.

And then the little body lets loose an enormous fart, loud.

"That's why bugaboo was fussing, huh, little one?" Rose Red smiles, which is the opposite of what I do when a stink bomb is loosed in my close vicinity, but okay, we'll go with it.

Quincy smiles. I can't help but remark. "Toddler life is good, huh, now that you've gotten that out of your system?"

She giggles.

Rose Red smiles. "Ah, look, she likes you. Are you her uncle?"

Red sure is attentive to me. "I'm her godfather. In a strictly non-Mafia sense."

"Well, she loves her handsome godfather. You do, don't you little bugaboo?"

She just called me handsome. Is something going on here that I'm missing? "I think she just likes playing with my keys." I fail to mention that I usually make Quincy wail.

"You get up to Toronto much?"

"We'll be back after the long weekend. We're filming for another few weeks."

"I live in Toronto. We could get together sometime. Couldn't we, little girl, huh?" She turns Quincy over again and holds her up, face level, gives her another little raspberry sound and a goofy face.

"Which are we talking about? Me and you, or me and the toddler and you?"

Rose Red laughs, a high peal. "You and me." She looks right at Quincy. "Your godfather's irresistible." She hands my goddaughter back to me, holds out her hand.

"Give me your phone, you handsome silly man."

I hand it to her. I don't know why. I just do.

She takes it and puts her phone number in, hands it back to me.

"I have to go lock the galley down before we land." She licks her lips slowly. "I look forward to hearing from you." She turns and sashays up to the front of the plane.

Quincy looks at me. She drools. I look at her, my mouth open, too.

"What just happened?"

Quincy blinks.

Here's what happens next: I get this queasy feeling in the pit of my stomach. I hold Quincy and rock her gently, and she closes her eyes, so I close mine.

In my mind's eye, do I see the storybook flight attendant, the one with the black hair and the red lips? The one who said I was irresistible?

Nope.

I see the woman with the fly rod in her hand, her eyes on the river, the gold flecks in her eyes glinting in the river light reflected, her smile broad.

That one. That girl, the one who hates my guts, who didn't call or text me back.

I open my eyes, and Quincy looks at me, tries to poke a wet toddler finger in my eye.

"This is a mess." That feeling in my gut is guilt, and the woman on my mind?

She's love.

Quincy and I spend some more time drooling and bonding, and finally the plane lands in Nowheresville, Idaho, destination Macy.

If she'll have me. I'm a little bit convinced that this return trip is a terrible idea, but I'm a lot convinced that I'm beyond hope and that I might as well listen to Kelly's advice and actually put up a fight and try to reach Macy.

Will she let me in? Who knows. I won't forgive myself if I don't make an attempt.

I'm Jeremy King, Smartest Guy in the Room, Agent of All Agents.

I win at everything. Usually.

I might have to lose a little bit to win with Macy, but I'm going to try. I'm definitely not a quitter.

"Are you speaking on this trip or is your big idea to remain mute?" Andy's rescued Quincy from me, thanked me profusely for letting him and Kelly sleep a bit. Now he holds her at his hip and interrogates me.

Quincy fusses, squirms in his grasp, looking around for her mama.

"My goddaughter doesn't like your tone." I've talked about myself more in the last month than in the whole last decade before that, and I'm getting tired of being the center of discussion. Center of attention and adoration, I'm totally on board with that. Center of talk, introspection, and inspection, possibly the center of a discussion of failings and shortcomings, no way in hell.

"He speaks!" Andy smiles at me. I hate that he can read me so well. That's a downside to actually having a friend. He knows me, and I can't lie to him as well as most people. And he calls me on it. What a pain in the ass.

"My big idea is to grovel, I think." I might as well be honest with him. Whatever I have left of my pride/ego/hubris is already catching a late bus to Peoria. No sense in trying to maintain dignity.

Andy nods. "I've done that before." We walk off the plane, make our way to the terminal. Quincy squeals in delight as the wind on the tarmac whips her little sundress around her legs. Andrew keeps his iron grasp on her.

"What do you mean? You're Andy Pettigrew. You don't grovel." I look at him. Guys who look like him don't ever have to grovel.

He looks at me and shakes his head. "You've got a short memory. I don't know another word to describe what I had to do to get Kelly back when I massively screwed that up. I thought I'd lost her." His face clouds over. He's serious. We usually don't get back around to this stuff.

"Dude. I didn't mean to bring that up."

"You didn't. Listen, J, you're doing the right thing. I can tell. If you can't trust your own instincts, trust mine. It's worth it. It's worth trying."

"But what if it doesn't work? What if she won't talk to me?" I hate the sound to my voice. I sound desperate. I feel desperate. God.

"What if she does? What are you going to say to her?" He pulls the door to the terminal open. We sneak inside, and he holds the door. "Hey, hold Quincy for one more minute. Kelly was waiting back to grab the stroller. I'm going to go help her." He hands the little one to me and jogs back over to where Kelly is trying to resurrect the stroller.

I look at the blonde Quincy. She's drooling again, but she doesn't fuss. She just hangs out with me. She raises her fat little hand and points at her mom and dad.

They've finally gotten the stroller to unfold, and hand in hand, they push it towards us. Kelly must say something to Andy, and he leans down and kisses her, wraps an arm around her shoulder.

They suck so bad. I look at Quincy, who plays with the end of my nose. She likes to pat it with the flat of her palm. I don't know why, but it keeps her happy most of the time, so I humor her.

She looks like she'll listen to me, so I rant. "Seriously, can your parents look at least a little miserable? Your Uncle Jeremy's dying in the midst of a total fuck-up on the love front here. The poster children for love might as well take a voodoo needle to my embroidered heart."

Quincy looks at me, seriously. "Poop."

I laugh so hard I almost drop her.

Andy and Kelly meet back up with us. Kelly looks at me askance. "What's so funny?"

"What words has Quincy said to you?"

"So far Mama and Dada and Bobo and Hunner. And birdy."

"Well, add on a classic. She's a peach."

Andy picks her out of my arms. "What? You didn't teach her the f-word, did you? You'll lose your godfather designation if you did."

Quincy chimes in. "Poop."

Kelly snorts. "Jeremy didn't teach her that. It's too clean."

Andy tucks Quincy into the stroller. "Let's go impress everyone at the picnic. Maybe that'll be your way in with Macy, a small child and her growing vocabulary."

I think again about how this is going to go. "I'll take whatever I can get."

THE GRIFTERS

And here we are, driving a Yukon down a dry road in Idaho. Sure, Kelly sits next to Quincy in the back seat, helping her drink watered-down juice and eat Melba toast. And yes, Andy knows the road better, but it's déjà vu all over again.

"How in the world did you manage to get the house again? It's the 4th of July weekend. No way was it just available." I resist the urge to chew my nails. Or hang my head out the window and scream from anxiety.

Andy smiles. "Way. It was available. The crew of football coaches due to come fish all just got fired when the A.D. at Carroll College cleaned house. No fishing and bonding for them, poor schmucks."

"I feel sorry for them and lucky for us. What about Tucker?" Tucker was with us in Toronto, and why he'd pass on the chance to come hang out with us, I don't know. I think he likes me okay, and his and Andy's bromance endures, movie after movie and premiere after premiere.

Andy sighs. "Poor guy had to cover some Nickelodeon girl at a baseball game. She was singing the National Anthem. It's almost as bad as protecting a boy band."

"Fewer ten-year-old girls squealing, but just barely. And then drunk idiots who don't give a rip chucking beers down on the field 'cause they want the game to start."

Andy looks at me. "You've done that before. Don't be all pious."

"I did that at a hockey game. And it was a squid, not a beer. And it wasn't about some tween singing, it was a show of support."

"Children, stop squabbling. I left Hunter and Beau at home with Tessa, I thought." Kelly chides us in a voice I'm positive I've heard her use with her boys.

"Careful, young lady. I'm tender." I turn and face her, pull a goofy face for Quincy.

Kelly nods barely. "Not tender enough for my taste, but I'll allow it. Now talk about something else."

"Honey, we're home!" Andy pulls the left onto the loop road off of the highway.

And my palms begin to sweat. I feel a sheen of nerves and nausea coat my tongue and my armpits.

"Jesus. This was a bad idea."

Andy turns into the parking lot of the lodge. I scan the lot for Macy's car. Nothing.

"This is the scariest best idea you've had in a while, Mr. King." Andy points to the main building. "Go check in for us. We've got about a ton of small child gear to unload."

I get out of the car and swallow my heart back down into my chest. Where is her car? Is she not here? Maybe some other guy rented her out for the day; she's out fishing with him, giving him all of her attention.

I shake my head hard. One thing I've never been is jealous. Okay, I've been jealous as hell, but with Macy, one of the most amazing things was the way it felt. No one else got us the way we got each other. No one can compete with me, I don't think, because we fit. We get each other. I've been with plenty of women who should've been my match. But when you meet yours, you just know. I think. Unless I'm so delusional that I'll realize this is all shit right about the same time they lock the door on my nice little padded cell.

I pull the handle of the door to the main lodge and hear raised voices. My mouth goes dry, and my pulse shoots into high gear. It's Macy. Macy and Richard, if I remember that voice.

"I did no such thing. I always have Irene or Daniel double count the front desk till, anyway. Every time. And most of the time I'm out on the river. I don't even touch money most of the time."

"All I know is there's a serious shortfall, Macy. You can't explain that away."

"I shouldn't have to explain it. I had nothing to do with it. I don't even believe this is happening! I didn't make the deposit that day. I was just back from Seattle, and I didn't even work a full shift. And I hardly ever handle cash, anyway. How could we be short?"

"Lots of ways to embezzle. And it's us, not you. You're not short. I bet if I checked your balance at D.L. Evans Bank, I'd find it has grown. A lot. Recently."

"Richard, come on. You know me. Why would I do that?"

"I can think of a lot of reasons why. Your car. It's falling apart. You owe money all over Teton County. I don't even fault you for it. I'd want a way out of this place if I were you."

"I'm done listening."

"That's fine. I called the prosecuting attorney's office. They'll be in contact after the long weekend."

"What? If they've got a reason to arrest me, why don't they do it now?"

"They don't have access to our accounts until Monday. Lisa's visiting her kids in Provo, and when she's back, she'll fax over the bank's statement of accounts. Then the attorney's office can open the case."

"I can't even believe what I'm hearing. You've got no proof."

I've been standing in the front lobby, trying to slow the rush of blood in my ears enough to hear the conversation. The back room behind the front desk is just out of my line of sight, but it's the same one where I first saw Macy. When she came out to check Andy and me in, and noticed me instead of the movie star.

But what the hell am I hearing now?

I need to get out. If she sees me, there'll be no hope we can even talk. I don't know what's going on, but I need to sort it out on my own before she sees me.

I push out the door, trying to figure out what to tell Andy and Kelly. My phone buzzes.

Sorry to make you wait, buddy. They left the house open for us—we just saw the sign on the door. Come over unless you're already fixing things with fishergirl.

I swallow hard. He can't know what I just heard. I've got to figure it out before he catches wind. He's supported me through all of this because he trusted what I thought of Macy. But I don't know if he'd forgive this. If it's true, Macy's sunk with my friends. Andy protects us, and he'd tell me to protect myself.

This royally sucks.

When I walk in the house, I immediately latch on to the little girl trying to waddle her way around the coffee table. "Q! Look at you, you big girl!"

Andy looks up from putting away bottles of formula. "Did you see her?"

I don't know how I get anything out, but I do. "No one was at the desk. I waited for a bit, but then I got your text. Guess I'll catch her later."

We settle in, eat dinner, entertain Quincy, and then Kelly puts her down for the night. I can hear her in the bedroom, singing to the little girl. Andy sits with me on the couch, and the TV's on, but we've turned the volume down so Quincy can settle.

"If we get any more domestic, I may as well check into the Golden Dawn Estates and hang it all up. I feel a hundred years old." I can't think straight, but I can't let Andy know there's a problem.

Andy smiles. "I can't get enough of it."

"All of it?" I look at him, wondering about this for real.

He considers, looks up at the big log beams of the ceiling for a beat. "Okay, croup, I got enough of that for a lifetime. If I could trade all of the sick baby worry for sleep—I do like sleep."

I can't tell him, but an idea lights in my sad, ridiculous brain. "So no Tucker, but what about Todd? He's missing out."

Andy shrugs. "I wasn't able to get a hold of him in time. He's still in LA, still saying it's all about the new album, but I don't know. He was way off his game the whole trip out here."

"He didn't tell you about the death in the family?"

Andy looks surprised. "No. What? Someone in his family died that week?"

Now I'm suspicious. Todd thinks of Andy as his BFF. He didn't tell him about the death? "Apparently not. Very surprised that I didn't get a straight story from Mr. Reliable." I can't keep the sarcasm from dripping off my tongue.

I get a jab to the ribs. Andy follows it up with a finger wag. "Now, listen. You know Todd's like a brother to me."

"I know, I know, the high school friend, the one who knew you when, who keeps it real. I'm with you. I must've misunderstood what he was upset about."

"So now the infamously impatient and judgy Jeremy King wants to give him a chance to redeem himself? Why the sudden altruism?"

I know exactly why. The plot I'm hatching isn't ready to crack its shell yet, so I don't say what I'm really thinking. "It's not altruism. I need someone to drink a 4th of July beer with, and it's certainly not you, oh squeaky clean one."

Andy shakes his head. "You're insufferable." He stands up and stretches, points to the bedroom where Kelly and Quincy are. "My wife has stopped singing, which means the wild wombat toddler's finally asleep. I'm taking my leave of you and going to where the wife is."

"Sayonara. I might call Todd if you're okay with it."

He nods. "Go for it. And let me know if you grow a pair and go looking for Macy. You know, the real reason we're here."

I swallow hard, put on the best poker face I have. "I got the feeling she's not working tonight. I'll track her down tomorrow."

"Okay. Maybe we'll get in some fishing before it gets too hot. You could woo her on the river again."

"Yeah, that went so well the first time. But yes, fishing I can do." I feel like shit for a minute. "Hey, brother, you've been amazing through this whole thing. I don't know why I've completely gone overboard, but thanks for sticking with me."

"You've apparently lost your mind." He lingers at the hallway for a minute. "But for a good cause. Many a man has lost his shit over a woman. You're not immune, which I find hopeful. So there you go. Good night, my insane friend."

I hesitate to admit this, but Andy might be the wisest person I know. And I owe him for it. "Good night."

I wait for about five minutes before I step out of the front door and call Todd.

"Hello?"

He actually answers.

"Todd, you need to come to Idaho and do me a favor."

"Fuck you, Jeremy. Anything else?"

"Look, you told me you had a death in the family, but Andy never heard a thing about that."

There's a long pause on the phone. "Don't say anything to him. It was my cat."

"For Chrissakes. Your cat. That was the death in the family."

He sighs. I can hear it through the phone. "I'm not lying."

"Fine. Sorry about Fluffy."

"Her name was Mrs. Nesbitt."

"You're giving me way too much to tease you about. I will try really, really hard to rise above. Now redeem yourself and get your ass down here. Andy would love for you to come hang with us, and I could really use your help. It's for Macy, so it's not even really for me. You'd be helping someone else."

"So this favor would be about what?"

"I'll cut your balls off if you leak this to Tucker or Andy, but the lodge owner, I heard him accuse Macy of stealing money from the company. Taking a deposit, skimming the hotel till."

"And?"

"I don't buy it."

"Based on what? That she's a good lay?"

"Now you may need to come here so I can kick your ass for that comment, you douche."

He breathes into the phone for a second. "Sorry. You know you and me, we could work harder to get along. We both like Andy a lot, and he seems to tolerate you, so maybe there's some common ground here."

"Right now the common ground we share has something to do with the day that you bagged out of fishing to stay back at the house. I think it might help get Macy out of this mess that Richard's accusing her of. Did you see her at all on that day?"

"I did, but I wasn't stealing if that's what you're thinking."

"I don't give a shit what you were doing, but you can vouch for Macy on that day, and that's the important part."

"Huh. I see your point."

"Are you getting on a plane, then?"

"I don't know, Jeremy, you're the big-time Hollywood agent. What plane are you putting me on?"

I grit my teeth. "Fine. I'll call Aaronson and see about his plane. If not that, you better take a first class ticket. I'll text you with the details."

He chuckles. "I like this. Jeremy King bending over backwards to spend time with me, of all people."

"I don't like it one bit, but I'll do what it takes to clear things for Macy."

"I'll go pack. Text me." He makes a loud smooching sound, wet through the phone. "Love you, J."

"Screw you, Todd." I end the call.

An alibi is a good start, but I've got to track the money. However, I don't need anybody's help around here for that.

LA is all about money. If I need to follow money, I know plenty of LA people for that. Money leaves a trail like a big ol' Seattle slug, and I can get someone to find it.

I just need a little time.

I spend most of the night on the phone. Eventually I come inside, and realize that I'm cold and sore and tired as hell.

And that Andy is up and humming in the kitchen. Cheerily.

"Morning, sunshine. What's the deal with you? You look like you were hit by a bus."

"Just trying to figure some things out. I need to borrow the Yukon this morning. I need to go find Macy."

His eyes widen, and his voice brightens. "That's what I want to hear. Some fighting spirit." He tosses me the keys. "You go, girl."

I punch him in the arm, keys in my hand. "Don't mock me. I'm cranky, and the 'let's tease Jeremy 'cause he's in love' shtick wears thin today."

He laughs. "God love you, Jeremy King. See you in a bit."

I drive over to Macy's apartment. It's ungodly early. Seriously, even on days when I run in LA, I don't wake up this early. Of course, I didn't really go to bed last night, so…

Her car is in front of the apartment, and I puzzle on why it wasn't in the parking lot of the lodge last night.

I get out and go and knock on her door.

The little dogs, Canadian celebrity impersonators Justin Trudeau and Pierre Trudeau, are comfortingly barking their little heads off on the other side of the door. That's a good sign.

She opens the door just a crack. Then, when she sees that it's me, she swings it wide, and the dogs come out and bounce around my ankles, and then Justin Trudeau gets too excited and flops over, snoring loudly.

"What's going on? Why are you here?"

I shove my hands into my pockets. "Listen. All my nerves from last night and the day before that and most of the time in Toronto are all shot and frayed and numbed by the lack of sleep and the stench of desperation. So I've got no game today, not a single tiny shred of it."

She purses her lips, thinking. "Okay, I guess." She's quiet.

"What I mean to say is that I came back to tell you I'm sorry, and I want you in my life, and then I heard Richard the owner talking to you last night, and I know about the missing money, and I want to help you."

She sucks in a breath. I don't know if she's shocked by my rambling honesty, or what. She takes a step closer to me.

"I need you to believe me. I didn't take that money. I swear to God." She looks up at me, the skin under her delicate jaw flushes pink, and I can see her swallow hard.

"I need to believe you. But you did steal my watch. You yourself told me you're a compulsive thief."

"Please. Jeremy."

She's never said my first name. To hear it come from those lips sends me into orbit. I bite my lip.

"Say something." She puts a hand out, and her eyes dip to the ground between us, and then she sets that impossibly soft hand, delicate as a bird, rests it imperceptibly, over my heart. Her palm warms the cotton of my t-shirt. I bite down harder on my lip.

I turn the hand over. It's the one she cut, the one that was bandaged that first night. The healing wound is pink and bumpy across her palm. I trace it with my finger.

I open my mouth, and the truth spills out. "I want you. I don't care if you stole it. I don't think you did, but I still want you no matter what."

She puts her other hand at the back of my neck and pulls me down to her. She kisses me.

I open my mouth to hers, and I push my body close to hers. I take her in my arms, pull her to me, lift her up to kiss her more deeply. She wraps her legs around my waist.

"God dammit, you better be telling me the truth." I carry her into her house, straight to the bedroom.

And the little dogs set out to eat the cushions of the living room couch.

We lie in bed, and I watch Macy. The sun's finally up, but Macy's fallen back to sleep. She's drifted off, her lips parted as she breathes, a little soft raspy sound on each intake of breath.

I wonder about her life, when she was younger. I wish I'd been here, met her earlier, maybe spared her some of the hard living she had to do.

I've never been one to look back much. I think it serves me pretty well. I can be sentimental or nostalgic, I guess, but I don't dwell on the past much at all, mostly because I don't see the purpose.

Plus, unless it's fond remembering, it just reminds me what a colossal dumb ass I can be. A lot. Often. Frequently.

I had a girlfriend once (briefly—I've been over this territory— I'm pretty sure she handed out flyers about my failings in the middle of a well-to-do street in Bel Air). This girlfriend, she could not only remember what happened on a specific day that was weeks, months, or years ago, she could also remember what day of the week it was, the weather, everything.

"You were wearing that red polo, the one I like so much, with the white trim on the collar," she'd say.

It hurt her feelings that I couldn't recall the name of her sister. It was Eugenia, which is weird, in my opinion, so I should've remembered it. We broke up at a polo match on the Coachella grounds when she implied that she could do all the remembering for both of us, as though I needed to marry her before I was reduced to a gravy-slurping simpleton in my old age. I told her at least I didn't already have an old person's name like Eugenia did, and that was that.

Anyway, the point of that is this: some days, I can't remember if I've shaved until I run a hand over my face. I think it's for good reason.

Maybe it's the pace I keep. Maybe it's true—I am a shark—if I stop and consider and ponder and hold on to the past, I'll suffocate and die.

Maybe that's why Macy and I, we click. Because as "unproud" of my past as I am, she can say the same.

Maybe we're both looking to the future because it's gotta be better than the past.

A clean slate is never more appealing than when your current slate is ugly, with black, deep marks from a whole lot of screw-ups and mistakes. Some ugly things are carved into both of our slates, gouged and messy.

So forgetting isn't a bad thing.

Except, right now, I'm looking at Macy, trying to soak this moment in.

This is the first time she hasn't fled the scene of the crime, so to speak. When we were together in Seattle, she didn't wake up with me. But here she is, sleeping next to me.

This moment, I wouldn't mind remembering this one. The sunlight through the blinds in her ridiculously pink bedroom lights up the wisps of hair around her face.

I can hear the dogs in the other room. They definitely did some damage, I suspect. Now one of them sounds like he's eating kibble in the kitchen, but the other one, probably Justin Trudeau, snores. I can hear his snorts loud and clear.

"Grandma Kitty. She's why I like pink." Macy opens her eyes and looks right into mine.

"What?" I stretch an arm out as she slides in close to me, rests her head on my chest.

"One of the times they took me away from my mom, when I was little, I went to stay with a foster mom. She was older. Her name was Grandma Kitty." Macy swallows hard, but continues. "Mom always painted my fingernails black."

"What? When you were little?" I reach out and touch her hair.

"Yeah. She painted a wall in my room black, too." She picks her head up and looks at me. "Let's leave it at 'she had issues'. But anyway, I ended up one night at Grandma Kitty's house."

She breathes in deeply, pulls her body closer to mine. "Her house was warm, and she smelled like lavender. The first thing she did was put me into a bubble bath. The whole bathroom was sparkling white, and the tub was warm and filled to overflowing with these silky sweet bubbles. And I soaked in the tub, and she helped me wash my hair, and then she took the black nail polish off my fingers, and she said to me, 'Princesses wear pink nail polish. Don't let anyone tell you you're not a princess.'"

"Princess. Definitely you." I smile and kiss her.

"So that's why the pink. She was one of the nicest people I ever got to know."

"What happened to her?"

"I think you're petting my hair. Can you not?" Macy reaches up and touches my hand.

"I was caressing your hair, comforting you."

"I don't like being petted."

"Think of it as more of a pat."

"It's still a no." She sits up and pulls her t-shirt down, turns to face me. "Everything else is a big hell yes, though."

"You've taken up swearing again, then?" I sit up and take her face in my hands, kiss her deeply.

"Hell yes, I have." She kisses me back. "Will you help me straighten this mess out?"

"I've already started. I hope that's okay."

She sits back and nods. "I'll give you as much information as I can. I've screwed plenty of things up in my time, but I'd never screw up the best job I've ever had. I swear."

"I think we follow the timeline and the money and it'll all come out. But this place, Macy, I don't know."

"Let's not talk about me leaving the river, okay? It breaks my heart to think about it."

I nod. "Fair enough. We'll get this figured out."

She kisses me and untangles herself from the bedcovers. "I'm gonna take a shower."

I lie back and look at the ridiculous Canadian flag on her ceiling. "Okay."

She waits at the bathroom door. "You coming?"

"What?"

She points at me; she points to the bathroom. "Shower. You coming?"

Hell yes, I am.

It's fair to say that the rest of the day is epic. But real life has a nasty way of rearing its ugly head. Macy and I need to solve her very big problem before the weekend ends, and law enforcement makes an appearance.

I've got calls out to my favorite money people in LA, and Todd is due to arrive here any minute. Between the money trail and what I hope Todd can attest to, I think I can make this work for Macy. I can fix this for Macy.

As the afternoon wanes, I drive back to the lodge to pick up the rest of the crew. We're all headed to the fairgrounds for the big 4th of July party. Macy plans to meet us there after she finds all of her bank statements from the last year. She got the marching orders from my agency's lawyer, who I of course corralled into helping me. Why do I employ these people if not to help the people I love out of a jam? I hustle to the lodge and try to ignore the fact that I love Macy and that I'm even admitting it now too.

The 4th of July in LA isn't much different than any other summer weekend. All the industry types jostle for invites to the best parties and worry about being seen. It usually ends up that someone has a Malibu beach house or downtown restaurant rooftop or Hollywood Hills pool where they host a party. There may be a sparkler or two, but mostly the party consists of young actresses (wearing tiny star-spangled swimsuits they spent a month's waitress or PA salary to buy) dancing around, preening and hoping someone will notice their spray-tanned selves. Kind of Coachella without the sunstroke.

I've begun to realize that in other parts of the country, the 4th of July is still associated with, you know, Independence Day and freedom and forefathers.

It appears that Teton County, Idaho, may be the epicenter of patriotic fervor. I pick up Andy, Kelly, and Quincy, and we drive to the county fairgrounds in Driggs.

It's not exactly what I pictured. I expected a country gazebo, maybe a town square with a big white bandstand.

This is a big dusty square of land, just past the Super 8 and the Seoul Korean restaurant. And the Teton County museum, which is more fancy and beige than I expected.

If it weren't for a huge white carnival-style tent, it'd be a million degrees here.

We get out to survey the area. The sun can't go down soon enough.

"It's hot." Andy slides on his sunglasses, but there will be no hoodie-wearing in this sunshine.

"Ya don't say?" I feel nervous and cranky.

"Da da da da da!" Quincy hits the ground wobbly, but running. Kelly chases after her, toward the sketchy-looking workers installing a wooden parquet dance floor in front of a stage under the cover of the huge white Tates Rents tent.

Andy stays back with me, ready to fill in as my counselor. "What's up? I thought things were all fixed between you and fishergirl."

"They are. Now we've got to fix a problem someone's hung around her neck."

"Are you planning on elaborating?" He looks worried.

"I could. Do you really want me to right now?" I might sound a bit snippy.

"I guess you could do the typical Jeremy thing instead."

"Which is what?" I'm sweating between my shoulder blades. If the sun would just freaking go down already.

"You know, you usually make a bigger mess of the problem and then fix it and then act as though you were in control the whole time." We finally make it under the shade of the tent, and I swear the temperature drops ten degrees.

"There's where I beg to differ. I'm always in control. That's the typical Jeremy King thing—control."

He smiles, but it's this weird, mom kind of "I'll humor you" smile. I think I'm not going to like what comes next. "Sit back. I'm about to get preachy."

I hold my hands to the heavens. "Here it comes. I'm ready to receive your wisdom."

He waves me off. "You scoff, you deride, you pooh-pooh—"

"I don't 'pooh-pooh.' Give me some credit." I sigh and sit on a folding chair. Besides the workers and Kelly and Quincy, the tent is empty. The smart locals knew it'd be too damn hot until the sun sunk under the horizon. Nobody here but us tourists.

"Let's talk about control."

"What about it?"

"The crazy thing about life—you can't control it. The crazy thing about human beings? They won't let you control them. As much as you want to be the smartest guy in the room, be the one in control, life won't let you run the show. How you respond to that, react to that, hell, how you roll with that—that's your quality of life right there." He points to Quincy, who at this moment trips over her own toddler shoes and eats it on the newly-installed dance floor.

But before Kelly can scoop her up, Q tripods back up to standing and takes off at a full run again.

"See?" Andy points at her. "You value dominance, control? Think that's what equals winning? No. Resilience. That is what puts a man on top. The ability to absorb the punches, roll with the punches, get back up. Just like Q over there. Never stay down when the thing side-swipes you that you never saw coming."

I chew on this for a minute. "Macy's life. She's been kicked in the teeth so many times. I just want to spare her some of that."

He shakes his head. I notice he's not taken his sunglasses off yet, even though we're sitting in the cool shade of the tent. "You can't spare her. She is who she is because she's resilient. Persistent. Relentless. It's not always about winning, Jeremy King-of-the-world. It's about coming back from defeat. Over and over again. That's life."

I get up from the steel folding chair and walk toward Q, watching her toddle in circles. "But it'd be so much easier if I could just win all the time. That's my zone."

Andy comes over and gives me the fatherly hand on the shoulder, with the added empathy squeeze. He uses it a lot in "listening scenes" in his movies, but I can tell it's genuine now. "Losing builds character. Losing control makes you human. We tell Hunter and Beau 'mistakes are for learning, losing is how you win at life' all the time. Seems to work. They've turned out to be mostly normal people."

"Now you're parenting me? Great."

He scoops up Quincy and carries her, fireman-carry, to her mom. "Oh, how the mighty have fallen, eh, J?"

I stand there and watch as Andy drifts over to his wife, surrounded by a slowly growing number of people and a whole lot of red, white, and blue.

Everything is drenched in it. Bunting, banners, streamers, lights—if it's stationary, it's been decorated.

Andy and Kelly take to the dance floor with Quincy in the fading light. There's a DJ now, and the music will clearly be all country, all the time. Quincy twirls in circles and squeals.

I would grab a beer, but there's a clearly marked "beer garden," and I know Andy won't go within eight miles of it, so I guess tonight's a bottled water kind of a night.

I come up to Andy, who's watching Kelly chase Quincy.

"Does she run on nuclear power? She's never still."

Andy shrugs. "Toddlers are powered by the sun. Or the moon. Or juice boxes."

We watch as Kelly follows Quincy, who weaves in and out of the people milling around the dance floor. It's too early for dancing, maybe. The Rotary Club is busy setting up long tables and roasting hot dogs for the picnic. Quincy seems to be making a real effort to ditch her mom in the crowd.

"Looks exhausting."

Andy nods. "Pretty much."

But then Quincy, as if on cue, notices Andy and me standing over here. She lets out a delighted squeal and comes careening over on her fat little baby legs.

"Daddeee!"

"Baby!" Andy kneels and opens his arms to the blonde whirling dervish. Her forward momentum propels her into his arms, and he scoops her up.

"How's Daddy's favorite baby?" He gives her a big kiss.

She giggles and grabs a big tuft of his hair.

Andy points to her and then uses the same hand to wrest his hair away from her. "Exhausting but absolutely worth it, my friend."

The sun's gone now, and the set-up crew turns on all of the strands of red, white and blue lights. As more people who are clearly from around here begin to show up, I feel self-conscious in my collared shirt and loafers. "One of us should've packed cowboy boots."

Andy nods. "Something faintly red, white, or blue would've come in handy, probably."

"I get my ass kicked in crowds like this. It rarely fails."

"You should get your ass kicked in all sorts of crowds, but you don't, so don't sweat it."

"I wish Tucker was here." I have a passing thought about Troy. It'd be nice to have Tucker around if Troy made an appearance. Tucker assures us Troy won't, but I'm the one who's paid to worry about all kinds of contingencies.

"Will I do?" Todd Ford slaps Andy and me on the back at the same time.

"Not really." I turn around as he gives Andy the bro-hug. I manage to put a hand out, and Todd shakes. I do need him to help Macy, after all.

"You made it. I'm glad but surprised." Andy smiles at him.

Todd shrugs a little. "Jeremy kind of made it sound like an emergency, so here I am."

"What's that about?" Andy asks me. "And if you've roped Todd into it, you might as well rope me in too."

"Fine." I try not to scowl. "I wanted to have Todd here to vouch for Macy."

"For what?"

Todd butts in. "The last day you all fished. When I stayed back at the lodge. I can vouch for Macy."

"About what?" Andy looks puzzled.

I speak up. "Richard says there's a deposit from that day that's gone missing, and that Macy took it. Said she was supposed to take the deposit to the bank, but it never made it there."

"Huh. That doesn't sound good."

I poke at Andy, trying to get him to hold off on making a judgment, and point at Todd. "But tell him why you matter in this."

"I saw Richard take the deposit bag to his car, and I knew she wasn't in the lodge when he said she was, because she was with me." Todd says it quietly, and his lips form a slim line.

Andy looks panicked. "You knew Jeremy was all about her. What were you doing?"

I shake my head. "No, it's not that. Give him a chance. And besides, there's absolutely no way she'd be interested in him."

Andy walks over to one of the long tables and sits down. We follow, but two teenage girls approach him for an autograph and a selfie first.

Todd squints at me. "'Absolutely no way'? You were pretty worried she might be interested in me the first couple days."

"Shut it, Todd. Just tell these girls to take a walk and tell Andy what happened."

Todd intervenes and sends the young girls, autographs in hand, on their way. He and I sit on either side of Andy to fend off any other potential nuisances.

"So what's the story?" Andy looks tired of us.

Todd sits back. "Macy came by since she was still benched from fishing. She was going to leave a note for lover boy here. But I was there, and she saw that I was upset, so she stayed."

"Upset?" Andy's confused.

I'm losing patience now. "You know how Todd was on his phone the whole week, and all distracted, and all 'I've got important band business'?"

"Yeah."

Todd looks at the table, avoiding our eyes. "It wasn't band stuff. It was Mrs. Nesbitt."

Andy's lost. "Who? What are we talking about?"

"His cat."

Andy starts to grin, and then purses his lips as soon as the grin spreads wide. He's trying not to laugh. "Your cat?"

Todd still won't look at either of us. "That whole week, Mrs. Nesbitt, my cat—the house sitter kept texting me and telling me she wasn't eating. She was worried about her, and she wanted to take her to the vet."

"Your cat?" Andy still has his lips pursed in a tight pucker.

Todd puffs his chest out, defensive. "Dude, she was all the family I had. I got her when I moved out of my parents' house."

"So you got her last month, you mean." I can't help it.

"Shut up, Jeremy. Try not to be such a dick. Do you want my help with Macy or not?"

Andy's regained his composure, and his mouth is back to normal. "What happened to Mrs. Nesbitt?"

Todd swallows hard. "I told the house sitter to just wait, that I'd get home and take her to the vet myself. She was sixteen."

I react. "My God, that's like zombie status."

"Jeremy!" Andy scolds me.

Todd looks up at the ceiling of the tent. "But she died, on that last day. The house sitter found her all curled up…" He lets the sentence trail off, and he turns his back to the both of us.

Andy coughs. "Sorry, man."

"Yeah, no wonder you were such a douche that whole week. Sorry."

Andy shakes his head at me. "Remind me not to invite you to speak at my funeral."

"You couldn't invite me, you'd be dead. But I'd say nice things, I swear."

We sit in silence for a minute, stare at Todd's back. He may be shuddering ever so slightly. Then I hear a sniffle, and he turns back to face us.

"Who do I need to set the record straight with? Are you going to confront Richard?" Todd's eyes look wet, but he juts out his chin, jaw set in determination. I almost feel for the guy.

Andy stands up. "Now I really wish Tucker were here. I don't know about this."

We follow him back to the dance floor, where it does appear that Quincy is showing some signs of slowing down. She stands on Kelly's toes, and Kelly sways with her in a circle to the music.

I finish the discussion up before we're within earshot of Kelly. "I don't know what I'll say to Richard. I need a couple more days for my people to connect all the dots. A holiday weekend is not a great time to track down bankers."

"We'll figure it out. Maybe not right now, though." Andy nods in Kelly's direction. And he's right, she definitely doesn't need to be dragged into this.

I check my phone and realize I haven't heard from Macy.

"On your phone, Jeremy? Maybe I should make some dick comment about it." Todd stands next to me.

"I see you're back to being one of my least favorite guys." I consider texting Macy.

And then, there she is. She walks into the tent at the far end, by the Rotarians. Her hair is down, wavy at her shoulders.

She wears a red top with white shorts and a blue pair of cowboy boots.

Of course she does. She fits here.

She's radiant.

I watch her as she makes her way through the crowd. These are people she knows. She gives a few small smiles here and there, waves to Kevin/Kramer, even talks to Evan the other guy for a minute.

Her eyes search the crowd. She weaves in and out of the masses on the dance floor, every so often craning her neck to get a better view.

Is she—could it be that she's actually looking for me?

I dismiss it as soon as I think it.

But, then, she spots me.

And here's the thing—remember when I wondered what it would be like to have that one person—not a huge crowd, just that one person—who lit up when I walked in the room?

Well, friends, she sees me, her eyes widen, her lips split into a grin, and

She.

Lights.

Up.

She pulls her petite frame up tall, and I swear she skips the last few feet through the crowd to me.

I don't care if she's skittish, I don't care if she's trouble. I pull her into my arms and look at this smile, this happiness on her face, that I think just might be there because of me.

"Hey."

"Hey."

I touch her face, gently run my thumb over her bottom lip. "What's this smile about?"

She tilts her head a little, considering, purses her lips. "What can I say, Mr. King. I'm happy to see you."

I kiss her then and hold her close to me.

And I swear to God this could be all there is and I'd be good.

"Mr. King." A cold voice from over my shoulder breaks the perfect moment into a thousand pieces.

I'd like to break the owner's face, for more reasons than one.

I turn around and face him. "Richard."

"Macy, you're making all kinds of choices I don't think are wise." Richard looks right through me and settles on Macy.

"Richard, his trip's over. Nothing happened while I was working with him on the river."

"Messing with the guests. And stealing."

Macy shakes her head, as though she's trying to cast a nightmare away. "No, no, none of this is right."

I step in front of her. I know she hates alphas, but it takes one to take another one down. "Richard, you better go. You made the mistake of pinning your mishandling on Macy. My attorneys are on it, and I am, too. The deposit, your bad choices, all of it."

He looks at me. He looks unsettled, maybe worried. "You know this girl for five minutes and…"

I step to him. "I would quit while you're ahead. Say another word, and I'll break your nose."

Andy walks up, with Todd in tow. "What's going on? Anything you need help with, J?"

Richard steps back, puts space between me and him. "We're fine." He stalks away through the crowd, on his phone to someone as he walks to the parking lot.

Macy leans in to me, her body going soft. "What am I going to do?"

I hold her. "Just trust me that I'm really close to fixing this. There's nothing to worry about." I stroke her hair.

"You're petting me."

I stand there with her, play with a few strands of the blonde with brown tips. "You know, to be honest, I don't understand your hair. If we're being straight with each other."

She punches my arm. "It's called reverse ombre. It's a thing." She pokes at me now, continuing to assault my arm. "And I'm serious. What am I going to do?"

"You could come with me. Get out of here for a while. There's no point in sticking around in a place like this."

"Except that I love it. And I love the river. But if I don't have my job…" She leaves off. Her eyes look misty, and her face reveals the fear of being lost, unmoored.

"Just come with me. Let me fix it. Just get out of here."

She stands there, twisting a red, white and blue hair tie 'round and around her wrist. "You want me to just bail out? That's what's supposed to fix this?"

"Right now I'm going to take you in my arms and dance with you close to me. But yes, after that, I'm the one who cares about you, and I think it'd be good to get away from here."

"You 'care' about me. I'm giving up on the only job I've ever really been good at to go with someone who 'cares'. That's some weak sauce there, if you're trying to convince me."

"Stop." I take her by the hand.

"Stop what?"

"Stop pushing for me to say something more."

"About what?"

"I'm not going to say I love you right now. You won't let me in. You want me to throw my heart at your feet, but you won't tell me who taught you to tie flies or where your mom went."

I pull her close and feel her through the damp of my shirt. She's quiet. Her lips are parted, but whatever words were poised on them, they stay put.

"Are we agreed, then?" I take her hand, slip my other arm around her waist to dance with her. I rub her palm in circles with my thumb, sway with her in my arms to the country music that's too soft to make the words out.

"We haven't agreed on anything since you showed up three weeks ago."

"Make it easy for me. From the second I saw you, I wanted you, but from the second you opened your mouth, you were dead-set on making it hard."

"You make it hard. You make it hard to not want to punch you in the mouth sometimes."

"Well, you've already done that, so can you just consider what I'm saying and set the physical beating aside?"

She rests her head on my chest and just dances with me. After a good minute, she looks at me. "I don't know. Let me think about it later. I don't even want to think right now."

Her eyes fill up, wet and uncertain. I can't push any harder, not tonight. "Fair enough."

And we dance.

I take Macy home, drop her at her front door.

"Think about it."

"I've already thought about it. I can't leave the river. It's the only place where I'm good at anything. Don't take that away."

"There are other rivers."

"Not near LA. Isn't that the point? That we'd be together?"

My head hurts. "I want your name cleared, and I want you to have a fresh start. There are other rivers."

"I like this one."

She drives me to drink, this woman.

I close my eyes, promise to pour a strong one when I get back the lodge, then take a slow, deep breath.

"Our main job right now is to clear the accusations up. Richard's nervous, so I think I'm on the right track. Then we can finish the discussion of where you're going to reign as fisherperson supreme. But the whole finance thing—I'll have it figured out and you cleared before the end of this weekend."

"I don't see how you can do that."

"Trust me. I'm good at meddling, remember? That's why you hated me for a while."

"Jury's still out." She counters. "I haven't totally let go of that."

"Point taken. I remain on probation."

We stand in front of her door, and I can hear the little psycho dogs whining on the other side of it.

"You better get in there. Justin Trudeau'll have an aneurysm."

She looks at me. Is she thinking about kissing me, maybe?

"Okay. Good night." She slips in the door and shuts it in my face. Guess not.

I get into the Yukon and start it. I sit there and check my phone.

There's a rap on my window. After I peel myself off the roof of the car, I put the window down for Macy.

"We could just drive around for a little bit. Maybe talk."

She's reconsidered. Maybe she *is* thinking about kissing me.

"Get in."

She gets in the car, and I back out, pull away from her apartment complex. The night is deep now. When it's dark in LA, it's never dark. The landscape is always bathed in the milky light of the city—parking lots, high rises, freeways, stadiums—they all cast a halogen glow over the whole valley, and you're never really in the dark.

Middle of nowhere Idaho dark is another story. Without the moon tonight, I can only see as far as my headlights' beams in front of the car.

Macy sits next to me and looks out the window. At nothing.

"How's the view?"

"Hmm?" She picks her head up, turns to face me.

"Were we going to drive and talk or drive and sulk or what?"

She bows her head. "Sorry. I just thought about how you're trying to help. I felt bad for shutting the door in your face."

"The dogs are probably eating what's left of your sofa for coming home and leaving again."

She smiles. "Probably."

We sit quiet for a minute as I try to decide what to say. I stare ahead of me, watching the road unfold in the pool of my headlights.

Somebody's brights glint in the rearview mirror.

"Great."

"What?" Macy turns to try to see behind us.

"Just some Mater from the Land of Tater trying to crawl up my ass." I give the Yukon a little gas.

"It's a truck." Macy sounds worried. The truck's right on me now. "Just pull over for him. He's probably drunk. Fourth of July brings out the aggro drunk rednecks."

I pull to the side, and the truck pulls to the left as if to pass us.

But when it's even with us, instead of cruising by, it holds steady, and begins to edge closer to us.

And I get a better look at the truck.

"Troy." Macy says it just as it registers with me, and I slam on the brakes, hard.

The truck shoots ahead, and our tires squeal as the Yukon shudders under the brakes.

"Oh my God!" Macy cries out, hoarse.

We're stopped, but the truck ahead of us has stopped, too.

"He's coming back. What's he going to do?"

I pull the Yukon around and gun it, trying to put some distance between us and the psycho behind us. "I don't know. Let's get back to civilization. Call 911."

Macy pulls her phone out of her purse. "No signal. It'll come back in range when we're closer to my apartment. You can drive straight through to town and City Hall. There's hopefully at least one deputy on duty." She turns around in her seat to check on the truck.

It's coming up behind us.

"Troy? What the hell?" Macy yells, as if he could hear her. "Why is he chasing us"

I push the Yukon, and we stretch out the length of road between us and him. I check the rearview and feel a surge of adrenaline.

"We're losing him." I turn back to Macy.

She screams.

A huge, brown animal is on the hood.

I open my eyes and feel something wet all over my face. And I can hardly breathe. Someone forces the air out of my ribcage in short, quick huffs.

"Stop." I force it out with the next push on my chest, force my eyes to focus in on the space above me.

"Jeremy? Hey, hey, Jeremy! Look at me, look right here!"

I blink hard and see Macy.

"Stop crushing my chest." It hurts to talk. Sharp pain stabs at my face and head. I'm thirsty; my mouth's parched.

"It's CPR. You weren't responsive." She holds my hands, both of them together, and she strokes them. It feels nice.

"I'm responsive now. Talking is responding. Let me sit up, damn it." I try.

She pushes on me again. "No! No, your neck might be hurt. Spinal cord and all that. Lie still."

"Let me sit up a little. I'm gonna throw up if you don't." I can taste blood down the back of my throat.

She slides a hand around my back and gives me a nudge, pulling me up onto her lap.

"Where's Troy?"

"Long gone. He got out, saw me crawl out of the car and got back in his truck and took off." She pets my hair now.

"Macy?"

She leans forward, still petting me. "Yes? Stay awake for me. Help's coming."

"Stop petting me. I liked the hand-stroking, though. You can do that."

She snorts. "Good lord. You're going to be fine, aren't you? And I'll pet you if I want." She leans over me and kisses my lips. "You're a bloody mess." She uses the hem of her sleeve to wipe my face. It comes away angry, wet crimson.

"I love you." I see my blood on her hands, and all I want to do is hold her, never let her go.

"What?" She leans over me. I can smell something sweet on her breath. Mint, maybe.

"I feel like I'm going to pass out. I want you to know I love you in case I die."

"For crying out loud, Jeremy." She kisses me again. "You're not going to die. I already saved your life."

"I like it when you call me by my first name. That's new." My head spins again, and I close my eyes, concentrate on the feel of her hands on my hands.

There's nothing wrong with contemplating mortality, I guess.

I don't want to go right now, obviously. I'd kind of like to have a chance to make peace and get my affairs in order.

I guess the best policy on that is to always be squared up. I mean, that the people who love you know that you love them, every day.

That you don't bitch and crab at somebody, and then you die and leave it all unsaid.

What is the whole point anyway?

I try to concentrate, and I feel cold, but I see the river, see Macy, see the moose crossing the river on that first evening, making ripples in the lilac night.

Maybe that's what this is all about. My mortality, not Macy's, mine. I've been so wrapped up in her life. But what about my life? It's my life. How do I want to live it? I'm afraid of a scary accidental death because I want to make sure when I go I've gotten it all said, gotten it all done.

What is it that I need to get done?

"Jeremy, open your eyes. Jeremy, they're here. The ambulance is here."

"You didn't say anything." I open my eyes.

"What?" She looks like she's crying. Her eyes look wet.

"You didn't say you love me back." I keep my eyes on her face even though the black night behind her spins a bit.

"What? Are we really?—Jeremy, I love you. Okay? I love you, of course I love you. And I hate you for living in LA and wanting me to live there, and I love you for trying to help, and I hate you for running into that stupid elk."

"He ran into me."

"It was a cow. A she."

"Of course it was a female." I try to reach up, touch her face.

"Nobody likes a chauvinist jerk, even when you're all bloody and hurt. Stop, just rest." She holds my hand in hers.

"Thanks for not petting me. Stay with me." I look at her, and everything gets very still.

"Always." She bends down and kisses me, briefly, and I can tell someone else is there because she lets go of my hand and whoever takes it has the hands of a longshoreman.

Then I throw up. But it's all okay because Macy and I, we said we loved each other and I feel warm and safe and she remembered her CPR, thank Jesus.

I close my eyes for a nap while we ride in the ambulance.

THE KING'S SPEECH

The nap must be a long one. When I come to, I'm in a bed. No one's in the room.

Great. I've been stuck in an institution.

Then I tilt my head, just a tiny movement, and it feels as though I've brought a Ping driver solidly through the front of my skull.

"Holy—" I can't even finish the thought, because opening my mouth has brought on another shooting bolt of lightning.

Macy pops up from somewhere. I didn't see her anywhere, but now I'm terrified to try to turn my head to see where she came from. "Don't talk. The doctor thinks you might have a hairline fracture in your jaw or cheekbone."

I'd nod, but Jesus. I blink a couple times.

"Concussion. The thing with your jaw. Lots of blood. But that's about it."

"And he broke his collarbone. And broke all his toes in his right foot. Did you tell him that part?" Andy comes into my line of vision.

"I think it hurts for him to talk. Is the nurse around?" Macy sounds nervous, worried. I want to say not to worry.

Because you know what? I don't care if my head's about to topple off the top of my spine.

Macy is here with me, and I do recall her saying she loved me.

As long as she said that, it's all good.

Okay, as long as I'm not about to die and she said that, it's all good.

"The poor elk, though." Andy says this for my benefit.

"And it completely shredded the Yukon. They won't be renting that one out again."

I try to nod again and suck air in through my teeth.

Macy leaps up. "That's it. I'm going to find LaDonna. She can't avoid me. She should know I'm not going to let her sit on her ass and play Bejeweled while Jeremy's in pain."

She flies out of the room, out of my line of sight.

Andy leans in front of me. "You should just rest. All that financial stuff you scanned and sent to Tucker, he took care of it—it was the data they needed. Richard, he set Macy up with that missing deposit. He's been skimming off the top for at least eighteen months. That's why, when you started sniffing around, he sicced Troy on you. But between Todd's alibi for Macy from that day when he skipped out on fishing and the money transfers you had your people track down, the attorney's office filed charges against Richard, not Macy."

"I—" Again, I have a lot I want to say, but the roofing nail that someone drove into my face and forgot to tell me about, won't let me.

Andy shakes his head. "Macy's gone to get LaDonna, nurse of the year and doser of the drugs. You rest. Next time you wake up I bet they'll have figured out the face thing."

I set my head back against the pillow and wait for Macy.

She comes back into view, towing a tiny Hispanic lady by the hand. "See, see how still he's holding his head? And he can't even talk, it hurts so bad."

LaDonna looks skeptical. She turns to Andy. "This true?"

Andy stands next to her. I try to will him to action. Use your superhero movie star charms for good, my friend.

Andy nods, folds his arms over his chest. "Trust me, Jeremy King is not a man of few words. I've never heard him so quiet. And as much as it pains me to relieve him of his suffering, I do think he's in some pain."

LaDonna relents. "The orders give me a little wiggle room. I can give him another dose now, and then when the doctor makes rounds, we'll get that cheek and jaw thing straightened out." She approaches me with a large needle. Before I can react, I feel something warm and then cold climb up my arm.

"You just rest, Mr. King. Everyone tells me I should be glad you can't speak."

Macy takes my hand and smiles at me, and then her lovely eyes go gray and then it's dark.

THE LAST WALTZ

The elevator. Another elevator, this one to the top of the CN tower in Toronto.

"Not long enough to get in any trouble, too long to not feel stifling." I try to ignore the smell of a day's worth of sweaty tourists.

Macy smacks my arm. "You do not get to be a killjoy. You know how long I've wanted to come here. Now is not the time for 'Jeremy King, disaffected agent who's seen it all' to rear his ugly head."

I frown. "I'm not disaffected, and my head's not ugly."

She leans in and kisses me. "You have a perfectly lovely head. You are jaded, though. Admit it, Mr. King."

The elevator stops before we can get any farther.

"I still don't get why you didn't do this sooner."

"It's money, and I didn't know about the passport."

"*No criminal or immigration-related convictions.* That's what stopped you." I hug her as we get off and head to the edge of the observation deck.

"I didn't know if that meant me or not. Now I do. Here I am. And the best part is, I get to share this with you." She weaves her arms around to my back and pulls herself close to my body.

Screw the CN tower. I'm ready to go back to the hotel. "We should hurry this up."

She grins. "I know your game. This is the Jeremy King experience. You're ready to pop me on a plane and send me on my way."

"Who told you about that? Was it Todd? I'll kick his ass."

She smiles. "Not telling."

"This is not the 'experience.' This is you and me, learning to act like a normal couple." I kiss her neck, brush an earlobe, work up to whispering some really suggestive sweet nothings.

"No, sir, don't go in for the kill." She slides out of my arms. "I want to see the view before I fall prey to your charms."

I watch her walk the perimeter of the deck, enjoy seeing her face light up with wonder at the blanket of Toronto and beyond spread out below us.

She pauses, waves me over. "Come see this with me."

I come close to her. "It's really beautiful. It's good that we came up here."

She smiles. "I told you."

Standing close to her, I touch her hand. "Hey, you remember when you said you wouldn't take gifts worth more than forty bucks?"

She looks curious. "Yeah."

I slip a ring on her finger, on the fourth finger on her left hand. It twinkles in the night air, thousands of feet above the land of both Trudeaus and poutine.

"What is this?" She gasps.

"I may have broken the rule."

"You can't have spent this kind of money on me."

I smile. "I found a loophole."

"What is it?" She's crying now, tears sliding down her cheeks as she grins and looks from my face to the ring and back again.

"I bought this with the swear jar money."

She tilts her head back and laughs. "You're too much."

"Yes, I am. I love you."

She kisses me. "I love you."

"And I'm safe to say you're a yes on the proposal?"

"As long as I get to spend summers on the river, I'm a yes. Per our discussion."

I hold her close and kiss her again. "Per our discussion. You're a piece of work, Macy Shea Summerlin."

"So are you, Mr. Jeremy King."

"Made for each other, clearly." I lead her to the elevator. "Let's go see what the Trudeaus got up to while we were gone."

We get back on the elevator and go to face the world. It's a pretty great feeling.

And that's not some mushy bullshit; it's just true.

ACKNOWLEDGEMENTS

Sometimes I feel more hot mess than hot ticket, and I am so lucky to have so many amazing people who support me in my life. You all are phenomenal.

To my family. My man and my boys put up with me and the perpetual whining/stewing that I lovingly call the creative process. And the Anderson, Lindsay, and Finn clans are my first and best cheerleaders. I love all of you.

To my Chix. Thanks for sticking with me and being my sounding board. We are a BA bunch of women, and I can't wait to see what's in store for us next.

To my work family, a whole organization of passionate and caring people! Thanks for all of your support for my "other" job.

To the ladies of the book world who have offered me such great friendship—the Jennifers (Lane and Locklear), Jessica, Nancee, Colleen, Nicki, Traci, Midian, Michelle, and Angy.

And to the Omnific crew. You started this great journey with one "yes." Thanks for backing an unknown!

ABOUT THE AUTHOR

Beck Anderson loves to write about love and its power to heal and grow people past their many imperfections. She is a firm believer in the phrase "mistakes are for learning" and uses it frequently to guide her in writing life and real life.

Beck balances (clumsily at best) writing novels and screenplays, working full-time as an educator, mothering two pre-teen males, loving one post-40 husband, and making time to walk the foothills of Boise, Idaho, with Stefano DiMera Delfino Anderson, the suavest Chihuahua north of the border.

Her first novel, *Fix You*, was a RWA Rita® finalist for Best First Book and Best Contemporary Romance. Learn more at authorbeck. com.